"You obviously don't like me," Bella said.

"That's not true." And it wasn't. Kyle simply didn't know how to handle Bella. Her temperament, her energy, her drive—they were all good things, professionally speaking, but they were nothing he was prepared to deal with. And that was what really bothered him.

"I came here to train with *you*, Kyle." Bella's words were as sharp and precise as a scalpel. Her composure was unexpected, and it threw him off balance even more. "Not with your staff, not in your gym. I came for *you*. But if you can't work with me, then all you have to do is say so, and I won't waste any more of my time or yours."

"That's not what I want." The thought of losing her because he'd misspoken—because he couldn't get over himself and deal with her— made him physically ill.

Dear Reader,

I can't believe I'm publishing my third Harlequin Superromance book! Part of me always thought I might sell two books at most before I dropped dead from exhaustion...the other part yelled at me like a drill sergeant to keep writing. And so *In Her Corner* was born.

I knew when I started writing my first book, *Her Son's Hero* (Harlequin Superromance July 2011), that I would later write about a female MMA fighter. There'd been a few successful female fighters, but it was widely believed that women would never make it into the wider professional arena for a lot of reasons. That didn't stop talented female athletes from trying, though.

I was thrilled that so many great historic milestones in women's mixed martial arts happened while I was writing this book, including the launch of Invicta Fighting Championship, a professional all-women's MMA promotion company; and the first female fight in the world's largest fight promotion, the UFC. It's been exciting seeing female athletes compete at this level, and I've met so many more female fans as the sport continues to grow.

In Her Corner isn't just about one woman's struggle for the right to fight; it's also about one man's struggle with himself. Kyle Peters was a flirtatious playboy in *Her Son's Hero,* but things have changed since, and the wrestling coach is having a hard time working with wannabe pro fighter Bella Fiore. Bella's part of MMA royalty, the only daughter of the world-famous Fiores who teach Brazilian jujitsu. Kyle can help get her career off the ground and break her away from her family's legacy, but he's wrestling with his own demons. He'll have to decide whether to see Bella as an opponent or an ally.

I love hearing from readers! Visit me on my webpage, at www.vickiessex.com; on Facebook, at www.facebook.com/vickiessexauthor; or on Twitter, @VickiEssex.

Keep fighting the good fight!

Vicki Essex

VICKI
ESSEX

—

In Her Corner

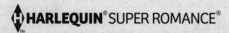
HARLEQUIN® SUPER ROMANCE®

Recycling programs
for this product may
not exist in your area.

ISBN-13: 978-0-373-60837-9

IN HER CORNER

Copyright © 2014 by Vicki So

Printed in U.S.A.

ABOUT THE AUTHOR

Vicki Essex couldn't throw a punch if her life depended on it, but she's been known to inflict injury accidentally, and suggests you stay out of arm's reach, just in case. She's a big fan of muscles and sportsmanship, and enjoys watching MMA fights while crocheting. She lives in Toronto and is an omnivore. Visit her at www.vickiessex.com; on Facebook, www.facebook.com/vickiessexauthor; and on Twitter, @VickiEssex.

Books by Vicki Essex

HARLEQUIN SUPERROMANCE

Other titles by this author available in ebook format.

Special thanks to Elizabeth Gonçalves for her help with the Portuguese language.
All mistakes are my own. *Muito obrigado!*
Vou fazer-lhe uma toranja boneco de neve!

A huge thanks to actor Tahmoh Penikett, who provided a perfect physical template for Kyle and happily played along when I asked him to pose for my cover.
(Check out my website if you want the full story. 8))

Thanks to my fantastic editor, Karen Reid.

Thanks to the lovely folks at Harlequin Enterprises, especially to the art and production departments, who put together the best covers.

For my friends and family, who've cheered me on.

And as always, for John, my schmoo.

CHAPTER ONE

KYLE STOMPED ON the brake and jerked the wheel to the right as the maniac on the bike barreled toward him.

The figure in black and red whipped by, his loaded backpack brushing Kyle's newly detailed convertible. Something metal bounced against the side of the car like a dud missile, rolling under the chassis. He slammed the heel of his palm against the wheel. *No one* touched his baby.

"Hey!" he shouted as a horn blared. The cyclist darted out of the path of another car, wobbling on its suicide trajectory against New Orleans traffic. "What's wrong with you?"

The bicycle skidded to a stop. The front wheel popped up and pivoted around as the rider deftly maneuvered it like a rearing show horse. A horn blared, and the driver of the car the cyclist had barely dodged rolled down the window, shouting obscenities. The cyclist studied the ground, frowning, eyes masked by reflective sunglasses. He looked up briefly and screamed an obscenity right back.

Jesus, the cyclist was a woman. All that lean muscle, plus the helmet and high-cut cycling top had effectively hidden any evidence of her femininity. Not that her being a woman subdued his temper. Kyle yelled, "Hey, lady, are you nuts?"

She ignored him as she walk-rode her bike back between the stalled lines of traffic, searching under the cars she'd passed. The driver who'd screamed at her started to get out of his car, swearing and waving his fist.

This was going to get ugly, and the cyclist had no idea the man was stalking toward her. "You're riding on the wrong side of the road," Kyle told her when she was within earshot. The driver from the other car continued yelling but was hesitant to stray too far from his vehicle. Kyle popped his seat belt, ready to intervene.

The woman scrambled off her bike and leaned it against the driver's-side door. "What are you doing?" He fought the urge to shove her bike off the side of his convertible.

"I dropped my water bottle." Her voice was smooth and sooty, tinted with an accent that definitely said not from around here. She got down on her hands and knees and reached under his car. Kyle got an eyeful of backpack, booty and muscular calves, and his ire was momentarily forgotten.

"Dammit." She crawled back up. "I can't reach it. Could you move your car?"

He blew out a breath. "Listen, lady, you can't ride against traffic. It's dangerous."

"No, it's not." She said it matter-of-factly, without the slightest trace of defensiveness or irony. "I can see what's coming, and so can you. I don't see what you're worried about—you're the one behind two tons of steel." She rapped on the side of the car.

Kyle's temperature peaked. "Don't. Touch. My car."

She blinked, gave him an apologetic smile and lifted her bike off the door. "Sorry. Can I please get my bottle now?"

Her flippancy reminded Kyle of his sister, Jessica. He frowned deeply. He was not going to let her get to him—or have the last word. "Listen. I don't know where you're from, but in this city, you ride on a bike path and follow traffic laws. Otherwise, I can't say what'll happen. Not everyone is as nice as me." He glared pointedly at the driver who'd gotten out of his car—the man looked like he still wanted to club her over the head. When Kyle narrowed his eyes at him, he stomped back into his vehicle.

The woman noticed the exchange. She lifted her chin a fraction, acknowledgment and challenge clear in her strong, stubborn jaw. He couldn't see her eyes behind the mirrored lenses but felt as if he were being studied by a predator. "Of course. You're right. I apologize." Her full lips tilted up.

A jolt of surprise hit him. He'd expected her to put up more of a fight, maybe scream at him in a fit of bipedal road rage.

The traffic ahead was moving again, and the

cars behind Kyle honked. He quickly buckled up and inched his vehicle forward, giving the woman enough space to retrieve her battered aluminum water bottle. She swung a leg over the bike and started to go with traffic, staying right next to Kyle's side-view mirror. When he finally regained his speed, she kept up with minimal effort, legs pumping. Flashes of her well-sculpted body danced in his peripheral vision.

He braked for a stoplight. She halted at his elbow. "Do you mind?"

She flashed bright white teeth. "No."

"You're following way too close."

"Don't worry. I won't touch your car as long as you drive predictably. Anyhow, it seems safer riding next to you than trying to get around everyone else. And you're obviously a good enough driver that you wouldn't hurt me."

He stared. He didn't know what this woman's problem was, but he was done with her. He was going to be late for work and he had an important client coming.

"I'm taking the next right," he said, then cursed himself for warning her.

"Me, too." She gave him an enigmatic grin.

Kyle gripped the steering wheel, suppressing the urge to yell at her to back the hell off. His heart thudded. Sweat dripped from his brow. The sweltering New Orleans heat was only slightly moderated by the thin cloud cover. He wished now that he'd put the top up and turned on the air conditioner. At least then he wouldn't have to deal with his cycling stalker. He'd have to shower again before his new client arrived. A Fiore was not someone whose hand you wanted to shake when you smelled like balls.

He tried to focus on driving, but the whole time he was ultra-aware of the pilot fish cyclist in her skin-tight cycling gear. She stayed so close that at stoplights, he could practically smell her—a strangely enticing combination of spice and something like fresh-baked bread. Like a hot-cross bun.

His eyes darted left as she slowed. Staring at *her* hot-cross buns nearly made him miss his turn. He yanked the wheel right. She arced away from the car, caroming into the next lane. Suddenly free of her, he floored it, speeding ahead and leaving her far behind as traffic closed around her. His tense shoulders relaxed as he pulled into the parking lot next to Payette's, the official Unlimited Fighting Federation's mixed martial arts gym he'd been managing for the past three years.

He grabbed his gym bag from the backseat and headed to the front door. His footsteps faltered as the cyclist coasted to a stop and alighted from the still-moving bike right beside him. She snatched it up as if it were broomstick.

Kyle stifled a groan.

"You left me behind." She took out a sturdy U-lock from her backpack and attached the bike to a stand in front of the building.

Kyle didn't say anything as he continued into the gym.

"Hey, wait up!" The woman's sooty voice dogged him.

"I have somewhere to be," he said without turning. He was used to dealing with hangers-on. Maybe she recognized him and wanted an autograph or something. If she tried to give him her number, he'd be sure to lose it as quickly as possible.

"We all have somewhere to be," she said as he reached the entryway. "It just so happens I have to be right here." She touched his arm. Something electric shot through him, and he whipped around. "With you."

She was shorter than he'd first thought—five-eight at most. But she was built like a brick house with thick biceps that showed through the stretchy biking top and a trim, tapered waist. He'd been wrong to say that the biking gear hid all her feminine assets, because he could see them clearly defined now. Her grin widened as she unsnapped her helmet and shook out her hair. Long, thick, wavy black tresses slick with sweat tumbled out, barely tamed by an elastic hair tie at her nape.

He shouldn't have been intrigued. Pushy girls weren't his thing.

She stuck out her hand. "Kyle Peters, right? I guess you don't recognize me."

He panicked, searching through his internal catalog of bedroom conquests. He tried to place her face—something about her seemed familiar, but he would've remembered a body like that.

She lifted her sunglasses to rest on the crown of her head. When he saw the glass-green eyes her family was famous for, he knew he'd made a huge mistake.

"BELLA FIORE." SHE extended her hand again, cooler now that she knew what Kyle Peters was really like. Any man who cared more about his car than a human life didn't rank high on her list.

It wasn't even a very nice car.

She watched his expression shift from embarrassment to frustration to regret and then, surprisingly, to anger. "You recognized me and didn't introduce yourself?"

"In the middle of traffic? I didn't think it was the safest place to do so." She kept her smile polite, even though she wanted to laugh at him. The guy was a lot more high-strung than his reputation suggested.

He opened his mouth as if to retort, but then shook his head and pushed into the gym. Bella followed, unable to resist a peek at his shapely behind. It'd been seven years since he'd wrestled professionally, but he still had the great glutes of an Olympic medalist. Actually, all of him was admirable—thick muscles on his upper body, a narrow waist, strong thighs and not an ounce of extra meat visible on him. He was the living portrait of a Greco-Roman wrestler, complete with broken Romanesque nose and dark brown Brutus-style haircut. She wondered idly if he'd ever wrestled naked like the pugilists of those bygone days.

The scent of rubber and sweat filled her nostrils as they entered Payette's. Some things didn't change gym to gym. The main reception area included a few café tables and a bar where a fridge supplied clients with bottled water, energy drinks and protein supplements. In one corner, UFF merchandise and workout gear—gloves, hand wraps, apparel and so forth—were displayed for sale. A faded sign proclaiming everything at 50 percent off hung askew from the ceiling.

Kyle paused at the front desk where a young woman with dark blond hair gave him a cursory smile. "Morning, boss. You got a call from Hadrian Blackwell." She handed him a slip. Kyle scowled at it as the receptionist—her name tag read Liz—turned a brighter smile on Bella. "Hi, how can I help you?"

"I'm early for my ten-o'clock appointment with him." She hitched a thumb toward Kyle, who continued to stare at the phone slip, his brow bunched.

The receptionist's face brightened. "You must be Bella Fiore. It's so good to meet you." She shook her hand vigorously. "We've been really excited about having you here. I'm a huge fan."

"Of my brothers, my cousins or my grandfather?"

"Of you," Liz said with a light laugh. "But of your whole family, too, of course."

Bella kept her smile modest. She couldn't walk

into a mixed martial arts gym and introduce herself without getting a lot of oohs and aahs over her lineage. The Fiores were like royalty in the MMA world.

"Liz, please show Ms. Fiore around. I need to make this call." Kyle barely looked at her as he strode away.

Bella watched him go, chewing on her lower lip. Apparently, Mr. Three-Time Olympic Gold Medalist didn't have to use his manners. But her oldest brother, Marco, had said Kyle Peters was one of the best wrestling coaches around. He'd helped a lot of MMA fighters, including the current UFF welterweight champion, Dominic Payette, for whom the gym was named, climb to stardom. That he was willing to make time for her in exchange for her working at the UFF gym was an opportunity she couldn't pass up.

Liz gave her an apologetic smile. "Sorry, Kyle's kind of a bear before his first cup of coffee. And he hates having his morning routine thrown off." She rounded the counter. "Let me give you the fifty-cent tour."

Bella had seen photos of Payette's, but they didn't do the state-of-the-art facility justice. The place was enormous, big enough to fit a full-size MMA cage and a boxing ring on the same floor with room for universal machines, free weights and other fitness equipment. The second floor housed a separate multipurpose martial arts studio covered in thick rubber mats. Mirrors lined one wall. Six men of various sizes worked on the heavy bags chained to the exposed metal beams. One of them looked up and shouted across the room to where a man slouched against a pillar reading a magazine. They both came at Liz's beckoning.

"These are our senior coaches," Liz said as they approached. "Tito's our physical therapist and Muay Thai instructor—" Bella shook hands with the stouter of the two "—and Orville's our judo teacher. Boys, this is Bella Fiore."

"I trained with your cousin Robert a few years ago in New Jersey," Orville said to Bella, a big grin splitting his face. "When I heard a Fiore was coming here, I thought it was going to be him."

"Sorry, you're stuck with me."

"Oh, I don't mean—"

She waved him off, giving him an understanding smile. She didn't mean to sound defensive or self-deprecating, but she knew what everyone was thinking: Why on earth was a Fiore training outside of a Fiore-run gym?

"Rob devotes most of his time to teaching at the family studio in Dallas now," she said. "I'll tell him hello for you." There was no need to explain herself further. No need to get into the details of her break from the family, though people would probably hear about it sooner or later.

Liz led her back downstairs and showed her the ladies' locker room. "I'll let you get changed while

I pull the paperwork together. Feel free to explore, use the equipment, warm up. This'll be your gym, too, for the next six months." She glanced toward the office at the end of the room, her lips pursed. "Kyle's probably going to be in his office for a bit."

"A bit" wouldn't hurt, Bella decided. She needed time to get her head into the game and figure out what Kyle Peters's problem was.

"BELLA FIORE, EH?" Kyle pictured the president of the UFF, Hadrian Blackwell, sitting back in his executive office chair. With his thick, dark hair and perpetual five-o'clock shadow, the man looked and sounded like the real-life Fred Flintstone. "A perfect 6-0 record, with three KOs and one submission. She's got talent, that's for sure."

"She does." Kyle had a YouTube video of Bella's most recent fight running on mute on his laptop. She'd dominated her opponent in the three-round matchup in April. She had a mean right hook and delivered a devastating roundhouse kick to the other woman's head that made Kyle wince. "But it's not as if she has a lot of competition in her weight class."

"She would if she dropped ten pounds. The women's 145-pound weight class has got some serious contenders and lots of up-and-comers."

"You're watching girl fights now?" The UFF president had once infamously said that women's MMA was an insult to the sport and that no woman would ever enter a UFF cage unless she was in a bikini and holding round numbers.

"MMA's my business. I watch everything that has to do with my world." Hadrian said it so sharply that Kyle's humor shriveled. "And speaking of business, what's going on with my gym?"

Kyle had been anticipating this conversation. He took a deep breath. "Economic downturn. People just aren't signing up for memberships."

"According to the numbers, people are *leaving* Payette's. None of the other gyms are losing business. What gives?"

Kyle's throat felt tight. "We're working on a new campaign strategy. I'll be forwarding details to you soon."

"I don't give a crap about ads and handing out free passes. The reputation and quality of the trainers speaks for itself. You've got what should be the crown jewel with all your heavy hitters. So what's the problem?"

Kyle dug his thumb into the knot of stress between his clenched jaw and his ear. "I can't say, sir."

"Can't say? Don't know? Don't care?" He let out a frustrated huff. "Shit, Kyle, I expected to hear a better excuse than that. Does it have anything to do with that thing that happened with what's-her-face?"

"No, sir." He clutched the edge of his desk. "She has nothing to do with it."

"And you're behaving yourself?"

"Yes, sir." Kyle's cheeks burned. He took a deep

breath to still the quivering in his gut, then exhaled, trying to purge the impotent anger gathering inside him.

"Anyhow, that's in the past. Let's look forward, all right? You have a Fiore in your gym now—you know they don't teach a lot outside of their tight little circle of friends. So don't screw this up."

"Yes, sir." Kyle hung up and sat back, attempting to regain his calm as he stared at the screen. YouTube had queued up another video about Bella, this one a cheaply produced feature with shots of her training at the Fiore Brazilian Jujitsu Studio in São Paulo, Brazil. He unmuted it. The video stuttered, the music was cheesy and the transitions rough. He watched it while fuming over Hadrian's humiliating dressing-down. As much as he respected him, the UFF president was the least sensitive man he knew. Next to his father, of course.

He pushed away from his desk and yanked his damp T-shirt over his head. He'd never gotten used to the humidity in NOLA. He applied another layer of antiperspirant under his arms and hung his street clothes in his private office locker to air, then pulled on a black T-shirt with the Payette's UFF logo printed on the breast. The heavy cotton grew damp at his touch and chafed his skin. He knew he should have gone with the more expensive moisture-wicking uniform tees, but he'd already had a thousand of them printed. It felt like a waste not wearing them.

Liz knocked and stuck her head past the door. "You decent?"

"What's the point of asking if you're going to come in anyhow?"

The receptionist bustled in, a cup of coffee and a clipboard in hand. She put them both on his desk and went around the room, drawing the blinds open so he could see out and everyone could see in. "Wayne's at a dentist appointment this morning. Root canal. We shouldn't expect him back at all today."

Kyle rolled his eyes. "He's such a baby."

She didn't comment. "I shuffled his clients between Tito and Orville. I've also got five potential members scheduled for tours."

"Maybe I should do those."

Liz regarded him archly. "Um, aren't you forgetting something?"

"No." He sipped his coffee, letting the caffeinated miracle nectar flow through his veins. His headache eased.

"Uh, yeah. Bella Fiore? It's her first day here." She planted her fists on her hips. "You were kind of rude to her."

Probably, but she was off-putting—and he didn't like off-putting. "She's crazy, you know. She was riding her bike *against* rush-hour traffic. I don't even know where she was headed—she was going in the complete opposite direction of the gym."

"She told me she likes to ride around the city before a workout to warm up. It gets her blood pumping."

It probably got her in the right frame of mind for punching things, too. The way she biked, it was as if she was aiming to piss off people so they'd yell at her to get her good and mad. Not exactly the Zen-like discipline the Fiores were known for.

"What did Hadrian say?" Liz asked after a beat.

He stalled by spinning his chair around and staring at his wall calendar, noting the dates of all the different MMA events the gym's clients were involved in. "Kyle?" Liz prompted.

"Nothing important. He was just calling in to check on us." *And tell me to behave myself. And sell more memberships. And be nice to Bella Fiore. Or else.*

Liz looked like she wanted to say something, but whatever it was, she held back. "Bella's warming up now. You need to go and greet her properly before she gets the wrong idea about you." With that, she departed.

Of course, Liz was right. He had to play nice with Bella Fiore. Her family name had been the only reason he'd agreed to train her in the first place, and he hated to admit it, but he needed her reputation more than she needed his.

He wasn't about to tell *her* that, though.

CHAPTER TWO

BELLA SURREPTITIOUSLY WATCHED Kyle Peters through the bars of the open vertical blinds covering his office windows. How long would she have to wait before he acknowledged her presence? Her temper simmered. She refused to be treated like a second-class student the way her grandfather and the rest of the family had treated her....

Calm down. You just got here, and Liz did say he's cranky. She couldn't take this slight personally. The guy didn't even know her, and she had come on strong—one of her less attractive traits, according to her grandfather Fulvio.

She should probably cut Kyle some slack. Maybe he was simply having a bad morning.

Yet with every minute he made her wait, her doubts about leaving Brazil grew. Her family all thought she was crazy to pursue her professional fighting career against Fulvio's wishes. Marco had been the only one who'd stuck up for her and suggested she go to New Orleans to work on her wrestling skills and take-down techniques.

"*Avô* will never give you what you need here," he'd

said. "You need to get away from the Fiore system. In the States, you'll have teachers who are willing to work with you, if for no other reason than your blood ties."

The Fiore name might open doors, but Bella wanted to be recognized as a fighter in her own right. She was more than the granddaughter of Fulvio Fiore, father of the Fiore BJJ system.

"Thought I'd bring you a T-shirt." Liz interrupted her reverie and handed her a black cotton tee. "Don't feel that you have to wear it—they're too hot to train in. I think Kyle's the only one who actually wears one on a regular basis."

Bella slipped it on over top of her moisture-wicking short-sleeved rash guard. It was stifling, but she wanted to show her new boss and coach she was willing to be a part of the team. T-shirt solidarity could be unifying, couldn't it?

"He should be out any minute. He'd never admit it, but calls with Hadrian Blackwell rattle him."

"Bad news?" Bella's question ended with a wry, speculative twist in her tone. She'd heard rumors about how phone calls with the UFF president often went.

"Let me put it this way. He doesn't call to ask how the kids are doing. A call from Hadrian means it's either horrifically bad news or stunningly good news." She glanced back at Kyle and pursed her lips, and Bella got the distinct impression they rarely got the latter.

Bella looked at Kyle, too. He was gathering some papers off his desk and taking his sweet time about it. "You ever meet him?" Bella asked.

"You mean Hadrian? Yeah, once, when he cut the ribbon on this place." She wrinkled her nose. "He called me 'sweetheart' and told me to get him a bottle of water."

Bella nodded. She'd met the UFF president on a couple of occasions when he'd visited the flagship Fiore studio in São Paulo in the early days of the UFF. He hadn't said much to her, either, but she'd only just started competitive fighting at the time, and with the rest of the boys around…well, being passed over wasn't anything new to her.

"Careful," Liz teased. "Your tongue's going to start hanging out soon."

Bella blinked. "Sorry?"

She tipped her chin toward Kyle. "You're not the first girl to look at him like that." Liz smiled wryly as Bella's cheeks heated. She hadn't even realized she'd been staring, much less drooling. "Pretty much every girl who walks through those doors falls for Kyle. He's like a freaking calendar model."

Bella chuckled. "I see the appeal, but I've been surrounded by muscly men my whole life. It takes more than a little flexing to get my attention." Though not much more where Kyle was concerned. She'd followed his career too closely to deny more intimate knowledge of his life.

Liz shrugged as if to say *we'll see.* But there was

something of a warning in her look, too. Was it for Bella, or was she warning her away from the boss?

Finally, Kyle emerged, a clipboard in hand. "Bella Fiore." He said it as though he were calling someone in line for a colonoscopy.

She stepped forward gamely and said, "Hi, Bella, I'm Kyle Peters." She met his cool look with a goofy smile. When his face didn't crack at her humor, she sagged and sighed. "Are we trying for a do-over? Because you really suck at them."

Lines appeared between his eyebrows, cracking his stoic mask. "Is everything a joke to you?"

"Just this conversation. But I'm all about second, third and fourth chances. I like to get things right. Let's try this again." She stuck out a hand. "Hi. *I'm* Bella Fiore. Sorry about scaring you on the road earlier."

He gripped her hand and slowly pumped it. "Kyle Peters." No apologies for his rudeness. No "very nice to meet you" as he practically crushed her fingers.

"You always hold a girl's hand this tight?" she asked sweetly, squeezing right back. "I usually get taken out for dinner first."

He let go abruptly and took a step back. She folded her arms over her chest to keep from flexing her fingers. "I hope you realize this is a serious place of business," he said, his demeanor icing over. "Our clients expect a certain level of professionalism."

"I think I know how to deal with clients." Wow. Who'd sucked the fun out of him? Marco had warned her that Kyle was charming and quite the ladies' man. Well, whoever he'd been talking about, it wasn't this cheerless drill sergeant. She didn't care how hunky he was—the guy was a *cuzão*.

He settled the edge of the clipboard against his hard, flat stomach. "I've got you scheduled to teach a few of the free classes open to new and potential members. I have the last teacher's notes if you need them, but you can design the programs however you like." He handed her a sheet. Apparently, they were jumping right into things. Which would've been fine, except…well, she hadn't been sure what to expect.

This wasn't a Fiore studio run by her family and close friends—it was an official UFF gym, backed by one of the biggest MMA fight promoters in the world. What were the rules and expectations here? Were they stricter about how employees used their time?

"We'll also be hosting a booth at a local health and fitness fair on the first weekend of November. You'll be expected to take a shift, give demonstrations and do the setup and takedown."

She scanned the schedule Kyle had handed her and scowled. "What's 'Bootyfit'?"

"It's a class primarily for high-impact aerobics and core strengthening. It'll be your responsibility to pull together the program."

"And this—'Girlicious Foxy Boxing'?"

"Women's-only kickboxing. Noncombative striking, aerobic focused. Tito helps out in that class. You two can put your heads together and figure out how you'll teach it."

"Why didn't you call it aerobic kickboxing?"

"Because guys who are serious about fighting would be disappointed by the class and girls won't join it at all. These classes are meant to attract members outside our core demographic. I don't know if you noticed, but this is an MMA gym. That label doesn't inspire a lot of women to come through those doors."

"And nothing reels women in like a class that teaches them to shake their booty while men gawk at them from the weight room." Most women she knew would be happy to simply work out in a fun class. They didn't need to be reminded that they had to be *foxylicious* or *bootytastic* or *tittytacular* or whatever.

His look grew stony. "The classes are held in the upper studio. And you should know that there are strict rules about harassment in place here at Payette's. All my employees and clients are expected to behave appropriately. No double standards." His viciously stern tone made her flinch. Bella did not like being talked down to. She was on the verge of snapping back at him when, thankfully, Liz intervened.

"Boss? Everything okay?" She glanced between them questioningly.

Bella hadn't realized they were standing toe to toe like two growling pit bulls. Kyle broke away and rubbed tiny circles into his right temple. "It's fine. It's nothing."

The receptionist gave him a look like a mother threatening a time-out, then went back to her desk.

Bella let out a breath. Less than an hour in and she was already picking fights with the boss. She knew she was antagonizing Kyle partly because it was too easy to mess with someone that uptight. Kyle reminded her of her grandfather—as unsmiling and unyielding as a stone gargoyle. The guy had to have a funny bone somewhere beneath all that tightly wound muscle. She could practically see his high blood pressure throbbing through the veins on his corded neck. What he needed was a long vacation.

Or a good lay.

But as much as she wanted to shake him up, she couldn't keep poking the bear. Bella folded her hands behind her and bowed her head. If she wanted to work with the best wrestler in the biz, she had to dial it back. "I apologize. Again." She had a feeling she'd be doing that a lot with him. The thought grated. "As long as there are people taking the class, it doesn't matter what it's called."

"It's half-full now," he said tautly.

He ran through the rest of the schedule with her. She would teach four classes a week and give physical assessments and personal training sessions. The rest of the time she could spend training.

"Don't expect my guys to drop everything for

you," he warned. "Some have their own fights to train for and clients on the side. Do you have fights coming up?"

She'd been looking, but opponents in the women's 155-pound weight class were few and far between. "No."

"Then you won't be a priority. We focus on the clients with upcoming matches as we get closer to the dates."

And just like that, he'd dismissed her again. "I'm still looking for my next fight. But in the meantime, I'm happy to settle in here, learn the ropes." She tried for a smile but was sure she was baring her teeth at him.

Kyle nodded. "Good. I'll have Tito start conditioning with you."

"And then?"

"And then we'll see." He started to walk stiffly away, but paused and said over his shoulder, "I wasn't scared, you know."

"Scared?"

"When you came up to me on your bike. I wasn't scared of you. But you messed with my car. If you'd been a guy, I would've probably punched you in the face."

Bella tilted her chin up unapologetically, not in the least intimidated. "This is going to be a thing between us, isn't it?"

His look was stone-cold. "Just don't touch my car again."

AT THE END of the day, Bella opened the windows in her apartment to let in the damp night air. If she closed her eyes, she could almost pretend she was back in São Paulo. Of course, there it would be getting hotter as summer encroached while in New Orleans, the summer season was tapering off. The idea of living through two winters in one year kind of depressed her—not that winter in New Orleans would be like anything she'd experienced when she'd gone to university in Canada. She was grateful for that.

She checked her watch and right on time, the phone rang. She picked up.

"Querida, tudo bem?"

"I'm good, *Mamãe*." Her mother, Ana, had called every day since she'd arrived in New Orleans. "I started at Payette's today."

"Did you make any friends?"

"I suppose." Except for Kyle, she thought acerbically. But that had been partly her fault. *"Cómo está o Papai?"*

"Your father misses you, but Fulvio keeps him too busy to mope."

"Is Fulvio still mad?"

"Your grandfather?" Ana blew out a breath noisily. "Who knows? He hasn't said anything, but that's Fulvio. You know what he can be like when he doesn't get his way."

"I guess the silent treatment is better than the yelling treatment." Though Bella wasn't entirely certain that was true. They'd parted on terrible terms, and the guilt of storming out on him ate at her conscience. She loved her grandfather—he'd taught her almost everything she knew about fighting. But she couldn't let him dictate her future.

She asked after her brothers, and her mother went on at length about their various clients, fights and adventures in the gym. Bella was content to simply listen. She could tell Ana missed having her daughter around to talk to. She missed her mother, too. But Ana understood why she'd had to leave.

"So, did you get your driver's license yet?"

"I told you, my bike is enough. I didn't go through the trouble of shipping it here so that I could buy a car."

"No one in America rides bicycles. Some crazy idiot in an SUV is going to get you killed."

She thought about her encounter with Kyle and smiled to herself. "I'll be fine. My apartment is barely a thirty-minute ride from the gym. I rode everywhere back home, and you never complained."

"You never *heard* me complain is all. Worrying about you took years off my life."

"I wear a helmet. Besides, I face worse every time I spar."

"Don't remind me." She sighed. "I realize this is your dream, Bella, even if no one here approves. But I want you to know I love you and all I want is for you to be happy and safe."

"I can promise I'll be one of those things. But probably not both. Not by your definition."

"Bella…"

"I'm taking all the precautions. I never do anything I don't think I'm capable of. I was trained by the best."

After they hung up, Bella was restless. Her first day had been a paperwork and orientation kind of day, and while her brain was tired, her body wasn't. She got dressed and went for a walk.

She wasn't too far from Bourbon Street, so she pointed herself toward the district. As she meandered along the famous strip, she was surprised by the number of people out on a Monday night. Weaving through the crowd, it was hard to imagine what the weekend would look like.

She peeked into the bars as she passed, then walked into one that suited her—clean, classy, with modern furnishings and an extensive menu. TV screens showed sports highlights, a baseball game and, more importantly, an MMA fight.

She parked herself at the corner of the bar closest to the screen showing the fight. She ordered a bottle of beer. She didn't normally drink when she was training, but it didn't seem right to order water.

She nursed her drink as she watched the fight, studying the two lightweights' techniques. She knew of one of them—Alessander Mortensen, an up-and-comer who specialized in judo. He'd trained briefly with her brothers in São Paulo. His opponent, Mike Bourne, danced out of the other man's reach, striking and weaving, but not getting any significant hits in. The guy was afraid.

"Oh, c'mon!" she yelled at the screen. The match ended to a round of boos. Bourne had let the clock run out, evading Mortensen as long as possible, scoring points with cheap kicks to the shins. Sadly, she couldn't say that Mortensen was doing any better.

"I didn't know chicks watched this stuff." A man slid up next to her. He smelled like uncooked ground beef. "Can I buy you a drink?"

She barely spared him a glance. "No thanks. I already have one."

The man asked the bartender for two beers anyway. "What is it about these fights that chicks like? Two greased-up guys mounting each other? That's pretty gay."

She turned cold eyes toward him. He might have been okay looking in a certain light, but the words coming out of his mouth spoiled any such illusions. "*I* like watching the fights because it's what my family and I do for a living. And as for your homophobic comment, I won't even dignify that with a response. Now take your cheap-ass beers and go away. I'm trying to enjoy the fight."

He slid closer. "Aw, don't be like that. I didn't mean—"

"Read between the lines, asshole." She raised her voice so everyone in the place would hear. "You insulted me. You blew it. Now leave me alone."

"Hey, buddy." A presence as oppressive as a storm

front pushed into her personal space from behind. The hairs on Bella's neck rose. "Is there a problem?"

The beefy-smelling man snatched up his beers and grumbled, "Dyke bitch," as he shuffled off.

"We're good here," she ground out, keeping one eye on the man. "Just giving this creep his walking papers." She challenged him with a level look when he turned and glared, but his eyes canted to her protector and he moved on.

"Were you planning on starting a bar fight here tonight? You don't want to get banned before you've tried their shrimp po'boy sandwiches." Kyle took the guy's place next to her, staying close until the man made it back to his table.

"If he started something, I would've finished it." She took a long pull of her beer to soothe her nerves.

"I don't doubt it. But I'd hate to have to explain to your family why I had to bail you out of jail when you haven't been here a week."

"Sorry. But I won't pretend to be nice to jackasses for the sake of being polite, especially ones who talk to me like I'm a dumb piece of meat."

He chuckled. The sound was pleasant, even human. "I can see that. I think you made everyone in the room cup their balls." His eyes shone with admiration and a bit of nervousness. "Do me a favor, and just say thanks for the rescue to salve my male ego."

She studied him carefully. He must've had a few drinks in him because he seemed a lot more relaxed. His shoulders weren't hunched up around his ears, and the lines on his face weren't so deep. He was actually smiling. As he was now, she could sort of see why Marco had warned her against his lady-killer reputation. "Thanks." She toasted him with her bottle. "I owe you one."

He flagged down the bartender while she let her attention return to the match. She couldn't concentrate on the commentary, hyperaware of Kyle's elbow resting an inch from hers. She thought he was watching her, but she didn't dare look. "What are you doing here?" she asked finally.

"Besides protecting your honor?" He paused and nodded toward a booth. "I'm here with...friends."

She glanced at the table. Three petite coeds sipping cocktails with umbrellas in them chattered animatedly. Bella stifled a snort. "A little young, aren't they?"

He smirked. "A gentleman doesn't ask a lady her age."

"You might want to, in case the cops come around asking for ID."

His lips tilted in a half smile. "Jealous?"

She didn't respond. She didn't want to admit she'd been feeling kind of lonely since arriving in the States.

"Hey...do you want to join us?" Kyle asked as if reading her thoughts.

"No." She shook her head emphatically. "I'm going to finish this and see where the fight goes, then head home."

"If you change your mind…"

She waved him off. "Go on. The Powerpuff Girls need their juice."

He gathered up the drinks in his big hands. "Stay out of trouble."

"You, too, Coach. Don't let them stay out past their curfew."

He chuckled and went back to the table. Bella was in a better mood as she watched the rest of the fight.

She kept an inch of warm beer at the bottom of her bottle as the next fight started. She heard the girls with Kyle laughing and giggling. She didn't want to watch them, but they were loud and boisterous, drawing envious looks from all corners of the bar. The girls hung on Kyle's every word. The blonde looked especially into him, gazing doe-eyed at him.

The bartender put another open bottle in front of her.

She looked at him quizzically. "I didn't order this."

"It's on the house. I liked the way you handled that jerk earlier. I've been looking for a reason to refuse him service and kick him out." He crossed his thick arms over his barrel chest. "Sorry I didn't step in fast enough."

"No need to be sorry, Mr….?"

"Neal." They shook hands, and he nodded vaguely over his shoulder. "I can see you're really into the game."

"Oh, I'm actually watching the fight."

"I didn't mean the Yankees game." He inclined

his chin toward the table. "I mean Kyle. Must be at least once a week he comes in with a date or picks up some chick and leaves with them. I've got my money on the one in the pink sweater tonight. You?"

Bella wasn't sure why she felt such disappointment. She'd been warned about Kyle's reputation, after all. "The blonde," she said decisively. "Look at those puppy-dog eyes."

He polished the counter top, chuckling. "I'll be honest, when he came over here, I thought maybe you were a contender."

"Oh, we know each other. He's my wrestling coach."

"No kidding? You're training at Payette's?"

"I'm working there while I train. Kind of like an exchange program."

They chatted awhile about her background. Neal was more into boxing, but he seemed genuinely interested in her. Platonically, she was certain, if the wedding ring on his finger meant anything.

"Oh, damn." Neal turned in time to see two of the girls get up from the table and hug their blonde counterpart goodbye. A couple of minutes later, Kyle and the blonde left. Bella's gaze snagged his as he passed. He averted his eyes, almost shamefaced. "Looks like you were right."

"What can I say?" She took a long pull of her second beer as the door swung shut. "She seemed his type."

CHAPTER THREE

KYLE GULPED DOWN the extra large black coffee, head throbbing. He'd managed a few hours' sleep, but ugh, why had he agreed to do shots of peach schnapps, of all things? He should have stuck to bourbon, but Penny—or Jenny or Patty or whatever the blonde's name was—had said it was an old man's drink.

He pushed into Payette's and came face-to-face with Bella. She flashed blindingly white teeth. "Long night?"

"How late did *you* stay out?" he asked, deflecting her question. "I thought you said you were going home after you finished your drink."

She lifted a shoulder. "I wanted to see the Chen-DaSilva fight." Speculation reflected in her eyes, but she didn't ask the question he saw there.

Not that he would have answered. His sex life wasn't anyone's business.

He changed in his office, downed two extra-strength Tylenol, then went over the schedule. The loud rapping on his door made his head throb.

"Hey, boss." Wayne grinned, then winced, holding his jaw. "I'm back."

Kyle acknowledged him with a wave. "How was the dentist?"

"Awful. I swear they were drilling into my brain. They put me on some pretty strong painkillers. I thought I'd let you know."

"Sure you don't need an extra day?" He'd fully expected the boxing coach to call in sick. Wayne was getting on in years, after all, even if he didn't want to admit it.

"I heard Bella Fiore started yesterday. I wanted to meet her, make sure she stays on top of her stand-up game. Don't worry—I won't use any heavy machinery today." He headed off.

Kyle watched from his office, tensing as the former heavyweight boxer introduced himself to Bella, shaking hands and talking enthusiastically with her.

He forced himself to look away. He didn't know why he was being so nosy. It wasn't as if Wayne would ever do anything to make anyone feel unwelcome. He was really a sweet guy despite his hulking frame and nickname, "Crusher."

In fact, if there was anyone he had to worry about, it was Bella. Thinking about how she'd dealt with that jerk at the bar last night, he should probably warn the boxing coach about her. He should probably warn all the guys....

What are you, their mom? Everyone knew the potential consequences of flirting with coworkers. It would be embarrassing and condescending for everyone if he had to reiterate the policy.

As the week went on, though, he became convinced he'd have to sit down with Bella and talk to her about *her* conduct. Besides being a very attractive woman and the first new female employee at Payette's in over a year, she was effusive to a fault.

She was too eager to please, dropping whatever she was doing to help a client or trainer. She'd step right up to clients that weren't hers and correct their techniques and forms without being asked. She boldly approached regulars and offered her training services. She didn't seem to understand that a lot of these guys came in for a simple workout, or else had trainers already. People might misinterpret her intentions.

Sooner or later, she'd start stepping on toes. If she scooped one of the other trainers' clients or had a misunderstanding with someone…well, he didn't want to deal with the interoffice fallout. He'd have a talk with her.

On Friday, she came to his office to show him the programs she'd put together for her classes. He only half listened to her as she outlined the exercises.

"So, with Orville and Tito doing conditioning with me, and Wayne filling in with sparring and stand-up, I was wondering if we could schedule some mat time on Wednesdays and Fridays."

"I'm sorry?" He'd only caught the word *we,* and it'd jolted him.

"I came here so you could train me, Kyle?" Her

prompt rose in a question. "I arranged the schedule with the others so we'd have time—"

"I'm kind of busy with these new recruitment programs," he interrupted, tapping the binder of marketing plans on his desk. "The week after next we can start."

Her expression closed, and her mouth firmed into a tight line. He thought she'd leave. People usually did when he put his foot down.

"No." She placed her notes on his desk and primly settled her palms on top, pressing down firmly. "That's not acceptable."

"I'm sorry, but that's—"

"Not in our agreement. I was promised one-on-one time with you. I've been here a week and you've barely given me the time of day." Her dark eyes held his, hard and unblinking as a jade statue's. "So, what's the problem, Coach? Did I say something to offend you?"

He took a deep breath. "I'm concerned about the way you conduct yourself around here."

She absorbed his words slowly before narrowing her eyes. "How's that?"

"You're too forward." It wasn't what he'd meant to say, but now that it had come out, he was committed to it. "You can't go around offering your training services to every single client. Most of the regulars already have coaches. They don't need you to confuse them, and it won't help you get along with the others. On top of that, you've been greeting clients at the door. That's Liz's job. It's what she's paid to do. You've only been here a week and I'm concerned you don't know enough about how things work here to give them the information they need."

Her blazing green eyes seared a hole right through him. "I think I said hello to two people who walked in. *Two.* And that was only because Liz was in the bathroom and they were standing there, looking lost. I didn't see any of the guys rushing out to greet them, so *I* said hello. Now you're telling me that's wrong?"

"You should've gotten a senior staff member. But that's not the only thing." He took a deep breath and plunged forward. "You're too friendly with the guys. Some of them might get the wrong idea."

He only realized how bad it sounded after the words left his mouth.

Her voice pitched down an octave. *"Excuse me?"*

"This is a gym full of guys, and some clients get it in their heads that… Well, see, there was this one guy who tried to ask Liz out, but she wouldn't date him…"

"And you blame Liz for that?"

"No!" He massaged his scalp. He was making a mess of this. "All I'm saying is, you're a…a woman, and if you act friendly…"

She slowly leaned forward in her seat. "I'm friendly because I'm actually a nice person. I talk to clients because I want them to get the most out of their time here. That's how a Fiore gym is run.

We learn from having lots of different trainers, lots of variety and techniques. We don't isolate every single student and tell them they're only allowed to work with one person. We certainly don't isolate the women from the men because we don't trust what they'll do to each other."

"Look, it came out totally wrong, and I apologize. Of course we want diversity in our trainers and clientele. That's half the reason you're here. But this is a professional gym. Some of the guys work on hourly fees, and they can't risk losing a client. I'd just appreciate it if you stepped back a bit."

She sat back and rolled her eyes. "No wonder you're losing customers."

He flinched as though she'd slapped him. "You need to remember—" *your place* "—that you're a guest trainer here. Temporary. Just because you've been doing this a long time at your family's studio doesn't mean you know what you're doing here."

She studied him coolly, glass-green eyes slicing him to ribbons. "You don't want me here, do you?"

A hard lump formed in his throat. "That's not it."

"You obviously don't like me."

"That's not true." And it wasn't. He simply didn't know how to handle her. Her temperament, her energy, her drive—they were all good things professionally speaking, but they were nothing he was prepared to deal with. And that was what really bothered him.

Bella's words were as sharp and precise as a scalpel. Her composure was unexpected and it threw him off balance even more. "I came here to train with *you,* Kyle. Not with your staff, not in your gym. I came for *you.* But if you can't work with me, then all you have to do is say so, and I won't waste any more of my time or yours."

"That's not what I want." He scrubbed his hands over his face and took a deep breath. "I've really messed this up."

She waited expectantly.

His chair creaked as he swung it to the left, tilting back with a long sigh. "I don't want you to go. I do have a lot to teach you, and I think you have a lot to teach our clients. You're a talented fighter, and you can bring a lot to this gym. I wouldn't have agreed to have you here otherwise."

"Except that I'm a Fiore."

"I won't lie to you. Your family name and reputation does have some draw. Since we posted that picture of you up on our website, we've had twice as many cold calls from guys who want to train here."

"And still you think I'm only here to flirt with your employees and steal clients?"

He grimaced. "I didn't mean for it to sound that way."

She didn't look impressed. "Answer me this. Will you or won't you make time to train me?"

He wiped a damp palm over his mouth. "I can spare you two hours this afternoon."

She nodded stiffly. "All right. Are we done?"

For now. "Yeah."

Her chair scraped back loudly, and she marched out of his office. The knot in Kyle's gut loosened. That had not gone the way he'd hoped. And he'd come off sounding like a complete asshole.

You let a girl push you around, his father's voice mocked from the back of his mind.

Kyle ground his teeth and pressed his thumbs against his closed eyelids. Whatever his issues, he couldn't afford to have Bella leaving with a negative impression of what Payette's had to offer.

He'd work with her. His job depended on it.

His sanity, however, was another matter.

LIZ'S JAW DROPPED. "He *said* that?"

"Maybe I'm making it sound like more than what he meant, and for his part, he did apologize, but I'm pretty sure he meant to tell me he didn't want me talking to, like, anyone." Bella sipped her iced tea, trying to wash away the bitterness Kyle's words had left behind. Liz had invited her out for after-work drinks. They were at The Spot, the gastropub she'd visited on Monday night. The other trainers were currently shooting pool, giving the girls a chance to chat. Kyle wasn't among the group.

"For the record, I don't have any problem with you talking to clients. I think everyone should take more initiative like you did," Liz said, and gave a disgruntled sigh. "So Kyle finally worked with you this afternoon?"

"He did, but mostly, he had me doing conditioning exercises. We never got around to any mat work." He'd been a taskmaster when it came to those endurance drills. They nearly had her puking a couple times, but she'd held it together.

"He does tend to go heavy on the endurance and strength training, but that's the way he works. I'm sure he'll get you wrestling soon."

Bella hoped so. After today's talk, she wasn't sure Payette's—or Kyle—was a good fit for her.

Neal, the bartender, set a plate of onion rings on the table in front of them. "For you ladies, on the house."

"Careful, Neal, or I'm going to start getting ideas." Bella winked at him, and Liz laughed as they reached for the plate.

He grinned. "I'll admit I came with an ulterior motive." They invited him to sit, and he took a chair. "A friend of mine runs a center for at-risk youth not too far from Payette's. She's looking for someone to come in and give her kids self-defense classes. I thought of you and said I'd ask if you're interested."

Bella hesitated. "I'd love to…but it's not my call to make. I'll have to ask Kyle." She looked to Liz, who gave her an affirming nod. "There are insurance questions and a whole lot of other issues he'd have to deal with."

"Here's my friend's card. You two can hash it out. I hope you'll do it, though—I read up on some of the stuff your family's done. I think you'd be perfect for this."

No pressure or anything, she thought as she pocketed the business card, and Neal headed back for the bar. She'd never stop being a Fiore, it seemed. But then, she'd never been able to turn down a call for help. If she could improve a few lives even just a little bit through martial arts, then there was no reason to deny this request.

The guys finished their pool game and joined the ladies, then ordered food. Tito and Orville sat on Bella's right in the semicircular booth, while Wayne perched on a tiny-looking bistro chair on the other side of the table. She liked the old boxer. His upturned smile and the lone furrow on his broad brow bracketed his cheerful countenance. They chatted about the upcoming UFF fights and the busy weekend ahead.

The door opened. Kyle walked in, and Bella's skin broke out in goose bumps. The guys all looked up and waved. She turned to give him a polite smile. Instead of joining them, though, he went to the bar and sat on his own.

"He doesn't drink with you guys?"

"Nah, not anymore. He used to, but then..." Orville trailed off.

"Then what?"

"He had one too many and banged our old yoga instructor."

"Tito!" Liz exclaimed.

"What? She's gonna hear about it sooner or later." He bit into his chicken wrap, eyes cast down.

Bella wasn't sure she wanted to hear more, but Liz explained quickly, "It was a bad scene. Kyle had the no-fraternization policy put into place after that."

"And turned into the biggest prick I know."

"Tito…" Liz pleaded.

"Hey, I like the guy. I really do. But he's nowhere near as fun as he used to be."

"Because he won't be your wingman anymore?"

"It's not that. For one, he doesn't hang with us. And whenever a girl walks into the gym, he acts like we're all gonna try to eat her or something." Orville sighed. "Man, Karla really did a number on him."

"We shouldn't be talking about this." Liz darted a nervous look at Kyle. "He's sitting right there."

But the guys had hooked onto the subject. "It wasn't his fault. Karla was bat-shit crazy," Wayne defended the boss valiantly.

Bella leaned forward, careful not to look too interested. "So…this Karla used to work at Payette's?"

"Karla taught yoga and Pilates and some of the other women's classes," Orville explained. "She was also a blue belt in krav maga. Really tough lady, like a blonde Xena on steroids.

"Anyhow, she was one of the gym's first hires—helped Kyle build and open the place. And I have to say, she was a good teacher. So we're celebrating our first-year anniversary at the gym after hours.

Champagne's flowing, music's playing. And Kyle, wouldn't you know, is there without a date—"

"Which is like showing up without a leg for Kyle," Tito added.

"—so what does he do? He starts hitting on Karla. They went home together, and she came back the next day in his car wearing the same clothes she'd been wearing the night before."

"Awkwaaaard," Tito drawled.

"After that, it got super weird. That office door was closed a lot when they were in there together, and we all had to pretend like we didn't know what was going on."

"And we didn't!" Liz insisted. "They could've just been talking about private stuff." Orville didn't let up, though, and she made a noise of exasperation.

"Two or three weeks later, it stopped. Things got arctic between them. My best guess is that he dumped her, and Karla didn't like that."

Wayne took up the story. "She started showing up to work drunk. She picked fights with all of the other trainers, harassed the clients. Anything to get Kyle's attention. One day, he takes her into the office, closes the door. I was standing right by the corner, and one of the blinds was half-open. I peeked in to see if they were…well." His face turned pink. "But then, she, like, punches herself. Wham! And then she screams and comes out holding her face and saying that Kyle hit her."

Bella flinched. "What?"

"'Course, I knew she was lying. We all did. You couldn't make the guy kill a bug." Wayne shook his head.

"Bitch be crazy," Tito said, then glanced at Liz, who glared daggers at him. "What?"

Bella saw his point but balked. She glanced at Kyle. Belts and training didn't amount to anything if you were caught off guard or you were emotional. Anything could happen. Though, Kyle was trained to fight, too. And if Karla had been in love with the guy…well, love did crazy things to people. It didn't mean *she'd* been crazy.

But then, Wayne had seen what had happened. He had no reason to lie.

She hated the doubt that nagged her.

Orville picked up where Wayne had left off. "He fired her then and there and called the cops when she refused to leave. See, if he'd hit her, you'd think she would've said something to the police, but she didn't. Anyway, we thought that was the end, but then she started calling every day. And she'd leave little gifts on the gym's doorstep—flowers and cookies and stuffed animals with notes saying 'I'm sorry'—"

"Guys, let's not talk about this anymore, okay?" Liz massaged the flesh between her eyes.

Orville and Wayne both looked like they wanted to say more, but they sipped their drinks furtively.

"If you ask me, it was a matter of time and statistics," Tito said. "Player's gonna be played eventually."

Bella's gaze drifted back to Kyle. He was talking to a pretty brunette at the bar.

So. He'd had a relationship with a coworker that had ended badly. It explained why he was so prickly about her being friendly, she supposed.

Not that it excused his behavior.

He could rest assured that she wouldn't get too friendly with *him*.

CHAPTER FOUR

BELLA GAVE IT a couple of days before she broached the subject of the Touchstone youth center's request for self-defense classes to Kyle. She was still sore about their exchange on Friday, but she wasn't about to let that interfere with her training. She had to remain professional.

She'd called Reta Schwartz, Neal's friend at the youth center, and listened to her ideas for classes to offer the young people who frequented the center. The social worker wanted something fun and practical to help boost their confidence. The center didn't have the space or equipment, so Bella said she'd ask Kyle if they could host the classes at Payette's.

"It would be a great opportunity for everyone involved," she told Kyle when she finally sat down with him. "We could do it in the evenings, right after the women's boot camp class."

He hesitated. "What kind of compensation are we talking?"

"Compensation? Kyle, this would be entirely pro bono. The center doesn't have money to throw around." He grimaced, and she continued, "You can write it off. Community outreach programs like this are vital to developing relationships with potential future clients, plus they're a great PR opportunity."

He pressed his palms together and rested his lips against them as if he might breathe patience into his cupped hands. "In theory, it sounds like a great idea, but as much as I'd love to take this on, we're already suffering from declining memberships. If we start inviting random street kids into Payette's, this place stops being a world-class MMA facility for serious fighters and turns into the local Y."

"That won't happen as long as the teaching standards are high. These kids will see that learning here is a privilege. We have to offer them something worth sticking around for, worth telling others about."

Kyle rubbed his forehead. He looked so much older when he did that. "I'm not sure I can convince any of the guys to run this class. They're busy enough...."

"I can take charge," she volunteered, sensing his crumbling resistance. "If you're not comfortable with that, I'm happy to take a co-teaching role, though if anyone leads this class, it should be you. We can put together a basic self-defense curriculum, mix it up with a few beginner Muay Thai and boxing lessons."

He regarded her with interest. "You're really into this."

"My grandfather Fulvio used to drive around the streets and hand his card out to kids in tough neighborhoods. He wanted to keep them out of gangs, get them to channel their anger into something constructive. The ones that came usually stayed and made something of themselves. It was Fulvio's way of doing something for the community. Plus, he got some of the most brilliant fighters off the streets."

She didn't mention that she thought this would be a good opportunity for her and Kyle to work together toward a common goal. As many times as she'd extended an olive branch, she'd also swatted him with it. She had to mend the rift between them if she was ever going to get that wrestling training she'd come here for.

"How'd they even afford the classes?" Kyle asked. "If they're street kids, I mean."

"Scholarships. Or he'd make them work their lessons off. He always figured something out. The money wasn't that important to him. All he cared about was the boys." She sat forward. "Kyle, if we want to get people to see that Payette's isn't just another gym, we need to reach out to them."

Kyle nodded. "All right. Let's do it. I'll lead the classes, but I want you there, too."

IT DIDN'T TAKE them long to put the hour-long class together. Reta had fifteen students signed up right away with a waiting list of ten more.

They started the class the following Wednesday. Six girls and nine boys ranging from age fourteen to twenty-two had signed up. Many of them didn't have proper gym clothes. Kyle handed out Payette's T-shirts to them as makeshift uniforms. In most cases, it was better than the clothes they had.

Bella watched as Kyle greeted everyone, speaking with the comfort and ease of someone used to interviews and large audiences. He joked around with the students, but his stance and the strong line of his back and shoulders told everyone he wasn't going to tolerate bullshit or goofing off. She wondered where he'd been storing this charming, confident, easygoing version of himself.

She surveyed the students. Most of them looked eager to learn, listening raptly as Kyle recited the gym rules. Her eye caught on one girl huddled in the far left corner with her knees drawn up to her chin, picking at her cuticles, eyes darting around as if someone was going to steal the mat out from under her.

"What's her story?" she asked Reta discreetly. The head of the youth program glanced over.

"That's Shawnese. She's…a special case."

"Special how?"

Reta hesitated. "She has trust issues."

Bella read between the lines and nodded. "I'll keep a close eye on her."

They went through warm-ups and conditioning— jumping jacks, pushups, burpees. Bella watched as Shawnese halfheartedly followed along. She sidled up next to her and smiled. "Hey."

The young woman turned a suspicious eye on her. "What do you want?"

"Nothing. Is it okay if I stand here with you? There isn't enough room on the other side."

She shrugged.

With Bella there, Shawnese followed along more closely. When Kyle told them to break up into pairs, Bella immediately partnered with her.

The exercise was to show the difference in strength using open and closed hands. One person would rest their arm over the other person's shoulder while they tried to bend it at the elbow. Invariably, the open-handed method always stayed straight.

"I don't get this," Shawnese said as she pulled at Bella's arm. The two of them stood eye to eye, but Bella easily had twenty pounds on the younger woman. "How can an open hand be stronger if people punch with closed fists?"

"There are different schools of thought with different martial arts forms, but we're teaching self-defense. Look." She held out her upturned hand. "If you strike out with the heel of your palm, you'll risk less injury to your own hand." She slowly pushed the hand out. "Even if you don't know what you're doing and you miss the bridge of a guy's nose, look at the damage you can do. Fingers in the eyes. Pushing the guy's head backward. Palm to their muzzle. You can grab their hair. Lots of things you can do with an open hand. Closed—" she made a fist "—and you cut off those opportunities."

Shawnese tilted her head, looking at her own hands as she flexed her fingers open and closed.

"The main thing," Bella emphasized, "is to get away. The best way to help yourself out of a situation is to walk away from it."

"Dunno if that's gonna be possible," Shawnese muttered.

"We're just giving you the basics. If you have questions, or you want to learn something specific, just ask." Bella hoped the young woman would do exactly that.

By the end of class, Shawnese seemed much more receptive to Kyle's instruction and to the prospect of more lessons.

"You did a great job," Reta said. "I'm kind of shocked Shawnese opened up to you so fast."

That was opening up? Reta must have read the look on Bella's face, because she chuckled. "Seriously, when she first came to the center, she barely said a word to anyone. Just sat in the corner to stay warm and safe. She tries to hide it and act tough— it's part of the armor. I think she's said more to you today than to anyone else all week."

After the students had gone, Bella went to Kyle. "That seemed to go really well. You were great."

He smiled modestly, dimples flashing in the corners of his mouth. Bella was struck by how much it changed his face. A little buzz zipped through her. In that brief glimpse, she saw the triumphant Olympic gold medalist, the heartbreaker playboy and the carefree youth she'd seen in old training footage. "You, too. Your assisting really helped move things along. The students show promise," he said. "Thanks for sticking by. I noticed you were spending some extra time with that one girl."

"Her name's Shawnese. Reta says she's got some trust issues. I thought it'd be a good idea to stay close to her. In a class of fifteen, there's always going to be one odd man out, and there's nothing worse than being the last person picked."

"Let's make sure we diversify when we pair them up," Kyle said. "It'll be good to get them to mingle."

"Good idea." She was almost certain this was the first time they'd agreed on something. It made her feel good.

"I know it's late," Kyle said, glancing at the clock, "but if you're free now, we could spend an hour on the mats."

"Absolutely." She nearly tripped on her own feet as she hurriedly stripped out of her Payette's T-shirt so she could work in her rash guard. Thanks to the class she was already warmed up. She stretched and shook out all her muscles while Kyle pulled off his own T-shirt.

Holy—

Bella froze as she caught the rippling expanse of his back. She'd seen him in videos wearing a wrestling singlet, but shirtless with an extra seven years was an entirely different matter. She knew all the technical names for the groups of bunching muscles—trapezius, latissimus dorsi, rhomboid major—but all she could think of was the lumps and wrinkles they would create beneath a satin blanket.

He grabbed a sleeveless black V-neck workout top from a gym bag and pulled it over his head, but not before she got an eyeful of his chest. She couldn't help but wonder what those pectorals would feel like.

"Okay, so you've probably got all the basics. I've seen your fights, and I think you have at least some techniques down."

"Let's not skip anything, Coach. Teach me the way you were taught."

Something flashed across Kyle's face. She wasn't even sure she'd seen it, but she thought it might have been resentment. He set his feet apart. "Okay. Show me your square stance."

Bella planted her feet shoulder-width apart, head up, knees slightly bent and elbows tucked at her sides. Kyle gave her a light shove to test her balance. Warmth snaked through her.

"Good. Now show me staggered."

She shifted her right foot back and lowered herself farther. "That's a little too low. You're way off balance, see?" He pushed her side to side, and she stumbled as she tried to stabilize herself.

"Well, I'm not going to stay in this position, am I?" Of course, it wasn't only his push that had tipped her off balance. "I thought the idea was to drive forward and attack. Like this." She lunged at Kyle and crashed into his middle, wrapping her arms around his waist and dragging him down. He was solid and warm, exactly as she'd imagined. And though they'd never sparred, this felt comfortably familiar.

He fell to his butt as she climbed on top of his chest. She was easily fifty pounds lighter than he was but kept him effectively pinned. She'd only managed that twice with her brothers. Heady triumph filled her as he struggled.

"Get off me!" Kyle roared.

She leaped off. Had she hurt him? He scrambled to his feet and took four big steps away.

"I'm sorry, I didn't feel you tapping out—"

He gave her such a nasty look she snapped her mouth shut. "Don't ever do that again," he snarled. "We don't have matches without refs, and we don't attack people who aren't ready."

"I didn't mean—"

"Lesson's over. Practice your stances. You don't have the basics down at all."

"Kyle—"

She watched him stalk off. She kicked at the air. *Porra!* She wasn't going to get anything right around him, was she?

HADRIAN BLACKWELL WHIPPED his cell phone onto the ground, and the pieces of shattered plastic case scattered across the hardwood floor. He forked his fingers through his hair and grabbed fistfuls at his temples, ready to tear it out.

Soft footsteps alerted him he was no longer alone in his home office.

"Babe? Something wrong?"

He looked up and his heart skipped a beat. He would never get used to seeing her like this—Quinn Bourdain in a silky cream negligee, her red-gold hair tumbling around her shoulders, barefoot and free of makeup toddling around his house. The sight of her nibbling on her lower lip worriedly made him ashamed of his violent outburst.

"I just got a call from Wendell McAvoy." He stooped to gather the pieces of the phone. "He's out. Torn ACL."

Quinn's hazel eyes snapped into focus and she straightened. "That's official?"

"Doctor said he'll be in recovery for months."

She left the office in a flutter of silk. Hadrian shook his head and followed her to the bedroom, where she was already pulling on her bra, panties and socks. She cradled her cell phone between her shoulder and cheek.

"Jason. Yeah, it's me. McAvoy's out of the UFF anniversary fight. ACL injury. Can you make room?" She paused, casting her speculative gaze on Hadrian. "No, I'm thinking more like a quarter page. Let me see what I can get first. I'll call you back."

"Do we really have to do this now?" Hadrian groaned.

She pulled one leg through her jeans. "I have to pay the rent somehow."

"That wouldn't be an issue if you just…" He trailed off at her pointed look and raked his fingers through his hair again. For months, he'd been asking Quinn to move in with him and quit her job, but she'd refused. She loved being a sports reporter on the MMA beat, even though it frequently put them on opposite sides of the table. Seeing her scramble back into work mode, so eager to leave their bubble of bliss, made him want to tie her down. Preferably to the bed.

"Stop, stop, stop." He took her by the wrists as she reached for her T-shirt. "What's the rush?"

"You don't want me to interview you topless, do you?" A single, plucked eyebrow arched. "You wouldn't be altogether there if I did."

"Hey, I've had to wheel and deal with guys running around with their junk hanging out in the locker room. I think I can handle a little boob."

"'Little'?" She feigned outrage and placed her hands on her hips, making her chest jut forward. Of course, Hadrian had seen bigger. But he opted for the politically correct response.

"No, perfect." He tried to give those perfects a squeeze. She evaded him.

"Sorry, babe. Mood's gone, and I've got a story to chase."

He moaned. "Damn it, I shouldn't have answered that phone."

"Told you so." She grabbed a pen and notepad

from her overnight bag then turned on a digital voice recorder. "Okay, so McAvoy's out of the big tenth anniversary matchup?"

He sighed. He should've asked her to go home and change into her reporter's outfit—the ugly almost ten-year-old burgundy pantsuit and white button-up shirt she'd been wearing to UFF press gigs since she'd started her career. That suit was as effective as a chastity belt.

He tore his eyes from her jeans and bra combo, and turned his back to her, mustering up his public voice. "The word from the McAvoy camp is that Wendell suffered a serious ACL injury and will be in recovery for at least six months."

"Do you have a replacement in mind?"

"Gimme a break, Quinn, I heard about this exactly thirty seconds ago."

Lips pursed, she waited.

"Fine. We're working on finding an appropriate match against Darren Dodge." He'd be making a lot of calls that weekend. He always had backups for the main event, but he'd already used four of them to fill other holes on the card.

"This is the fifth fighter to drop out of this event. People have said the anniversary is cursed."

"Off the record, people are idiots." When Quinn gave him her "be serious" look, he went with the company line. "Injuries happen, and the health and welfare of my fighters is important. A torn ACL is nothing to take lightly."

"But the last three cancellations—DePolo's doping scandal, Vasquez's battery and assault charge against McCaffrey, Brown's controversial remarks about—"

"I read the news, Quinn."

She sucked in a lip and plowed on. "These infringements are indicative of something more pervasive and widespread in the UFF. You've got bigger prizes, more at stake, and more fighters and gyms competing with each other every day. Is the increasing pressure to perform driving fighters to justify unsportsmanlike behavior?"

Hadrian stared at her, trying to sort out her eye-crossing question. "That's a lot of ten-dollar words to be throwing around on a Saturday, Quinn. Sounds like you've been holding on to that question for a while. When were you planning to spring it on me?"

"Sunday night, probably." She shrugged. "It's just business, babe."

He stuffed down his irritation and the resentment that her answer had tweaked. "I have a deep respect for these fighters," he said, clearing his throat, "and I put all my confidence in them to behave appropriately. Whatever beef they have with each other, whatever they're doing to their bodies—legal or otherwise—that's their deal. I can't control them every second of every day. They know the rules. They should know how to conduct themselves."

"But you have to admit, you've made the stakes such that the UFF is the only game in town."

"That's not true. There are dozens of other leagues—"

"That can barely compete, and you know it. That's why you've been buying them up, isn't it?"

He threw his hands in the air. "I thought this weekend was supposed to be about having fun."

She shut off her recorder. "I'm not attacking you, Hadrian. I'm asking a valid question."

"Yeah, but why the third degree? What story are you working on, exactly?"

"It's a feature," she said vaguely. "I'm freelancing it out."

"About what?"

"I have an idea, but it's all about research right now. I don't have a bigger picture yet. Just some ideas. And I won't say any more until I know exactly what I'm going to write about."

He set his jaw, eyes slipping back down to her chest. If he didn't know better, he could have sworn she'd planned the whole topless inquisition. Not that he really minded.

"Will you stay for dinner?" he asked, trying hard to keep hope out of his tone.

"Better not. I have to get to the office, make some calls and see who has the pulse on McAvoy." She pulled her T-shirt on and grabbed her running shoes. "Besides, you're going to be preoccupied, too, finding a replacement. If I finish early, maybe I'll come back, okay?" She gave him a peck on the cheek and left without saying goodbye.

Hadrian sighed. Well, there went his weekend.

CHAPTER FIVE

KYLE WATCHED THROUGH his office windows as Bella shadowboxed, pummeling her invisible opponent with the grace and power of a pro. She had perfect form—Wayne had praised her discipline and skill—and what she lacked in strength she made up for with finesse.

Something she obviously lacked when it came to working with him.

He knew he'd overreacted the other day when she'd tackled him. He'd lain in bed awake—which was no new thing—mad at himself and at her. Of course, it was always dangerous pulling stupid stunts like that. She should've known better. But he wasn't about to admit that the real reason he was so pissed off ran much deeper. No, she'd been in the wrong.

Sometime later, Orville joined her, along with Tito, and they began a few grappling and take-down exercises. He noticed she had no difficulty or awkwardness working with either of the men. Apparently, things only got weird when she worked with him.

And whose fault is that? His self-recriminating thoughts always took his father's berating tone. *Stop trying to put the blame on everyone else. This is all in your stupid head.*

He put down his file and rubbed his tired eyes. He had to try harder. He'd been unfair to her, and he was treating her like…well, not kindly, and it was entirely *his* problem.

The phone rang. Liz rarely transferred calls that weren't important, so it was with some trepidation that he picked up. "Hello?"

"Hey, killer." The soft, husky voice that beckoned from the other end of the line had him sitting up. He'd know that siren's call anywhere. "How's it hanging?"

"Bree Hannigan." A broad smile spread across his lips. "I thought you were in Australia."

"I was. I'm in California right now, doing some photo shoots for Chanel."

"Fancy. How are you?"

"Lonely," she whimpered. "Henri and I broke up a few months ago."

"I'm sorry to hear that." He wasn't. Not really. Bree had followed the photographer to the other side of the world almost two years ago. She'd been crazy about the guy.

They caught up with each other's lives. Bree told him about the dozens of exotic places she'd visited, complaining about how she'd had to live out of a suitcase and eat out all the time.

"Woe is me," Kyle teased. "Touring the world first-class as a fashion model? What a trial."

"You laugh, but you have no idea. All I really want is to relax and unwind in a big, comfy bed with a big, comfy man. Speaking of, I'm going to be in New Orleans in February. I was hoping we could… get comfy together."

Heat rolled lazily south through his chest and lower. The last time they'd been together, they'd spent most of that time in her hotel room. It had been an unforgettable weekend. "I'd like that…."

A sliver of doubt pricked his libido, and he hedged. His performance of late had been subpar. He didn't want to risk a misfire. "Let me know what your schedule's going to be like. Things have been busy here."

"Too busy for me?" He could hear her pout. "Kyle, have you been working too hard? You know stress only makes you tighten up."

How she managed to make everything she said sound like sex, Kyle didn't know. His gaze snagged on Bella as she tackled Orville, throwing her legs around his waist and dragging him to the ground. "I'll make room in my schedule."

"Good. I'll see you soon."

They hung up. Kyle was still smiling, but inside, threads of anticipation and dread tangled into a tight, messy knot.

BELLA SANK HER fists into the heavy bag, driving frustration into the leather and sand with each blow.

Wayne made her take a break. "You're going at it a little hard today. Everything okay?"

"I want to get a good workout." She took long, deep, calming breaths as she shook out her limbs. She was still frustrated by what had happened with Kyle. He'd been avoiding her since that incident, and part of her couldn't blame him. She'd behaved irresponsibly—Fulvio would've turned her over and spanked her if she'd tackled an unprepared teacher the way she'd attacked Kyle. She couldn't even say why she'd done it—it was that reckless impulse to mess with him she couldn't control.

Still, she didn't deserve the silent treatment.

Obviously Kyle had issues, and that thing between him and Karla was probably at the root of it. But it wasn't as if she was going to put him into a compromising position and get him in trouble. Anyhow, how was she supposed to grapple with other men under his rules? She couldn't jeopardize her training because Kyle was afraid of cooties.

At least the other guys had been generous with their time. Tito and Orville both took turns working with her, and Wayne had given her some terrific tips on her footwork. If it wasn't for them, she might have packed up and left a week ago.

"Excuse me, are you Bella Fiore?"

A man in white shirtsleeves flashed a smile big enough to carry a logo. His thin black tie was loosened and he carried his dark gray suit jacket slung across one shoulder. She got the distinct impression he had to make a real effort to look that casual. He pulled his hand out of his pocket and handed her a business card. "Ryan Holbrooke. I'm a fight manager and agent."

She wiped her arm across her sweaty brow and took the card with a gloved hand. "Is there something I can help you with, Mr. Holbrooke?"

"Call me Ryan, please. I'd heard you'd come from Brazil to train here and I wanted to stop by and meet you in person. I'm a big fan. I was hoping we could grab a drink sometime and discuss what your future might look like."

She scratched her nose. "I appreciate the offer, but my family's never used managers or agents. We take care of our own careers and book our own fights."

"Oh, so you have a fight coming up?"

She bit her lip. "Well, no…"

"Because I happen to know of an upcoming event, and you're exactly what their card needs."

She gave him a skeptical once-over. On the surface everything about him seemed legit, but he gave off a vibe she couldn't quite put her finger on. "What's the fight?"

"I won't lie, it's local. Kind of small, but it's a well-stacked league. Ever hear of Fury Fights?"

"Vaguely."

"Well, they do a convention and exhibition card

mid-November. Your opponent's from Kansas—
Betty The Hammer."

"Yeah, I know of Betty Heimer," Bella said. She'd
fought and lost against one of Bella's opponents a
couple years back.

Ryan nodded. "I've got plenty more details. I'd be
happy to discuss them with you."

He was earnest, and he seemed open. It wouldn't
hurt to talk. If nothing else, she'd get free drinks.

They agreed on a time and place, and then Ryan
left with a wave.

"Was that Ryan Holbrooke I saw walk out?" Tito
asked.

"Yeah. Do you know him?"

"He's a sports agent. He works with a lot of MMA
fighters and boxers. You were talking to him?"

"He wants me to meet him for drinks. Says he
might have a fight for me."

"Huh. Interesting." Tito folded his arms.

"What? You don't think I should?"

"No, no. He's an okay agent, I guess. He's helped
get his clients signed with some pretty big sponsors."

"I hear a 'but' in there."

Tito lifted one thick shoulder. "It's nothing personal. For me, anyhow."

"But it's personal for someone…like Kyle?" she
ventured.

His lips flattened out. "They have a *thing*."

Bella scoffed. Were they in high school or something? Regardless, talking with Ryan Holbrooke

shouldn't be any concern of Kyle's. If he had issues, he could bring them up with her. He was good at that.

"Do me a favor. Be careful around Ryan," Tito warned. "He's a smooth one."

RYAN HOLBROOKE WAS smooth, all right. He met her at a swank restaurant in the Garden District where they started with drinks at the bar, then, as their conversation lengthened, moved to the restaurant for dinner. If she didn't know any better, she would've thought it was a date.

She had to admit she was flattered by his attention, how he hung on her every word. Then again, if he wanted to snag her as a client, she didn't expect him to ignore her the way Kyle did.

She'd done a quick internet search to check Ryan Holbrooke's credentials, and he seemed to be the genuine article. He was good-looking, too, with flirty blue eyes, jet-black hair and a cocksure smile. He knew MMA, and had even competed for a while, so they didn't run out of things to talk about. He didn't challenge her or make her work too hard to like him. She'd forgotten what it was like to be with someone who appreciated her for who she was rather than someone who tried to mold her into something she wasn't.

Ryan paused and regarded her frankly. "I have to ask…how is it a girl like you is still single? You are single, aren't you?"

Her cheek ticked. "I'm not comfortable talking about it." It wasn't that the story made her particularly sad, but she'd just met Ryan, and sharing this kind of intimacy with him didn't feel…natural. Besides, it wasn't any of his business.

"I'm sorry. I didn't mean to upset you." He sounded as though he were the offended party. He was rubbing his left thumb against his bare ring finger, and he held up his hand when he noticed her looking. "Three years divorced," he confirmed with a wry twist of his lips. "My ex didn't understand the demands of my job. We didn't see eye to eye on a lot of things. Honestly, I'm better off without her."

"Tell me more about this fight," she said, hoping to change the subject. They hadn't gotten around to it with everything else they'd been discussing. "You mentioned Betty Heimer, but last I checked, she was in the 145-pound division."

"She had a kid and put on some weight. This'll be her first fight since she's been back. I think it'll be an easy one to win."

"I don't take fights because they're easy to win," she said, irritated he'd even suggested it. There was nothing worse than a mismatched opponent.

"That's not what I meant. Like I said, it's a convention with a small-time exhibition. More to showcase local talent, drum up publicity. Probably two or three hundred spectators, tops, which, at this stage in your career, is pretty good."

"I've fought for bigger crowds."

"But that was when you were fighting under your family's banner. Their backing got you sponsors. Do you have sponsors now? Don't answer that, I already know." He named them. He'd done his research, apparently.

"Everyone knows the Fiore name, but as a fighter, you need to build your personal profile. Get on social media, get your face in magazines, market yourself, that kind of thing. A fight right here in New Orleans will drum up some good publicity to start."

"And you're the guy to help me?"

"I wouldn't have come to Payette's to see you if I didn't think you were worth it. I don't know if anyone told you, but Kyle and I don't have a great working relationship. In fact, I'm thinking you could do better at a place like Star Gyms."

She knew of the national chain of high-end, full-service boutique fitness centers. They had a price tag to match the facilities, but that wasn't her issue. Bella fixed her mother's patented listen-to-me glare on Ryan. "I'm staying at Payette's. I signed a contract to stay on for six months. Besides, we're working with an at-risk youth center, and I won't give up on them."

Ryan raised his hands placatingly. "Hey, no sweat. I'm just here to offer my services to help you become a champ in all the aspects that your coaches can't train you in. What you're doing at Payette's is admirable—plus that community outreach stuff is PR gold." He flashed those billboard teeth again. "Listen, I'll be totally up-front. I like you, not only as a client, but as a person. In my business, that's rare." He shifted forward in his seat. "You're twenty-six, right? How many more years do you want to fight for?"

She shrugged. "If injuries don't slow me down? Realistically...I dunno...till I'm thirty-three? Thirty-five?" She hadn't thought quite that far ahead. She knew she'd have to stop for a year or two if she had children. And some fighters continued well into their forties, though she wasn't sure she'd be one of them. Quite frankly, it was hard to envision the future beyond the next match.

"Let's say you decide to quit at thirty-five. That means you've got less than nine years to scrape together enough for whatever you want to do afterward. There *is* an afterward, you know, and a lot of athletes don't realize that unless you get a sweet deal with a big-name brand, sponsorship money dries up pretty quick. Do you have any idea what you'll do once you quit fighting?"

"Train others," she said automatically. It was what her family had always done—pass on their teachings and raise new fighters on the Fiore system. "Work in my family's gym, I guess."

"Okay, so picture this—what if you could have your own gym?"

Bella admitted she'd thought about it. She'd always been resigned to the fact that she'd end up working for her father and grandfather and brothers for the rest of her life. But now that she'd broken off from her family tree, she could have dreams of her own.

The idea of that much freedom and autonomy saddened her a little. She missed everyone in São Paulo. Even Fulvio. At the same time, the chance to build and own something that was hers and hers alone was almost too sweet a dream to contemplate.

A gym. She'd call it Bella's. Her name would finally be featured ahead of the Fiore family name....

"You're starting to see it, right?" The glow of his smile reflected the stars in her eyes. "If you become the star you were born to be, you could have it all. Retire at thirty-five. Open your own gym. Your own restaurant. Whatever you want." He leaned toward her. "I want to see you succeed, and I know you will. I can help you move to the next level—won't you let me?"

"So you signed with Holbrooke?" Kyle sat back and carefully put down his coffee mug, afraid he might crush it in his hands or throw it at the wall.

Bella nodded. "He got me onto an exhibition card next month with Fury Fights, and he's working on getting me some sponsors."

"You should have talked to me first." He rubbed his temples, feeling a brand-new headache coming on. If he'd seen Ryan within ten feet of Bella, he would've...

You'd have what? His father's voice mocked. *Told him to get away from your girl?*

He pressed his palm onto the top of his desk. "I'll be honest with you. Ryan's scooped some of our clients before. I think he gets commission or something for bringing new clients to Star Gyms."

A look of understanding dawned on Bella's face. "He did try to sell me on switching gyms, but I made it clear that I won't leave Payette's."

The knot inside him eased a touch.

"Why do you even let him in here if he's stealing clients?" Bella asked.

"Our more serious fighters like that agents poke around here. I can't really ban the guy for searching out new talent." Of course, that wasn't the only reason he didn't ban Ryan from the gym. Bella had every right to look skeptical about his answer.

The truth was, Kyle didn't like Ryan, and it wasn't only because of his slimy business practices. The man was friends with Karla. And while he'd never said anything to suggest he knew about what had happened, he leered at Kyle whenever they saw each other.

If he banned the agent, who knew what the guy would say?

His irritation ratcheted up. "Tell me something." Kyle leaned forward. "What did he do to convince you? Fancy dinner? Promises of fame and fortune?"

"You say it as if I'm gullible. I didn't agree to it right away. I went home, did some research and talked to a few people. The guy has some serious fighters on his roster who've all moved on to the UFF."

"What you probably haven't heard is that he's had more burnouts than superstar successes. Ryan pushes hard, Bella. He's only interested in making money, even if it means making his clients do things they don't want to."

"You mean steroids?"

"I mean anything."

Bella shook her head. "I won't do anything I don't want to. I'm not that desperate. I know what's best for me."

Kyle had seen her kind of cocky conviction before. Usually in overconfident guys who thought they'd be the next Dominic Payette. She might be a Fiore, but he wondered if she knew how far she'd have to go to become a star.

"Look, it's done. Ryan will help me do some marketing and PR stuff. But you're the one who'll make me a good fighter."

But why Ryan? he wanted to whine. Not that it was his business. It was her career, after all. But that didn't mean he couldn't warn her.

Bella leaned forward suddenly, her eyes softening. "Look, I know things have been tense between us. I know you don't like Ryan, but he believes in me. I really need that." She glanced down. "I need *someone* to believe…" She trailed off.

His eyes widened. Suddenly, he got it. She'd

signed with Ryan because he supported her in ways Kyle hadn't. Ways her family hadn't. Why else was she here and not at a Fiore gym? Marco Fiore had mentioned something to him about a falling-out. Kyle understood that feeling of desolation when no one had faith in you. The ache spread as he realized his cold attitude hadn't helped. He'd practically pushed her toward Ryan.

"I believe in you," he blurted. Too little…but maybe not too late. Wry cynicism lurked in her eyes, but there was a spark of hope there, too. He swallowed thickly and leaned closer, trying desperately to infuse his words with sincerity. "I'm here for you, Bella."

"I really need to believe that, Kyle. You're the one I came here for. I want to bring something new to the cage. Betty Heimer has some major takedown skills, and I don't want to be unprepared. Will you help me? Please?"

He bit down on the inside of his cheek. As wildly infuriating as Bella could be, right now, she was vulnerable and she *needed* him.

He couldn't say no.

AFTER BELLA HAD finished with one of the fitness classes she taught, a young guy named Joe who'd been training at Payette's for over a year joined them on the mats at Kyle's request. At eighteen, he was a gangly kid who weighed a few pounds more than Bella did. As before, Kyle started from the beginning with basic wrestling stances. It never hurt to check a fighter's habits. It seemed Bella had taken his advice and adjusted her staggered stance. Joe was more sloppy, but he was still new to MMA.

They went through the basic takedowns, and Kyle found Bella's techniques a bit rough. Brazilian jujitsu and wrestling were separate disciplines with different rules and goals, but in MMA, the two were more fluid. He stopped the pair as she pinned Joe to the mats.

"Bella, you're still not cutting the corner fast enough," he said. "Betty's going to be fighting you off, so you'll have to do this in a snap. Don't give her time to readjust."

She shot him a look as if to say *duh*.

He raised an eyebrow and subbed in for Joe, getting into position.

Bella's lips curved. "Do you want me to fight you off?" she asked wryly.

"You can try."

Joe took another step back. Kyle said, "Go," and lunged forward. He snagged her wrist and hooked one hand behind her head, controlling her so she couldn't strike him.

But Bella was strong, and she'd had years of training with the first family of BJJ. She reversed their positions, dropping to her knees with one arm hooked under his thigh.

"That's good," Kyle said, grappling with her, keeping her close. "Using your height difference as an advantage definitely throws off a bigger opponent. But—" He shot his legs back and dropped his hips. He landed on her, then went for the full mount, straddling her chest. "I'm still bigger and stronger. From here I can get you into a lot of different submission holds."

"*If* you can hold on," she gritted. She lifted her hips and rolled and twisted beneath him. He lost his grip and slammed a hand down to stabilize himself. His nose ended up buried in the crook of her neck. The smell of hot-cross buns assailed him.

Before he could regain himself, she'd wrapped her muscular legs around his waist, ankles hooked into the small of his back. She pulled him down on top of her, gaining control despite still being pinned beneath him.

Her face was flushed, and strands of dark, curly hair stuck to her sweaty face. The combination of her piercing green eyes and the way she squeezed him between her thighs sent electricity across his skin. Blood pounded through his temples and made its way south.

"Nice guard," Joe said.

Kyle startled. He'd practically forgotten about Joe. He tapped out hastily, discreetly adjusting himself as he got up. "In wrestling, your opponent will be fighting against you all the way. The name of the game is domination."

"Well, I guess it's a good thing the name of *this*

game is MMA." Bella rolled into a sitting position. "That would've been a perfectly legal move."

He couldn't fault her for that. And he had to admit he was impressed. "Let's refocus on your takedown. Do the double-leg again. Joe, stand in for me."

The hour slipped by quickly as they ran through the exercise several times. He realized too late, though, that having the amateur spar with Bella had been a bad decision. The kid's technique was sloppy, and didn't provide a real challenge for Bella. Kyle itched to replace Joe, but getting that close to her again was a bad idea. He was still shaking off the tingles running figure eights through his groin. He'd *felt* her, and whatever went through him made him wholly aware that she was an attractive woman.

Apparently, he wasn't the consummate professional he thought he was.

CHAPTER SIX

"So what'd I do wrong?"

Kyle glanced up from his paperwork and frowned. After yesterday's session with Joe, it was clear to Bella she'd messed up somehow. The moment she'd established her guard, Kyle's eyes had clouded as something like anger flashed through them. After the lesson, he'd become distant and hidden in his office the rest of the day. And he'd hardly said hello to her today. "Does *anyone* around here remember how to knock?" he grumbled.

"I was thinking over the drills yesterday. I did something wrong, didn't I?" She stepped farther into his office and gripped the back of the visitor's chair.

His gaze remained fixed on her, but she detected a slight twitch in his jaw. "You did fine. You just need practice."

"But—"

"You did fine." He sent her a half smile that did crazy things to her insides. "I know you're eager to do more, and I think that's great. Just keep conditioning. Joe'll be in later. We'll train then."

Bella left unsatisfied. She was used to getting a lot

more feedback, but she reminded herself yet again that this was Payette's, not her family studio.

As the days went on, Kyle concentrated mainly on her takedowns and getting her opponent on the ground. There was a definite pattern to his coaching style, and it only got more intense as she drilled. His shouted instructions rang in her ears as she lay in bed, his demands that she move faster, watch her form and keep her guard up made her muscles twitch just as she thought she was drifting off to sleep. He was bent on perfection. And while she appreciated his tenacity, it made training tedious.

She kept her mouth shut, though. She wasn't about to jeopardize their tentative truce. This was what she'd come to New Orleans for, after all. Every day they worked together, she got another "fine." Maybe it was all he was willing to give.

At least her time as a trainer at Payette's was proving successful. She'd made the classes she was teaching more challenging, and the students appreciated being pushed harder. Her reputation as fair, fun but hard-assed circulated, and a few of the bodybuilders who regularly pumped iron at Payette's joined the classes. Kyle had been impressed and had rewarded her with a recruitment bonus.

On Wednesday evenings, the students from the Touchstone youth center came for their weekly lesson. Shawnese had slowly warmed to Bella. She no longer glared as if everyone was out to get her and even worked with her fellow classmates without hesitation. Reta was ecstatic about how much she'd opened up since she'd started the self-defense class.

It was the first week in November when Ryan showed up with a square-chinned, redheaded woman wearing an ill-cut burgundy pantsuit. She smiled broadly as she introduced herself. "Quinn Bourdain, *Las Vegas Sun News*. Ryan's told me a lot about you, Ms. Fiore. I'm looking forward to interviewing you."

Bella kept her smile fixed, but she snagged her manager's arm in a tight grip. "Um, Ryan, can I talk to you a minute?" She pulled him aside. Kyle hadn't arrived yet, and she had no idea how he'd react to seeing him there. "What's going on?"

"I told you, this class for at-risk youth is PR gold. I invited Quinn here all the way from Vegas. She owes me a favor. She's going to do a feature on you and this class you're teaching."

"I'm not teaching this class. Kyle is. Anyway, I don't think it's such a good idea. These kids haven't given their permission."

"We're not filming them, and we don't need their consent to observe. Anyhow, the article will be about you more than them. You know, local girl does good and breaks faces, too. That kind of stuff."

She shook her head. "I'm not local. And I'm not sure Kyle will approve."

"Approve of what?" Kyle asked as he walked into the gym. His entrance reminded Bella of a shark gliding through the water, deceptively innocuous and full of bloody intent. He looked down his nose.

"Ryan." The frost in his greeting crystalized in the air between them.

Ryan smiled, though it didn't reach his eyes. "Just the man I wanted to see. Have you met Ms. Bourdain?" He explained the reason for Quinn's presence. Kyle took it in, lips pursed.

"I don't know…" he began.

"C'mon, Kyle. It'd be good publicity for Payette's, not to mention Bella. You want to make sure you associate the gym with the future women's champ, don't you?" He clamped his hands over Bella's shoulders, his thick fingers digging into her flesh. Ryan jerked his chin at the gathering of young people. "It'll be good for them, too."

Kyle's eyes narrowed with suspicion. "Ask Reta first. She's the best judge of what's good for these kids. Some of them might not appreciate being talked about."

"Quinn's a top-notch journalist," Ryan said dismissively. "She'd never exploit someone for a story. No one who isn't asking for it, anyhow."

So Kyle grudgingly explained the situation to Reta, who had no problem with the reporter's presence. Neither did the students—they seemed excited by the idea of being in the newspaper. Kyle started the class, and the students were extra attentive. To everyone's surprise, Quinn changed into a T-shirt and trunks, took notes and snapped some pictures, before joining the class, too.

Ryan left twenty minutes into the lesson. Apparently he had better things to do than sit around and watch a client spar with a bunch of kids. Admittedly, Bella breathed a little easier without the tension stretching between her agent and her trainer. She might have been a pugilist by trade, but she'd always hated emotional cold wars.

As the class wrapped up and the kids went to get changed, Shawnese hung back. "Miss Bella, can I talk to you?"

"What's up, Shawnese?"

She gripped her bony elbows and glanced around nervously. "I was wondering..." Her voice dropped. "Can you teach me how to stop a guy with a knife?"

Bella sucked in her cheeks. "Um...I can. But it's not easy. The best way to get out—"

"Is to run away, yeah, so you guys keep saying. But sometimes you can't, and I don't want to turn my back on a knife, you know?"

She scratched her hip, a little unsure of how to handle this. "Listen, knife fighting and evading knife attacks is really advanced. It's not like the movies. I can't teach you everything, and you know what they say about a little knowledge."

"I'm not trying to be Superman. Just teach me what you can." Her voice quavered. She looked almost ready to bolt. Bella had a feeling that even if she asked, Shawnese would run away rather than explain herself. Bella couldn't deny her request.

She gave the girl a quick demonstration, using the lessons the students had already learned in class. The young woman took it all in calmly, following along as best as she could. She was by no means weak or small, but against a knife, all opponents, no matter how skilled, were at a disadvantage.

"Shawnese, what are you doing?" Reta called from the doorway. "The bus is leaving soon. You should get changed."

Shawnese waved her fingers at her as she left, smiling weakly. Unease rolled through Bella's stomach.

"A little extra tutoring?" Quinn sidled up next to her, hefting her bag.

"She's a special case."

"Special how?"

Bella hesitated. She wasn't about to share Shawnese's story with the reporter. "She just wanted a few tips."

"Well, forearmed is forewarned."

"I think it's the other way around."

"Depends which side of the hurting you're on," Quinn replied grimly.

Bella gave a wry smile. Maybe she should say something to Reta. She'd know how to handle Shawnese's situation *if* there was one. Plus, it wasn't really her business. She didn't want to put her nose where it didn't belong and risk losing the young woman's trust. She'd talk with Reta later.

Bella and Quinn went to The Spot for dinner where they conducted the one-on-one interview. They sat at the bar and ate. Quinn asked questions about Bella's background, her dreams and her current training. Bella did her best to answer them, but when it came to explaining her current relationship with the rest of the Fiore family, she glossed over a few details. Frustrated though she was with the way they'd treated her, she didn't want to hurt Fulvio or the others.

"So how's your relationship with Kyle Peters?" Quinn asked.

Bella nearly sucked her water down the wrong pipe. "I'm sorry?"

"Kyle. He has a reputation as a harsh taskmaster. Gets it from his father, David Peters. Has he treated you differently?"

She shifted her bottom on the suddenly too hot seat of the bar stool. "He's been…" She tried to force out a lie. Telling a reporter she didn't feel she was getting the best performance out of Kyle would not make him or Payette's look good. "He's been very good. I've learned a lot from him."

Quinn watched her carefully and turned the recorder off. "Okay, totally off-the-record. How's your relationship with Kyle, *really?*"

When Bella didn't answer her right away, Quinn pressed on. "I'm not trying to write a gossip piece or anything. That's not my style. You look like you want to say something but you're afraid of the repercussions. I'm asking as a human being, now." She lowered her voice. "Has he been inappropriate toward you?"

She blinked rapidly. "What? No. Why would you say that?"

Quinn fidgeted with the straw. "Rumors. He's got a reputation when it comes to women, you know." She paused, likely waiting for Bella to respond or ask for more details. When she did neither, Quinn shrugged. "They're probably nothing. Forget I even said anything."

TWO WEEKS LATER, Kyle was forced to admit that Ryan knew what he was doing with Bella's career. Quinn Bourdain's flattering article was syndicated in the *Times-Picayune* and had helped generate a lot of cold calls to the gym. People were interested in signing up for memberships and in supporting the gym's good works with the community. And within three days of the article, he'd added a women's self-defense class to the schedule.

Word about Payette's was spreading.

At the health and wellness fair, which took place at a plaza mall on the northeast end of town, Bella drew a hefty crowd, signing photos and copies of Quinn's article at the Payette's booth. She helped with demonstrations and sparred with various members of the gym. Her looks and skills combined seemed to have converted quite a few eager young men to the sport of MMA, and a few ladies, too. They signed up a record number of new members that day.

This was how it was supposed to be, Kyle thought with a broad smile. Fun. That was something coaching and running a gym used to be before he had to worry about membership dues and customer service and budgets and getting flyers printed and circulated around the city.

He remembered the day Dominic had asked him to manage the place. It'd only been a few weeks after Dom had won the belt. Kyle couldn't have been more honored and excited. The opportunity to run his own gym, even if it was owned by the UFF, had always been a dream of his. A chance to show everyone he was a winner beyond the podium.

He watched as Bella smilingly handed another on-the-spot sign-up over to Tito. Bella's presence had boosted revenue *and* morale. The guys laughed and joked with each other more. The clients were sticking around. And no one had complained about Bella in the least. He'd been wrong to think she'd cause any trouble.

The only drawback was Ryan's continued presence at the gym. He hung around Bella an awful lot for a guy who claimed he was a busy, important man with numerous clients. He'd even rolled up his expensive shirtsleeves and trained with her once or twice. The guy knew what he was doing, so Kyle couldn't boot him—though he could have called him on his lack of proper gym attire.

You sure you're not jealous? The thought echoed through his mind in his father's voice. Dad had goaded him frequently in order to incite a reaction, make him lose focus and catch him off guard while training. David Peters had believed the constant barrage of criticism and digs built character and forced Kyle to suppress emotions that would otherwise upset his game. As far as Kyle could tell, all it had done was give him a permanent complex.

I'm not jealous, he told himself firmly. *I'm concerned about Bella.*

After all, she needed someone to look after her in place of her father, grandfather and brothers. Maybe that was stupidly old-fashioned, but he didn't like to think of any woman on her own in a strange place. She needed a guiding hand. It didn't have to be his, but he'd rather it not be Ryan's.

"So tell me something, Coach," Bella said as she helped disassemble the booth at the end of the day. "How is it that you're not signing autographs or getting on the mats for these things? I mean, you're the one with three gold medals."

His smile was stiff. "That was a long time ago."

"Not that long. You stopped competing…what, seven years ago?"

"The leg still gives me trouble sometimes," he said. "I try not to aggravate it."

"It was the knee, right?" She studied him carefully, probably saw that he had no difficulty lifting the folding table or squatting for boxes. "Must've been pretty bad."

"I had to go in for a few surgeries, so, yeah." He didn't want to talk about it.

"If you're interested, I know some exercises you

could do to strengthen your knee. Marco hurt his knee a while back, too. It took a lot of rehab, but he's walking on it fine now."

"The problem isn't walking." Kyle snapped, and immediately regretted it. Bella was only trying to help him. He had no reason to bite her head off. "I'm past my prime now, is all. Wrestling or performing for anyone else…that's not my deal anymore." And neither was pleasing anyone else. "Thanks for the offer, though."

She gave him a strange look but went on stripping the booth.

In the mall parking lot, Kyle went to get his car. The sky was low, the clouds boiling with an impending storm. He pulled out of the space in time to see Bella unlocking her bike from a post. The first fat drops splashed against his windshield. In seconds, the sky opened up, and the rain roared against the soft top of his convertible.

Bella stood with her bike under the plaza mall's overhang. She stared up at the sky infuriated, as if daring it to come down and fight her. He smiled to himself. She'd probably challenge the storm cloud if it looked at her funny.

He couldn't leave her standing there. Kyle pulled the car up next to the curb and rolled down a window. Rain splashed him violently as he stuck his head out. "Need a lift?"

"I'll be okay," she shouted over the storm. "It's just a little rain. I'll wait for it to pass."

Thunder crashed through the sky, making them both flinch. The rain poured down harder.

"C'mon, get in."

"But...where am I going to put my bike?"

He was about to tell her to leave it locked up at the plaza mall, but it was a nice bike, and he didn't quite trust the neighborhood. "I'll pop the trunk."

He got out and wished he hadn't. The rain fell so hard it hurt. An inch of water flooded the pavement and seeped into his sneakers. He was drenched by the time he walked around to the back of the car. Bella had finagled her hybrid in, but the trunk wouldn't close, so they spent another few minutes bungee cording the trunk shut and making sure it was secure.

"Hurry up and get in." He dove into the driver's seat and they both shut their doors at the same time. Water ran off them in rivulets, dripping all over the leather interior.

Hastily, he grabbed his gym bag from the backseat and yanked out his towels and clothes. "Put these under you."

"I'm okay, I'm not that far."

"No, put these under you. I don't want the seats to get ruined."

She stared at him as if he was crazy but took the towel and slipped it under her. He did the same with his T-shirt and shorts, then buckled himself in.

"You really love this car, don't you?" She pulled her ponytail back and looked as though she was about to wring it out. She must have seen his murderous look because she stopped.

"I've had this car since I was twenty-one," he said, wiping his hands dry so he wouldn't get the leather steering wheel grip wet. He'd have to clean and wet-vac the interior after this.

"A little present to yourself after your first gold medal win?"

His lips lifted. "A gift from my father, actually. He promised he'd buy it for me if I came home with gold, and I did."

"Ah, I see now. It's all sentimental value."

"Are you kidding me? Do you know what kind of car this is?"

She glanced all around her, taking in the lines and surfaces, the sheer masculine perfection of the convertible. "It's…an old car. With a leaking roof." She pointed up at the drip slowly penetrating the fabric of the soft top. Kyle almost screamed.

"Start driving," she suggested. "It's probably a puddle gathering up top." She poked the ceiling. Water clung to her finger and leaked down her arm.

Kyle quickly put the car into gear. She gave him directions across town to an address off Bourbon Street. The rain pounded the pavement, sending pedestrians scurrying. He was glad he'd caught Bella before she'd tried to ride home in this.

Her apartment was located above a convenience store, with an outside entrance leading onto a wrap-around balcony. He helped her unload the bike and insisted on carrying it up the stairs for her.

"I can do that," she protested. "It's slippery on these steps."

"Which is why I should do it. The last thing either of us needs is for you to fall and hurt yourself before your match." He carried the bike up easily and parked it on the landing. Bella locked it to the post.

"Want to come in for a cup of coffee?" she asked. "I can get you a towel, too."

Kyle looked down at his car in the rain. If the roof was leaking, he should drive home and get it under the carport. But part of him—the part he used to listen to a lot more—said it'd be fine, that a little water wouldn't hurt. He'd have to get the interior cleaned anyhow, and the towels and clothes he'd left to soak up the excess water should handle any more drips. The rain seemed to be letting up, too. "Sounds good," he said, even as his instincts told him he should be doing anything but following Bella into her lair.

CHAPTER SEVEN

As HE CROSSED the threshold, instinct seized him, urging him to be cautious.

It wasn't fear, he told himself, but the topsy-turvy feeling in his chest grew as he inhaled that scent that was Bella—cinnamon, sugar, cloves and baking.

Her one-bedroom apartment was small but serviceable. Clothes were strewn on the back of the couch, over chairs, hanging off doorknobs, but she didn't rush to pick up and clear a space for him. In one corner, a fake many-armed cactus displayed an assortment of colorful underwear. "Laundry day?" he asked wryly. An electric-blue thong snagged his gaze and he was having the damnedest time not thinking about how Bella would look in it and nothing else.

"The dryers in the Laundromat up the street aren't very good. I swear they eat quarters." She started the coffeemaker and cleared a space on the sofa, tossing him a towel from the back of a chair. "Here. It's clean. Don't worry about making anything here wet. None of it's mine."

"It's a nice place," he said, rubbing his hair dry.

Her unique scent permeated the towel. She'd probably rubbed this towel against her naked body at some point.

Stiffly, he draped the towel across his shoulders.

"It reminds me of home." She plucked her panties off the cactus and dropped them into her basket as if they were fruit.

Fruit of the Loom, maybe. Wokka-wokka! Kyle smirked. His inner comedian hadn't spoken up in a long time.

"How's it like home?" he asked, refocusing on her.

"Well, the heat, for one. No A/C in here. But I like the way it feels. Lived-in. Like it's been here forever and will always be here."

"Well, it's a pretty lucky neighborhood you picked. This was one of the areas that Katrina didn't get."

She nodded. "So a lot of folks keep telling me. It's interesting how much people talk about it but also *don't* want to talk about it."

He kind of got that. The ravaged landscape still hadn't totally recovered all these years later. Reminders were everywhere. And yet, those who remained were stronger than ever. He envied the people of New Orleans and wished he had half their resilience.

The coffee finished percolating, and she brought him a mug. Black and strong, the way he liked it. She puttered around her tiny kitchen, and he felt oddly content to simply sit and watch her as she put a plate of munchies together—carrot sticks, cubed cheese, cucumber slices.

He didn't want to be impolite, but a peek inside her open fridge told him she wasn't well-stocked. A proper diet was important for training. He'd seen her eat at The Spot, so it probably wasn't a money issue. Maybe she just hadn't bought groceries in a while.

"Do you have dinner plans?" he asked before he could think better of it. "I have a hankering for hush puppies."

She gave him a strange look and glanced back at her fridge. Had he been too obvious? "I mean, we could order in," he clarified. But that sounded weird, too. "There's a place I know that delivers real Creole food. Have you had any yet?"

She shrugged. "I've had some. Nothing to write home about."

"Then you haven't had the real stuff. I'm buying." He dismissed her protests with a wave of his hand as he called his favorite eatery. He had the number on his cell phone's speed dial.

"You really didn't have to do that," Bella said once he'd hung up. "You already drove me home."

"If you don't eat with me, the delivery boy is going to give me his pity look."

"You mean, you can't find a nice young coed to share a rainy night in with you?"

"They don't like going out in the rain. It makes their hair frizzy."

Bella snickered and shook her head, her own

thick black curls and all their frizziness bouncing. "Their loss."

Within the hour, the restaurant delivered five large take-out bags. Recognizing Kyle, the delivery boy's smile widened, and he gave him a sly look as his gaze slipped past him to Bella. Kyle tipped the kid and shut the door.

"How hungry are you?" Bella exclaimed as he carried the food to her kitchen. "What is all this?"

"All the best things on the menu." He placed the bags on the table. "What can I say? I don't like doing things in half-measures, and I'm starving."

They opened container after container, and Kyle named each of the steaming, mouthwatering dishes. Jambalaya, gumbo, hush puppies, boiled crayfish, rice and beans, and for dessert, a greasy bag of powdered-sugar-covered beignets.

"Good thing I'm below weight right now," she said with a laugh. "Otherwise I'd have to turn down all this food."

"Don't worry. We'll work it off somehow." He snapped his jaw shut. He hadn't meant it to sound like a come-on. "Anyhow, you could use the calories. Today was a tough day. You can hang on to the leftovers, too. Most of this stuff is healthy…ish."

"Twist my arm, why don't you?" She reached for a plate and loaded it up.

They chatted about the gym, keeping things light. Bella told him about some of the things Ryan had been doing for her. Apparently, her agent was working on a big sponsorship deal with Silverstreak, the energy drink company that also sponsored Dominic Payette. Kyle was instantly suspicious. It seemed pretty early in her career to get that level of sponsorship.

"So how are things with your family?" he asked casually, trying to keep conversation flowing.

Bella paused, a spoonful of rice and beans in her mouth. She chewed slowly and replied, "Fine, I guess."

"You haven't talked to them?"

She swallowed. "I talk to my mother every night, but otherwise, no. We had a bit of a fight before I left. By *we,* I mean my grandfather and I. And when Fulvio puts his foot down, so does the rest of the family."

"Oh." He felt guilty for asking. He could imagine the pain this was bringing up. "I'm sorry to hear that. We can talk about something else."

"It's okay." She sighed. "Mom keeps me up-to-date on what's happening back home. Business as usual, according to her." She sounded sad about that. Though she'd left *them,* knowing life went on with the rest of the clan couldn't be all that comforting to hear.

Silence dropped between them as they chewed. The air grew close, and Kyle shifted in his seat. He felt as if he were on an awkward first date. Which this wasn't.

"So, do you have a boyfriend back home?"

His eyes bulged and he slammed his lips shut, while Bella stared at him as if a roach had crawled off his tongue. Why, oh, why had he asked *that* question? "Sorry. That's too personal...."

She raised a hand, looking almost relieved to be talking about something. "I came off a long-term relationship a little over two years ago. Then I got busy training and...well, I haven't found anyone. I mean, I've gone on dates, but no one's stuck."

Kyle's toes curled. He tried to look casual as he picked up another crayfish. "Can I ask what happened? Between you and the long-term boyfriend, I mean." He told himself that he didn't really want to know, he was just making conversation.

Her lips curved in a small smile. "Antonio and I knew each other for years before we started dating. He was close to my brothers and trained at my grandfather's studio. He was practically part of the family. Probably would've been, too, except he wanted me to stop fighting."

"Why?"

"He said he didn't want to see me get hurt. He kept going on about how it wouldn't look right and how our kids would be affected." Deep furrows appeared between her eyes. "When it came right down to it, it was him or fighting. I chose fighting."

"Your family must've been proud of you."

She snorted. "Not even a little. Antonio left the gym after we broke up. My grandfather was furious because he'd spent years grooming him to be a

Fiore teacher. And my brothers…well, Antonio was practically one of them, you know? They all thought I should've done as he wanted. They thought I was being selfish."

"Seriously? They sided with *him?*" A tight knot in his throat kept him from saying more, which was probably a good thing. He didn't want to speak ill of the Fiores. But he didn't understand why Bella's family would disapprove of her following the family legacy.

He saw she was hurt, too. Her eyes had lost their sparkle. He wondered if it was because of her family or because of this jerk Antonio. He hoped it wasn't the latter. If the guy really had cared about her, he wouldn't have asked her to give up her dreams.

She turned her head to catch him staring. "Something bugging you?"

He startled. "What makes you say that?"

"You were cracking your jaw. You do that and rub your tension points when you're stressed." She peered at him. "Still worrying about membership?"

He decided to divert the conversation. "A little. The numbers are up, though, which is good, and today was terrific. We have you to thank for that."

She batted her lashes. "Aw, that's sweet of you to say."

"It's the truth. I only sweet-talk people I'm trying to sleep with…"

He cringed. What was wrong with him? That was the old Kyle talking, the cocksure Kyle who could make a woman jump into bed on command. But Bella wasn't the type of girl to do that, and she certainly wasn't the woman he would have chosen to use that particular line on.

"I'm sorry, I didn't mean for it to come out that way. I should—"

She punched him in the shoulder hard enough to rock him in his seat. "Relax, Coach. I know what you meant. You don't have to play boss all the time." She smiled broadly, picked up another boiled crayfish and ripped its head off, sucking the brain-filled cavity noisily as juice dribbled down her chin. Kyle didn't know he could be revolted and intrigued at the same time, but he was.

He didn't know what this weird feeling was—it was like dancing on the tip of a knife hanging over the edge of a skyscraper. Exciting. Dangerous. Forbidden. But he was getting too close. He couldn't make the same mistake with Bella as he had with Karla. But he also couldn't deny that he was attracted to Bella.

Why was he even still here? He'd made sure Bella had gotten home safe, fed her and stocked her fridge. He'd done way more than what was expected of a coach and an employer. The closer night crept, the more danger he put himself in.

"I should go," he said abruptly. "I…I have some things I need to take care of."

"Oh." Bella looked surprised. "I'm sorry. I hope I wasn't keeping you."

"No, no, not at all. I lost track of time. I was supposed to meet someone…"

She raised an eyebrow. "Someone who isn't afraid of frizzy hair?"

Damn, he wasn't thinking clearly. "I should get showered, cleaned up…" He was acting as if he were sneaking out after an awkward morning after. He tried for a smile. "This was fun. Thanks."

"Hey, you paid for dinner." She sucked the juice from her fingers with a happy grin. "Least I could've done for you was let you get to first base."

His jaw slackened, and she laughed. "I'm joking, I'm joking! Man, Kyle, you need to lighten up. It's not as if you're *trying* to get in my pants."

"Good night." He bolted out and took the slick stairs two at a time, nearly slipping and going butt-first down to the ground. When he climbed into his car and slammed the door, he gripped the wheel tight and breathed deep.

His head cleared, and the southbound surge of blood eased. He did not need this. And he had to make sure his body knew it, too.

February, he told himself. *Bree will be here soon, and then you and she can get it on like rabbits in heat.*

First, a hot shower. Then he'd do exactly what he'd let Bella believe was on his agenda tonight—find himself a hot date, frizzy hair or no. If that didn't pan out, he'd go for a light jog in the cold rain and then read the gym's financials. That would kill his unwanted libido.

He turned the key in the ignition. The car sputtered.

He gave it another go. The engine whirred, coughed and died.

He sat back. No. No, not his baby. His head fell back against the headrest, making a wet, splashing sound. He glanced behind him, looked down and moaned.

An inch of water flooded the floor in the backseat.

"YOU'VE GOT TO be kidding me."

It wasn't the reaction Hadrian had hoped for. From the moment Quinn had spotted him waiting for her at the airport arrivals terminal, she wore an expression that danced between pleasant confusion and dismay. "If you're worried about being recognized with me, don't worry—this is a private rental."

"Yeah, but a *limo?*" The driver of the white stretch limousine smilingly took her rolling carry-on from her and placed it in the trunk. "You couldn't have come in a cab?"

"I have long legs," he said, keeping his smile bright despite the dimming happiness inside him. "Besides, what good is money if I don't spend it?"

She gave him that look—the one that told him she was neither impressed nor happy; the look that said she'd suffer his attention but only because he was so damned good in bed it was hard to say no.

"Hop in," he said, shooing the driver away from the door. He wanted to be the one to attend to her.

He watched her shapely behind shimmy in, and despite the poor fit of The Suit, he couldn't help reaching out and giving her butt a light slap before crawling in after her.

"Back to my place, Jeeves," he told the driver before rolling up the privacy screen.

Quinn was busy opening and closing every compartment in the limo. She'd done the same thing when she'd first entered his home. Compulsively curious, she couldn't help but stick her nose in every room and cupboard. He thought it was adorable, even if her insatiable curiosity was sometimes inconvenient when it came to his business or personal history.

He opened the minibar. "Drink?"

"Water," she said. "Is there chocolate in there? I can never eat airplane food, and I'm starving."

"I've got dinner waiting at home. I had Chef cook your favorite—spaghetti and meatballs."

She gave him a wan smile and stopped rummaging to give him a peck on the cheek. He slid an arm around her waist and pulled her closer, settling his lips over hers. The kiss deepened, and she sighed.

"Mmm, I missed you."

"I've only been gone a week."

"Too long." He undid her top button. "Take off The Suit, will you?"

"Hadrian, are you nuts? He'll hear." She indicated the driver with a nod.

"You think this is the first time people have made out back here?" He tugged at her burgundy blazer. He wanted to rip the thing and force her to let him buy something new but knew she wouldn't appreciate that.

She slipped off the blazer and shimmied out of the pants so that all she wore was the white shirt and cotton panties. *So damned sexy,* he thought, undoing the top buttons as she straddled him.

Things were just getting good when he felt a buzz in his pocket.

"Oh." Quinn arched an eyebrow. "That's different."

"Ignore it." He knew he should have turned his cell off. It buzzed again, and he reached down to yank it out. He might've rolled down the window and tossed the phone out, but Quinn grabbed it and looked at the number. "It's Blake Ames."

Blake was the card manager for the anniversary fight. Hadrian's stomach pitched. Reluctantly, he took his cell phone from Quinn and answered. She slid off his lap and waited.

A minute later, a headache pounding through his skull, he tossed the phone onto the seat and pinched the flesh between his eyes.

"What is it? What's wrong?" Quinn draped an arm across his back and ran her fingers through his hair, raking her nails lightly across his scalp. He groaned. "Maybe I can help you." She leaned over and nibbled his ear.

He closed his eyes and sank into the sensation. "Dodge is out."

Her stroking stilled. She drew back sharply. "You're kidding me."

For crying out loud. Hadrian was his own worst cockblocker. "Broke his arm. He fell off a ladder while putting up Christmas lights."

Quinn winced. "Someone should've told him to wait until after Thanksgiving." She studied him. "What are you going to do?"

"Move the Smith-Burton fight up to the main event, I guess. They're not as big a draw as Dodge is, obviously, but what choice do I have?"

"Are you telling me that off the record?"

He frowned. "I'm telling you because I thought you cared about my problems."

"Don't get snippy, Hadrian, I'm only doing my job." She reached for her pants and knocked on the privacy window. It rolled down a few inches.

"Yes, ma'am?"

"Sorry, change of plans." She gave him the address of her apartment.

"I thought we were going to have dinner, Quinn. Spaghetti and meatballs."

"I need to go home, get cleaned up and do some laundry." Her cool tone got cooler as she donned her armor, pulling her arms through the sleeves of her blazer and buttoning her shirt.

"You can do all those things at my place." He was tired of her running out on him, of her putting her job before him.

She flicked him an amused look. "You need to deal with this latest crisis. I'll give you time to figure things out before I hit you up with questions. You'll let me have the first kick at the can, right?"

He scoffed. "Don't I always?" He wasn't about to beg her to stay. She needed him more than he needed her, after all.

They dropped her off in front of her building, drawing a few odd looks from the residents loitering outside.

Without Quinn to share his dinner, he had no desire to go home. He told the driver to take him to the office instead.

It was going to take a lot of long hours to pull a miracle out of his ass and keep the show running.

"I DON'T KNOW about this," Bella said, picking at the tight blue-and-green-sequined gown clinging to her.

"You don't like it?" Ryan studied her as if she were some kind of rare exotic flower, turning her this way and that, one hand on her hip. He adjusted the straps and gave the low-cut dress a downward tug, exposing yet more cleavage. The moment he let go, Bella tugged it back up.

"I think it's a nice dress, just not for me. It's too flashy."

"It's perfect. It evokes Carnival. It catches the eye."

"It makes me look like a half-plucked peacock. Besides, my parents would have a fit if they saw me in this. I wasn't even allowed to wear makeup until I was twenty-one."

"Do you really care what your parents think?" Ryan smirked and tugged at her above-the-knee hemline. "Maybe we can take this up a little."

Bella didn't answer him. Of course she cared what her parents thought, to a point. Regardless of that, this dress was not her.

She swatted Ryan's hands away. "I'm changing." She went back into the dressing room, peeled the dress off and pulled on her street clothes. Her skin was chafing from trying on so many obscenely impractical dresses. She'd just pulled her T-shirt over her head when the change room door burst open. A hot mess of red, orange and gold flew at her.

"How about this one?" Ryan brandished the gaudy dress like a sword.

"Ryan," she snapped. "This is a ladies' change room."

He tilted his chin to one side and his lips twitched. "Relax, sweetheart, you were already dressed. And even if you weren't, it's not like I haven't seen *that* before."

She folded her arms and stared him down. He relented at her diamond-hard glare and gave a melodramatic sigh. "Fine, I'm sorry. I shouldn't have barged in like that. But if you don't want to be seen, lock your door next time." He whirled back out, as if he'd been the wronged party.

As far as she was concerned, a closed door was a clear sign that she didn't want anyone intruding. But she let it go. He was already in a mood, and they'd been in that shop for over an hour. It wasn't her fault none of the dresses suited her—she'd told him so forty minutes ago. But he'd insisted on making her try them all on anyhow.

They walked out of the high-end boutique empty-handed, the saleswoman glaring at their backs.

"You have to wear *something* to the UFF charity ball. It's not as if you can show up in a rash guard," Ryan said.

"That event is weeks away. I don't see why we have to shop for a dress now, much less go."

"The only way you get out there is by being seen, networking and making connections. If you want to leave an impression, you need to flaunt yourself. Make people notice. You know, dress for the job you want."

"What job is that? Slutty clown?"

"The dresses weren't that bad. Look, I'm your agent. Trust me, okay? I've been doing image consulting and PR for years. I'm not picking the skimpiest dresses I can find for you."

She'd hate to see what the *skimpiest* dresses looked like. "Well, it's not as if I could've afforded them anyhow."

"You don't worry about that. I would've bought it for you."

She gave him a quizzical look. Maybe he had a budget for wardrobe or something.

After a too-pricey lunch at a fancy restaurant, Ryan insisted on driving her back to her apartment.

"Thanks, but my bike's back at Payette's," she said.

"About that… You need to learn how to drive."

"I *know* how to drive, but I don't *need* to. I get around fine on my bike."

"It's not safe. And it makes you look ridiculous. You're a powerful woman. You should be driving a powerful car—something that makes a statement." He glanced her way. "It's all part of the image, sweetheart."

A powerful car. Like Kyle's convertible. She snorted, remembering how he'd humped back up the stairs and asked to use her phone to call Triple A. Poor Kyle had looked like someone had shot his dog as he watched his car get towed.

"Where do you live?" Ryan prompted.

"Take me to Payette's."

"I'm taking you home. Tell me where you live."

"And I'm telling you, drop me off at Payette's." She wouldn't give on this. She was tired and cranky and she needed to get away from Ryan's smothering attention.

He glared at her for a beat, brow lowered. He yanked the car sharply left, tires squealing, and wove through traffic at high speed. At one point, he drove within a few inches of a guy on a bicycle, then cut in front of him, making the cyclist wobble and nearly tip over. He rang his bell furiously, and Ryan swore at him, even though the guy probably couldn't hear him.

Bella shot Ryan a look of disgust, gripping her knees tight.

As he pulled up outside the gym, she opened the door before he even put the car in Park.

"Not cool," she said, getting out. She didn't want to be with him another minute.

"Wait, Bella…" His eyes flicked down. Maybe he'd realized his asinine behavior wouldn't earn him any sympathy, apology or leverage. "I'm sorry, but I have a temper when it comes to this kind of thing. I'm concerned for your safety. You should know I'm only doing what I think is best for you."

She frowned. Some apology.

"I'll see you tomorrow for the photo shoot?" He gave a tentative smile.

She looked him up and down, the way her mother sometimes did when she was displeased with one of her children. Forgiven but not forgotten, she thought. Still, she had to work with the guy, same way she did with Kyle. "Yeah. I'll be there."

He was her agent, after all. Her success was his success, and he wouldn't get paid until she did. And maybe he really was concerned about her career and welfare.

She headed into Payette's, trying hard to relax her face. No need to let Kyle see her irritation and have him interrogate her.

"How was the shopping trip? Did you buy anything?" Liz's face fell when she saw Bella had returned empty-handed.

"Nada. I don't even know why Ryan insisted on going out today."

Liz opened her mouth but then clamped it shut as Kyle walked in. He gave Bella a questioning once-over.

"No, we didn't buy anything," she said.

"Waste of a day." He looked strangely pleased, giving her a wry smile. "Joe's here. You wanna wrassle?"

Music to her ears. After the morning she'd had, getting back on the mats with Kyle was exactly what she needed.

CHAPTER EIGHT

THE PHOTO SHOOT was for a magazine feature about up-and-coming female athletes. Although Bella didn't know which publication it'd be for, Ryan had told her several times that he'd pulled a lot of strings to get her featured.

"The guy working on the piece owes me. I helped him a couple of years back when he needed interviews with some of my clients. He made his name on those stories."

Weird. She would've thought Ryan would appreciate *any* exposure his clients got.

The photographer, Jamie, shook hands with her, appraised her carefully and then showed her the change room where a rack of clothing awaited. A young woman with thick-framed glasses fixed her hair—which basically involved adding extra hairspray—and applied a heavy layer of makeup with candy-red lips and thick black mascara. It wasn't Bella's usual palette, but this was a photo shoot.

She donned the trunks and rash guard provided, and did a few quick warm-ups to get her blood flowing. The photographer had her do tough girl poses and action shots. Ryan watched pensively from the far corner until his attention wandered back to his smartphone.

They moved on to a tank top and zip-up hoodie with shorts. Jamie had her do more brooding shots. Then he started joking around, telling her stories about other athletes he'd photographed. It was a lot of fun, actually. Bella liked the guy. He did his job well.

"Okay, I'm gonna take a quick smoke break while you put on the next outfit," Jamie said, and ducked out while Bella went back to the change room. The hair and makeup girl met her with a hanger. A bunch of what appeared to be fat shoelaces hung from it.

She held it out with a nervous smile. "You might need help putting this on."

"Putting what on?" She stared at the shoelaces. The makeup girl took it off the hanger and spread it out. Bella's eyes went wide.

It was a bathing suit. Barely. The thin white strips of fabric radiated from three tiny triangles. She could barely figure out how anyone would put this on, much less swim in it.

"Boobs go here. Your arms go through these holes, legs through here." The hair and makeup girl tried for a reassuring smile. "Don't worry, it'll look fantastic on you. You've got the perfect body for this."

Bella looked from the suit to the girl and back, her good feelings about this shoot melting away. "Ryan!"

The agent strolled in casually, smiling. "Yes, sweetheart?"

"Did you see this?" She snatched the suit from the girl, who skittered away like a mouse from beneath a lion's paw. The laces tangled into a knot in her fist.

He looked calmly at the suit, then at her. "What's the problem?"

"What's the— Are you blind? I'm not wearing this."

He gave a light laugh. "Sweetheart, this is a photo shoot for *Brash*. Do you have any idea how big that is?"

Brash? The monthly glossy was barely more than a soft porn rag masquerading as a men's life-style magazine, with articles like "How to Tell Her Breasts Are Real" and "Three Steps To Dumping Your Long-Term Girlfriend."

"I don't care. I told you yesterday I'm not comfortable in revealing clothes. This counts as revealing."

"Sweetheart, it's okay—"

"No, it's not okay. And stop calling me sweetheart." She threw the suit onto the floor. "You're my agent. Do your job."

A storm boiled into his face. "*Do my job?* Listen, you. I have been doing my job. I've been working my ass off, even neglecting some of my other clients, so that you can make something of your little career. I deserve some respect, but all I get from you is your smart mouth."

She stared at him, shocked by his hateful tone. "This is unacceptable. I'm walking away right now."

He grabbed her, pinching the muscle between her

shoulder and neck so tight she yelped. He pushed her hard against the wall and pinned her there. His nostrils flared as he got up close. His cologne stung her eyes. "You do not walk away from me when I'm still talking. *I* came to you. There are hundreds of fighters who'd kill to have me as their agent. If you want to be a star, you do what I say. You give the camera what it wants, and you do it with a smile. You dress the way I tell you to, and you do it happily. Otherwise, I'll make sure you never get another fight anywhere."

Her heart rate ramped up, pushing blood into her head and hazing her vision. The expensive suit and fancy meals, the easy smile and casual airs—they'd all been stripped away to reveal the bully beneath.

In the three seconds it took her to rein in her temper, Bella could've broken his arm, smashed his nose and wrapped him in a headlock. She'd been trained by the best. But her training also meant she knew how to keep her cool. She looked him up and down and smiled tightly. "You know what, Ryan? You're fired."

"What?"

"Fired. Out. Off the payroll." She brushed off his suddenly limp hand and pushed past him. "I don't need you."

"You think you get to leave me?" His fingers wrapped around her wrist, and he jerked her back to face him. "You're just like *her*."

Okay. Bella twisted her grip, catching his hand

and pulling him against her. She spun, rammed her elbow into his solar plexus, pivoted on her heels, kicked his shin and slammed a right hook into his jaw. He collapsed to the ground, groaning.

Her harsh breaths stung her throat. "Don't touch me again. Ever."

"I think you better do as she says." Kyle's low, rough voice startled her. He stood in the doorway, massive arms folded over his chest, thunder in his face. She could see his fingers gripping his biceps tight, as if he were trying to contain himself. "I saw it all, Bella. Heard it, too."

"You…both of you…" Ryan got up slowly. His lip was bloodied and he limped a little. "You think you can get rid of me?"

"Leave, Ryan. Or I'll call the police and report you for assault."

"Assault? I didn't— She—" His face turned a shade of puce. He cut them one last glare before hurrying past Kyle. "This isn't over."

Bella started trembling. Her heart pounded in her ears. She felt light-headed.

"Easy, easy." Kyle was at her side instantly. He sat her down in a chair and pushed her head between her knees.

Her vision cleared as she breathed deeply to calm the jackhammer of her pulse. What the hell was wrong with her? She fought for a living. She'd fought against women and men tougher and better trained than Ryan. Why was she freaking out?

Kyle brought her a bottle of water, made her take small sips. "Do you want me to call the police?" he asked gently. "I heard everything. We could file a report."

"No. It's not worth it. He didn't...*do* anything." She was cold all over. Kyle must've had a sixth sense because he draped a big beach towel he'd found somewhere over her shoulders, then rubbed her arms roughly. She knew he was only trying to warm her up, but what she really wanted was his arms around her.

"Sorry." She wiped at an errant tear, angry that she looked like she was crying when she wasn't. It was frustration moisture. "I'll be fine in a minute."

"You did good," he said. "I mean, you really decked him, but you stopped at the right time. If it were me, he wouldn't have walked out of here at all."

"I didn't quite pull my punches, I'll admit," she said on a half laugh. She looked up at his grim smile. "You always seem to be around when I'm in trouble."

"I'm not stalking you, if that's what you're thinking."

She frowned. "Wait a second. Why *are* you here?"

"I couldn't get through on your cell phone, and Ryan was screening my calls." He wiped a hand across his mouth and glanced away. "It's... Oh, hell..."

"What? Tell me."

He gave her a pained look. "The hospital called. Shawnese is in the E.R. She's been stabbed."

THEY LEFT THE studio with barely an explanation to Jamie. Kyle drove Bella to the hospital in a rental car. She hadn't even realized she was still clutching the beach towel around her shoulders until they arrived at the E.R. A few queries later, they entered a postoperative recovery room. A police officer stood inside.

Shawnese lay in the bed, eyes shut, breathing deeply. She was hooked up to several monitors and IV bags. Her hands were heavily bandaged, and her face sported several puffy bruises. Bella pressed a fist to her mouth.

"Oh, my God." Kyle leaned against the door frame.

Bella looked to the officer. "What happened?"

"Bella Fiore?" The compact uniformed woman approached. "I'm Officer Sheila Jackson. I work in the Sixth District. I was the one who found Shawnese." Bella shook the policewoman's hand absently, unable to tear her gaze from the girl in the bed. "She was semiconscious when I found her. She said your name several times, and we found this card on her." She handed her one of Payette's business cards. One corner was stained with dried blood. Bella nearly dropped it.

"Shawnese is in a self-defense class I teach at Payette's," she explained, finding her voice.

"I wondered. I'm a fight fan. I recognized your family name."

Bella appreciated that the officer didn't make a

big deal of it and stayed on task. "What happened to her?"

"When I found her, she was cut up pretty bad. Her hands and arms, mostly. She'd lost a lot of blood. Looked like whatever happened, she put up a really hard fight."

Bella's stomach churned. She blindly sat in the chair by the bed. "Who did this?"

"Well, I have a few theories, but I can't say for sure until she wakes up and tells me exactly what happened. The problem is, I'm not sure she will." Bella questioningly stared up at Officer Jackson. "Shawnese is…known to us."

Code for she had a record. And, judging by the officer's sad look, a bad one. "A while back, she asked me to teach her how to defend against knife attacks," Bella said. She had told the same thing to Reta but hadn't yet heard back from the social worker.

The officer flipped open a notebook. "Did she mention why?"

"No. I thought maybe she was afraid in general. She has trust issues."

Officer Jackson nodded. "I thought if you were here, she might be more willing to talk. You're obviously important to her. She doesn't have anyone else."

"I'll call Reta and let her know what's happened," Kyle said, and hurried out.

Officer Jackson shifted her stance. "Listen. This looks like an attempted murder and aggravated assault case, and we want to open up a criminal investigation. But if she doesn't tell us what happened, a dangerous criminal walks free." She pocketed the notebook and rubbed her eyes. "I'm going to get a cup of coffee. If she wakes up, talk to her, but be gentle. Let me know if she says anything."

Seconds after the officer left, a raspy voice whispered, "'M not sayin' nothin'."

"Shawnese." Bella inched closer. "How are you feeling?"

The girl swallowed thickly and her eyes cracked open just barely. "Like shit." Her cracked lip twitched. "Y'should see the other guy."

Bella brought her a cup of ice and helped wet the girl's lips. "What happened?"

Shawnese's demeanor shuttered and she sank into her pillow. "Got jumped. Guy took my money."

"But…your hands."

"Fell into a pile of scrap metal."

Bella sucked in her lip. "C'mon, Shawnese. You want to let whoever did this get away with it?"

"He already has." She lifted her hands and made a face. "Better than being dead, I guess."

"Who's *he?*"

She turned her face to stare at the wall. Bella tried another tack. "Why did you ask for me? Why not Reta, or one of the other Touchstone kids?"

"I'm just a junkie to them. You think they care what happens to me?"

"Of course they care. Kyle's talking to Reta on the phone right now."

"You don't get it. I'm off the stuff, but they won't think that. I was trying to earn some quick money. I…I want to take more classes with you. Real classes to learn how to fight." Tears brimmed in her eyes. "No one's gonna believe that."

All the pieces snapped together, painting a gritty, ugly picture of Shawnese's life. Bella had a pretty good idea how the girl had intended to earn her money, and it made her mad and sad all at once. "Who did this to you? I want to know the bastard's name so I know whose ass I'll be kicking when I'm training on the heavy bag."

"Nuh-uh. You'll tell the cops."

"I won't." She gently placed both hands on her bandaged ones. "I swear."

Shawnese closed her eyes and let out a long breath. "Andre." It came out of her as though she'd been wrung out like an old washcloth.

Bella wrapped the name up in her mind and added it to the collection of pain and anger she kept tightly sealed away. She would think about this Andre on those days she needed to push herself past restraint. It was a dangerous practice, fighting angry. For Bella it was like hitting a turbo button on a Formula One race car—anger added a boost of power that could cost her her control.

Emotions made her lose focus, made her get sloppy. But for Shawnese, she would do this. She would make Andre a mental target and spend the rest of her life beating him into submission.

"You should rest. You were really brave." Bella choked on her words. "I'm proud of you."

"Don't let them give me any dope," Shawnese murmured. "I'm clean now. Don't need any dope. I'd rather feel the pain than have to get clean again."

"I'll let the nurse know." She had a feeling she was already on some kind of painkiller, though, probably morphine. She could only imagine what kind of agony she'd be suffering otherwise.

In a few minutes, she heard Shawnese's deep, steady breathing. She left the room and found Kyle by the nurses' station, quietly talking with Officer Jackson. "Reta's on her way over," he said.

"Shawnese woke up for a bit, but she's sleeping now."

The police officer straightened. "Did she tell you anything?"

Bella hesitated and shook her head. The officer sighed. "I'll start my report. I don't think I'll get anything more out of her tonight. But if she happens to say anything to you…" She handed her a business card. "She might not realize it, but I'm on her side. I know things have been tough for her. She lost her whole family in Katrina…" She tugged on the brim of her hat as she looked away, clearing her throat. "I'd better go. Thank you for coming down."

"Thank you." She watched the officer walk off,

saw how straight she kept her spine despite the slump in her shoulders, the tired shuffle of her feet.

"Hey." Kyle nudged her. "You okay?"

"I want to wait until Reta gets here. I don't want Shawnese to wake up alone."

He nodded. They stayed for another forty minutes. Reta arrived. Bella shared what Shawnese had told her, knowing Reta would understand her dilemma and keep her confidence. The social worker frowned.

"Andre comes around sometimes for the needle exchange and to pick up condoms. We've never been able to deny him service because he always follows the rules. I know he's bad news, but…" Her sad look said it all. She couldn't control what happened outside of Touchstone's walls. Her hands were tied unless Shawnese pressed charges.

Kyle looked confused. "I don't understand. The guy tried to kill her. Why wouldn't Shawnese want the cops to know?"

"She's afraid they'll arrest her. It may not look like it, but prostitution is frowned upon in NOLA." Reta paused, seeing Kyle's confusion. "Andre used to be Shawnese's pimp."

Kyle blinked. "Oh."

"She was barely fifteen when the cops first picked her up. After they processed her, they sent her to us. She's been in and out of trouble ever since, but she finally got herself clean and ditched Andre. I thought she was doing really well."

"Is there anything we can do to help?" Bella asked.

"Legally? No." She gave a wry shake of her head. "Believe it or not, we got lucky tonight. Shawnese is alive. I'm sorry to say this kind of thing happens more often than you think." Reta placed a hand on Bella's shoulder. "Whatever you taught her probably saved her life."

Within the hour, other workers and volunteers from Touchstone joined Reta. They'd spell each other off and keep Shawnese company. Bella wanted to stay, but Reta insisted she go home, since nothing more could be done. Weary to the bone, she let Kyle escort her back to the car.

"I wish I could do more for her," Bella said as they walked out to the parking lot. The sun had set and even though the pavement still radiated the day's heat, the air was damp and clung to her skin. She rubbed her arms, wondering where that towel had gotten to. She must have left it at the hospital...

A flash of Ryan's steel grip on her shoulder sapped the strength from her limbs. She pushed away the memory of the photo shoot, angry at herself for dwelling on her problems when Shawnese was so badly hurt.

"You did more than what was called for," Kyle said. "If you hadn't taken the extra time to teach her those techniques, who knows how much worse off she'd be?"

But regret had set its hooks into her, and she couldn't help the flood of self-recrimination. "I should've asked her why she was so afraid. I should've called the cops. I should've—"

"You did all you could reasonably do. Don't beat yourself up about it."

It didn't feel like nearly enough.

They arrived at Kyle's rental car. The ground suddenly pitched her to one side. In the grip of vertigo, she leaned heavily against the door, resting her forehead against the roof.

"Hey…hey!" Kyle was at her side. "Whoa, there. Breathe. Stay with me."

Bella found herself sitting in the passenger side seat with her head between her knees again. "I haven't eaten today," she mumbled, hands trembling. Ryan had told her not to eat before the photo shoot to keep from looking bloated.

Kyle opened the glove compartment. Several energy bars tumbled out. "I always keep a stash of these on me. Here. Eat."

Shakily, she wolfed down a granola bar, then sipped the water he brought her while eating a second bar. The hard ball of emotion compacted in her chest loosened. Tears poured down her cheeks. She wiped them away hastily, disgusted she was crying when Shawnese was the one who'd been through hell. And the girl hadn't shed a single tear.

A sob bubbled past her lips, then another. *"Merda,"* she said, whipping the empty wrapper on the ground and covering her face with her hands.

She hated crying, especially if someone were there to witness it.

"It's okay." Kyle knelt by the open car door and wrapped his arms around her shoulders, pulling her into his chest. He smelled a bit like a new car, but it was comforting. She buried her face against his shoulder and let herself cry. Kyle stroked her hair and shifted until he shared the seat with her, nearly holding her in his lap.

"Men suck," she said, once the sobs had subsided and she'd blown her nose. "I mean, not you…"

"Oh, I have to agree. Men do suck." He rubbed her back. "And I haven't exactly been a model of chivalry."

She gave a mirthless laugh. "Well, you can't be all bad. You let me snot all over your nice clean T-shirt." She drew back and grimaced. "Sorry."

He shrugged. "Trust me, boogers aren't the grossest thing that's been on this shirt." He still held her, stroking strands of hair away from her tear-streaked face. "Better?"

She nodded slowly, her heart thudding hard. His eyes were a deep, soft brown with slivers of gold. His thumb brushed her cheek, and his gaze canted down. "Good."

Her blood and breath went still.

They leaned in at the same time, lips meeting.

CHAPTER NINE

KYLE TASTED BELLA, felt her firm, warm flesh beneath his hands, but while everything in his body said, *More please,* his brain screamed, *What are you doing?*

And it wasn't because she had all the appeal of a damp tissue. Her red-rimmed eyes and runny nose should have been a total turnoff. But whatever part of him was reacting to her, it wasn't his body, which was what got him into trouble most of the time. And it wasn't his brain, which was bombarding him with a thousand reasons why this was wrong.

All he knew was that he had to kiss her. It was an instinct as deep and inexorable as the need for warmth on a dark, cold night.

Bella tasted like salted caramel—likely from the granola bars and tears, his brain pointed out with ruthless logic. Their mouths fit together perfectly. Her tongue darted out briefly, testing, meeting his.

He slid deeper into the roomy sedan's passenger seat, and she straddled his lap. Softly, then with increasing fervor, their lips met, parted, and crashed up against each other again, passion surging like the sea's powerful tides. Her fingers raked through his hair as she pressed closer. He glided a hand along her hip. His fingers slipped beneath the hem of her top, touching the silky soft skin in the small of her back. He was instantly hard, and his hands clutched her waist.

She gave a soft moan and wiggled her bottom, grinding down.

He sucked in a breath. It was too much—too fast, too soon, too Bella. Blindly, he leaped out of the seat, dumping her from his lap as he swallowed a strangled groan. He nearly staggered to his locked knees as the tide of heat ripped over him. Gradually, the stars cleared from his eyes.

"Kyle?"

He trembled, every nerve in his body on high alert as he felt the damp evening air on his skin. He turned away from her, mortified.

"I'm sorry. We…we shouldn't be doing this." He gripped the corner of the car door and rounded the hood, hoping the dampness in the front of his pants didn't show through. It was like the worst of his teenage years all over again.

Bella didn't say anything. He couldn't even look at her, but he knew she was watching him, confused and probably appalled. "I'll drop you off at home," he said, getting behind the wheel.

They didn't speak on the ride back to her apartment, but the questions and regrets were as suffocating as the humidity. What kind of man would ravage Bella in the front seat of a car after the day she'd had? He knew better than to take advantage of a woman in an emotional state.

He was a horn dog. Worse than that, all things considered.

He could only hope the falling darkness would hide his shame.

IT WAS AMAZING how interesting ceilings were at three o'clock in the morning.

Bella could still taste Kyle, could still smell him and feel the imprint of his palms on her skin. She'd eaten, showered and lain in bed for nearly four hours, all while replaying that kiss. On the one hand, Kyle's lips had managed to wipe out the day's drama and worries. On the other hand, she now had a whole new set of issues to contend with.

How could he mess with her like that? If they'd gotten down and dirty in the backseat, at least it would've taken the edge off. But no. He'd left her riled up and panting for more, and hating herself for every stupid minute of it.

Not that it was entirely his fault, she supposed. Mostly, she was ashamed of the fact that she'd acted on her feelings at a vulnerable moment. What did he think of her throwing herself at him when she was still in shock over the day's horrible events? *He must think I'm an insensitive…* She thought hard about the word she'd first learned from reading romance books. *Wanton*. Yeah. That sounded better than the only other word she could imagine people using.

Desperate to escape her thoughts, she covered her face with a pillow and squeezed her eyes shut. Her grandfather had a saying: emotions are like blood—the more you let them out, the weaker you got. Keeping yourself centered and levelheaded, containing your anger and fear—that was how you stayed strong, kept your opponents at bay.

Well, she'd certainly failed at that. If Fulvio had seen her bawling, he'd have used it as proof against her abilities and commitment as a fighter.

Would Kyle think the same? That she'd allowed herself to be compromised?

She pushed those self-defeating thoughts away, but her mind didn't stray far from Kyle. She didn't want to admit to herself that she'd been thinking about those lips since the day she'd arrived at Payette's. Didn't want to admit that the distant crush she'd had on him as a starstruck youth had turned into full-out lust the moment they'd touched. She was a professional, after all, and fighting meant a lot of full-body contact. Working with Kyle should've been an asexual exercise.

But things between them had changed. She'd learned Kyle was as skilled a kisser as he was a wrestler. She wondered what else he could teach her....

She turned over and sighed. Nothing, that's what.

She wasn't about to give in to her libido. Not if it meant losing Kyle as a coach.

The following day, Kyle didn't show up at Payette's. Instead, Tito came with instructions from Kyle for Joe and Bella to practice a series of takedowns and submissions.

"Where is he, anyhow?" Joe asked as they stretched.

Tito shrugged. "Didn't say. He left a message with Liz saying he'd be away for a few days."

"Maybe that old car of his has to be junked and he's in mourning," Joe said on a half laugh.

For some reason, Bella didn't find that funny. That car meant a lot to him. She couldn't imagine he was quite that preoccupied with his convertible, though.

Perhaps he'd gone to check on Shawnese. Or maybe he was filing a complaint against Ryan. Thinking about her agent—ex-agent, she corrected—brought a sour taste to her mouth. She'd considered going to the authorities about Ryan, but there was a chance he'd sue or press charges against her, too. That wasn't something she needed for her career. Maybe it was best to leave it alone.

For now, she had to focus on the fight. It was less than two weeks away, and she didn't feel anywhere near ready. She couldn't afford any more distractions.

Especially from Kyle.

KYLE STARED AT the steering wheel, willing his heartbeat to slow, his fingers to unclench from around the wheel. He'd been sitting in the parking lot at Payette's for almost five minutes now in the stifling heat. If he didn't get out of the car soon, he'd get heat stroke.

It'd been three days since that…*thing* had happened with Bella. Not to mention all the other ugliness of that single strange and terrible day. He chewed on the inside of his cheek. Was she laughing at him? Disappointed? Angry that he'd left her twisting in the wind? She'd probably figured he was avoiding her. That wasn't entirely untrue…but it also wasn't the whole truth. Even so, he couldn't keep shirking his responsibilities to the gym.

When he walked in, Liz looked up and smiled lopsidedly. "The prodigal coach returns."

"I had some things to take care of." He didn't need to explain himself. Things had to get done, and he knew no one would approve if he told them what he'd been up to.

"You weren't out stalking Ryan Holbrooke, were you?"

He whipped his head up to stare at the receptionist.

"Bella told me." The solemn look in Liz's eyes indicated she knew the whole story. "I never liked him—he's a serious creep."

"I should've banned him a long time ago. If he comes in, you scream for me or the guys. He's not likely to show his face here, but he's not welcome."

"Yes, sir." Her reply rang with approval.

He was barely at his desk for five minutes before the phone rang and Kyle picked up. Liz said, "Your sister, Jessica, on line one."

Now what? His shoulders ratcheted tight, sending pain through his neck and scalp. It'd been months since he'd spoken to Jess, and even then, their conversations had been entirely about Dad's will. Maybe she was calling about Mom—he hadn't heard from *her* lately, either. Palms sweating, he picked up the line.

"Hey, squirt," she greeted cheerfully. "How's it hanging?"

"What's wrong? Is it the inheritance?"

"Inheritance? What are you talking about? We took care of all that. Nothing's wrong." She sounded genuinely confused. "I called to say hello. I'm in New Orleans for a business conference. I thought we could meet up for dinner and drinks."

His muscles relaxed and he let out a breath. "Jesus, you scared me."

Jess's laugh was boisterous and full throated—and always great to hear. She hadn't laughed much as a youth. "It's fabulous here in the French Quarter. Why haven't you invited me to stay here before?"

He massaged the back of his neck. "I've been busy."

"Not too busy for dinner, I hope."

He hedged, searching for an excuse. "Hang on a sec." He put her on speakerphone as he moved around the room, searching for something to occupy his hands. He picked up the clipboard with the day's schedule and flipped through it noisily. "I've actually been out of the office for the past few days, and I have this important client I've been neglecting. She has a fight coming up and I need to work with her...."

"Well, a fighter has to eat, right? Bring her along."

"Oh, I don't know if she—"

"Remember how you used to fight with Dad about how important R & R was?"

He blew a breath through his nostrils. Bringing up Dad was not going to sway him. "I've got responsibilities to her—"

"Hey, don't let me interfere with your social calendar," Bella piped up from the doorway. "You talking to your sister?"

Kyle stilled. The sight of her made his chest tighten. She wore a green-and-white tank top, and her trunks were only a couple of inches above the knee, but it was more skin than he'd seen up to now. Her bronzed, muscled shoulders gleamed with a sheen of sweat. He waved her—and his unwanted libido—off.

"Was that her?" Jessica asked. "She sounds cute."

He glanced at Bella's retreating back. "I guess. If you like that sort of thing," he said before he could censure his thoughts.

"My brother the Lothario is ambivalent about a woman's looks?"

He lowered his voice. "I don't have the luxury to think about her like that."

"Ooh, touchy. So you like her, huh?"

Heat shot into his face. "No."

"Yes, you do. You're never this serious when it comes to women."

"Things change." She didn't know about Karla—all that had happened after Dad's funeral. "Anyhow, she's not my type."

"Whatever you say. So how about dinner?"

"I can't. I have a ton of work to catch up on." That wasn't even a lie.

Jess gave a melodramatic sigh. "Oh, well. I guess I'll have to eat all by my lonesome."

"That never used to be a problem."

"Pre-op, sure. But now…" She sighed again. Kyle couldn't help but feel a little guilty for not being a better brother. He only had himself to blame, too. Dad had forbidden everyone from even speaking to Jess, but Kyle could've called. Could've emailed pictures and kept in touch. But he hadn't. Jess was Jess and…well, things were different now.

"I'll be here all week," his sister said. "Promise you'll come see me?"

"I'll do my best." After he took down her number, he hung up and slumped in his chair. He was shaking out two Tylenols from a bottle when Bella entered.

"I heard what you said." She leaned against the doorjamb. "Am I really that important to you as a client?" Her lips slanted, parallel to one skeptically arched eyebrow.

"Of course you are." Were they really talking about this? He'd been away three long days, and she was acting as if nothing had happened. Not Ryan, not Shawnese, not that kiss...or the way he'd—

"Come on. You don't have to lie."

"I'm not."

"Humph." She didn't comment further but crossed her arms, pushing up her breasts. He shifted in his seat, remembering exactly how they'd felt pressed against his chest. "You know my fight's next Friday, right?"

He nodded.

"Good. Because considering no one else has any fights as close as mine, I was hoping to shamelessly monopolize your time."

Was that a threat?

He ground his teeth. Did she think he owed her something? That what they'd shared was more than a momentary lapse in judgment?

He fumed silently. He knew he'd regret that kiss.

They should sit down and talk about what had happened. He should lay it out for her, let her know he'd been...what? Blind with lust?

He gripped the edge of his desk, his thoughts running away from him. *Calm down.* He was freaking out for no reason. He was a professional, dammit, and he'd show her that was all he would be with her—professional.

"C'mon." He got up from his desk. "We need to nail your mounts."

"I know you'll be able to help me there," she said with a smirk, and followed him out.

CHAPTER TEN

THE DAY OF the Fury Fights exhibition match, Tito and Orville escorted Bella to the event. They would stand in as her cornermen. Kyle had called and told them he'd be late—he'd been held up by a call from the national manager of the UFF gyms.

"That can't be good news," Tito said nervously as they browsed the vendors' displays at the MMA convention. The two-day event took place in an arena complex outside of New Orleans and drew a few thousand MMA enthusiasts. "Maybe we should've brought résumés to hand out."

"I'm sure it's the usual money matters," Orville said. "Kyle'll pull through. He always does."

Bella saw the worry lurking in his eyes, though. He glanced at her and gave her a reassuring smile. "You ready?"

"As I'll ever be." She tried to narrow her thoughts down on her opponent, Betty Heimer. The match wasn't for another two hours, but she had to be weighed and checked by the doctor, then she'd need time to warm up.

Stupidly, all she could think about was why Kyle

was late and whether he'd even show up for her fight. She shouldn't care about having him here—this was only an exhibition. But he was her coach. She wanted to prove that she'd gained skills despite all the distractions and drama around them. She wanted to show him she was serious about her fighting career.

After taking a stroll around the convention, Bella signed in and was directed to the "locker room." Two bikini-clad girls applying a fog of hairspray and a couple of random employees occupied the washroom.

"Bella Fiore?" A woman in her mid-thirties with tightly bunned dirty-blond hair waved at her and gave a grim smile. "I'm Betty Heimer."

She blinked. *Oh, crap.* Bella brightened her smile and nodded, but they didn't shake hands. They'd tap gloves in the cage. That was where she'd really meet her. "Hi, Betty. Nice to meet you."

"Guess they didn't figure we'd need separate rooms," she said on a nervous laugh.

"Guess not." She could be polite and respectful, but she didn't want to get too friendly with a woman whose face she'd bust up shortly.

Betty scratched her nose. "I'll let you get changed. Good luck to you."

"You, too."

Slowly, Bella stripped out of her street wear, pulling on her rash guard and trunks. She turned and faced the corner of the locker room, trying to drown out the background noises, the flushing of the toilets and the cage girls' inane chatter. Meditating helped her find her center, to bury all the softest and most vulnerable parts of her psyche while donning her mental armor.

But as she sat there, trying hard to push the world out, thoughts of Kyle pushed in. She thought she'd put aside her personal feelings. After all, he'd made it clear his curiosity had been satisfied. Still, that kiss lingered like a ghost on her lips, and while that night shouldn't have meant anything, she couldn't help replaying it over and over.

Angry at herself for caring so much, she hastily wrapped her hands, put on her hoodie and running shoes and stepped out. Tito and Orville took her to a curtained-off area padded with rubber mats that served as a green room. Her fight with Heimer was fourth on the card, so she warmed up while they waited. Every time someone stuck their head in, her hopes shot up. But it was never Kyle.

"Head in the game, Twilight," Orville barked when she glanced over her shoulder yet again.

Bella scowled. "Y'know, it used to be my name meant *beautiful*." She threw a hard right hook at the mitts Orville held, making him grunt.

"You'll be lucky if the name doesn't stick," Tito commented. "You ought to pick something."

"How about 'the Beast,'" Orville suggested, and got a hard left jab he nearly didn't catch.

"Too cliché." Tito rubbed his chin. "Maybe 'the Babe'?"

"'The Brat'!"

"How about 'Bella Bootylicious Fiore'?"

"Will you two shut up?" Bella laughed finally. "You're messing up my mojo!"

Orville tsked. "Oh, this isn't good. She's laughing, Tito."

"Nerves," he agreed solemnly, and tickled her in the ribs, sending her into another fit of giggles. She punched him hard in the arm, and he hissed and rubbed his shoulder. "There you go. She just needs to loosen up."

"You'll do all right, Bella." Orville looked toward the entryway again, and his mouth tightened. "He'll be here soon."

KYLE CIRCLED THE parking lot a third time, tires squealing, but it was no use. The place was packed. He checked the clock again and swore—why had Vinny called right when he was about to leave? The guy had the worst timing. But he'd absolutely insisted on going over the marketing plans Kyle had sent him, saying it'd only take a minute—it had taken forty. It might have gone on for another forty except that a real emergency had interrupted the call: a client had dropped a dumbbell on his foot, and

Kyle had to drive him to the hospital. He dreaded the paperwork to come.

He ended up parking two blocks away from the stadium and jogging to the entrance. Inside, he could hear the crowd shouting and hooting. It took an interminable five minutes to get through backstage security.

"I'm sorry, you're with who?" the bald security guard asked.

"Bella Fiore," Kyle shouted again over the audience's catcalls.

The beefy man scowled at his list. "Is she one of the ring girls?"

"She's fighting Betty Heimer," he said impatiently.

"Oh, you mean the chick fight. That's happening right now."

"What?" He couldn't see past the partitions. The place wasn't as big as he thought it'd be, but the stands were packed. The guard stopped him as he started toward the cage.

"I need you to sign in and get a badge," he said.

"I have to get in there *right now*." He deked around the guard and hurried through the maze of partitions. Finally, heart pounding, he joined Tito and Orville in their corner.

Tito barely glanced at him. "About time," he bit out. "We're two minutes into the first round."

Bella bounced on the balls of her feet, bobbing and weaving and keeping in constant motion. Kyle recognized Wayne's techniques in action. Betty Heimer moved more slowly, conserving her energy, testing Bella with strikes she easily dodged. She was circling, waiting for an opening. Her face was fixed in pure concentration.

"C'mon, Bella," he shouted, beating his palm against the edge of the mat. "Keep it grounded. Don't tire yourself out."

The moment the words were past his lips, everything fell apart. Bella looked away from Heimer—a rookie mistake. She met his eye as her feet shifted into a staggered stance, preparing for a wrestling takedown, leaving her guard wide-open.

It seemed to happen in slow motion. In the split second it took for Bella to transition her footing, Betty slid forward and walloped her with a right hook.

Bella's eyes blanked, her mouth guard protruding from her lips.

She hit the floor with a resounding boom and didn't get up. And Kyle knew without a doubt it was his fault.

"BELLA. BELLA, CAN you hear me?"

The world shifted and spun around her. She heard people talking, but the voices faded in and out between the strange ringing and hooting sounds.

A man was kneeling next to her, snapping his fingers, calling her name. She felt as though she were trying to swim to the surface of a murky lake in the dark.

"Bella." Kyle's voice cut through her stupor. Her eyes snapped open, and she remembered.

The fight. She'd lost. She'd been knocked out, and she'd barely started that first round....

She pushed herself up, realized she was still in the cage. "I'm fine." Pain shafted through her head and a wave of dizziness rolled through her. Someone checked her eyes, asked her questions, then stood back.

"You'll be all right. Don't get up too quick."

"Yeah." She staggered to her feet and shook herself off. If she was going to lose, she was going to do it gracefully. The announcer declared Betty Heimer the winner and raised her hand. The crowd's mild applause and boos sank into Bella, who focused on keeping herself from swaying.

"I'm glad you're okay," Betty said in her ear as they hugged.

"It'll take a lot more to kill me." Bella forced a smile. "Congratulations."

Betty clapped her on the back and left, but she looked far from satisfied. Bella wouldn't be happy about a victory like that, either. It seemed more like a fluke than an actual win.

She was still in a daze as her corner ferried her off to the doctor's examination room. The physician, a middle-aged woman, made her lie down as she checked her over. Kyle, Tito, Orville and some official crowded into the tight space, looking grim.

"Don't move," the doctor ordered her sternly. "I

have to make sure you haven't suffered any major effects apart from a concussion."

"I'm fine, Doc."

"Don't argue with her." Kyle sounded angry. "She needs to do a full exam. It's the rules."

Bella heaved a sigh and stared at the ceiling. *Cristo,* she wasn't a fragile little bird. The only thing that hurt was her pride. How could she have made such an amateur mistake? She'd shut out the booing and catcalls, she'd closed off her mind to everything, even her corner's cheers. But the moment Kyle had walked in...

Her skin erupted in goose bumps and she shivered.

"Are you cold?" Kyle asked, then barked, "Someone get her a blanket."

"Will you leave me alone?" she snapped, eyes burning. "I'm fine. I don't need a blanket. I don't need anything." She could feel heat radiating off her cheeks. She was humiliated.

With a quiet, steady voice, the doctor ordered, "Gentlemen, please wait outside. I need to see my patient privately."

They stumped out in silence. The physician carefully checked her face. "That's going to be a hell of a shiner."

Bella didn't say anything. She wanted to crawl into a hole and die.

"On the upside," the doctor added, "at least this won't count toward your record."

But it did, she thought bleakly, hugging herself. Bella had lost more than an exhibition match. She'd lost everyone's respect.

CHAPTER ELEVEN

IT HAD BEEN a bad fight and everyone knew it. Maybe that was why the staff tiptoed around Bella for the rest of the week. No one could even look her in the eye without wincing, and the bruises weren't improved by the angry scowl she wore. It got especially awkward when footage of the spectacular knockout made it onto YouTube. By the time it reached Kyle's laptop, "Hot chick gets KO'd" had been viewed over 150,000 times.

It was hard when you lost, but it was especially hard when you knew it could have been easily prevented. Kyle felt bad for her. He felt bad for everyone. Tito, Orville and Wayne had worked hard with Bella. They'd all been expecting results. But one moment of distraction, one little slipup…

He dug his thumbs into his jaw and pressed his fingertips into his temples. This was his fault. He hadn't adequately prepared Bella for this match. He'd done nothing but ignore or distract her since she'd arrived. That the loss didn't count on her record hardly mattered. The video footage had made the highlight reels of many MMA websites. Bella had become a laughingstock.

Five days after the fight, the day before Thanksgiving, a call came for Bella.

"It's your grandfather," Liz said, her face a touch pale.

Bella stilled, and her lips compressed into a tight line. Kyle offered her his office, and she marched in, chin held high.

He didn't mean to eavesdrop, but he ended up using a table just outside his office to fill out some insurance forms. At first, it seemed like Bella was having a normal conversation with a family member. But since it was entirely in Portuguese, he had no idea what she was saying. Then her voice rose, and her objections came out in harsh syllables. She looked up to see him watching her from the doorway.

Her shoulders were bunched up to her ears, and her face was pale. She held the receiver an inch away from her ear. The stream of abuse pouring from the phone was unmistakably scathing.

His hands flexed into fists. Kyle wanted to take the phone from her and yell at the old man to give her some slack.

Her voice grew rough, defeated. *"Sim...sim...sim, Avô."* She glanced at him. "I have to…" Her lips compressed and she gently hung up the phone. She took a deep breath and hugged her elbows. "My grandfather heard about the match. He's so mad at how bad the loss was that he's threatened to disown me."

Kyle suppressed the choice insults he had for Fulvio Fiore, but instead he said, "He'd be wrong to. Everyone has bad fights."

She nodded but didn't look convinced. "So what's the word, Coach? You gonna fire me?"

"Fire you? Why?"

"Because I'm a loser. Because I'm obviously not qualified to teach anything after that match." It was clear from the deadpan way she said it that she was parroting what Fulvio had told her. But the slight tremor in her voice told him she'd fully expected him to obey what he assumed were her grandfather's wishes.

"If anyone's at fault, it's me." He glanced out the door. People milled about, trying to catch lingering bits of their conversation. He marched to the door and slammed it shut. "Sit."

She slid into a chair and slumped back, unable to meet his eye.

"Listen. I'm not going to fire you. That fight was an anomaly. You know anything can happen in the cage. If you need to blame someone, blame me. I didn't give you what you needed. And you paid the price because I neglected your training. I failed you."

And he had. Utterly. Admitting it and seeing that look of defeat in Bella's dull green eyes brought it home. He'd let this happen. He'd let his personal feelings interfere with his work.

He planted his palms on the desk. "From here on in, I'm giving you 100 percent. You lost because I didn't take you seriously. I didn't give you the right tools or enough of my time. I promise I will now."

She sank deeper into her chair. "I don't even have a fight coming up."

"That doesn't matter. It shouldn't matter. Your goal was to become a better fighter. I've been teaching you wrestling techniques all this time, and I ignored the fact that you're not a wrestler. You were going to go for a takedown, weren't you?"

She nodded.

Kyle thought as much. Replaying the fight in his head, he knew that the moment he'd opened his mouth, Bella had shifted because his voice had triggered her into taking a staggered stance. It was a Pavlovian response: the same thing had happened to Kyle whenever his father had pitched his voice in certain ways. They'd drilled that way, too, with Dad shouting instructions and Kyle going through the motions like a trained monkey.

"I'm sorry, Bella," he said. "I promise you, this is not the end."

Her weak smile didn't reach her eyes. Skepticism haunted them instead.

Don't you give up. Don't you dare give up. Defeat is for people who are too lazy to try anymore....

His fingers clenched as his father's voice rang in his ears.

He had no intention of giving up on her. Not by a long shot.

PAYETTE'S WAS CLOSED for the Thanksgiving holiday weekend. Bella spent that time exploring the local tourist attractions. She could have stayed home and trained, but after the Heimer fight, she wasn't in the mood.

At Liz's insistence, Bella had turkey dinner with Liz's family. The Gonçalveses were a happy bunch who'd come to the States from Portugal more than four decades ago, and they were thrilled to speak with Bella in their native tongue. The following day, Liz took her Black Friday shopping. It seemed Liz was bent on cheering her up.

Bella wasn't usually one to throw herself a pity party, but there was something more to the malaise that had invaded her. Maybe she was homesick. Or maybe she should've sat down and talked to Kyle about that kiss. If she'd brought it out into the open instead of letting her thoughts fester…

No, that couldn't be what was bothering her. This was about her confidence. She had to accept the defeat and move on. She couldn't let one mistake at an exhibition match define her career.

"Hey!" Liz waved a pair of socks in front of her face, tugging Bella from her thoughts. "Everything okay? You haven't bought a single thing."

Bella shrugged. "I don't see anything I need."

"This isn't about *need,*" Liz said, laughing lightly. "It's about crass consumerism. Contributing to the economy and providing jobs, something, something." She gestured vaguely with her hands and grinned.

"If you're going to return half this stuff next week, why even bother?"

"It's tradition." They elbowed their way through a crowd. "And it's a good workout. Trust me, it'll get your blood pumping."

She was right about that. Eventually, Bella picked up a few T-shirts and a dress marked down almost 80 percent, but her patience hung by a thread by the time they were lined up at the cash register. There, she yelled at a guy who was pushing an old woman with his cart. She told him to knock it off. When he yelled at her to mind her own business, Liz joined her and soon, the whole lineup was shaming him until he abandoned his purchases and left the store.

"That was horrible," Bella said as they piled into Liz's car.

"But you had fun, right?"

"Actually...yes." She laughed. It had taken her mind off her gloomy thoughts. And seeing how awful other people could be made her feel less bad about herself. She told Liz and laughed. "I must be crazy. And a terrible human being."

"Black Friday and Boxing Day shopping are as close to competitive fighting as I'll ever get," Liz said, pulling out of the lot. "It's the only time I'm not afraid of being punched in the face because I'll probably punch right back."

They went to The Spot for dinner and drinks. They were talking and laughing and enjoying the evening when Kyle walked through the door.

"He didn't go home for Thanksgiving?" Bella asked, trying to hide her sudden breathlessness with her whispered question.

Liz sucked in her lip. "He hasn't gone home for the holidays since his dad died."

"His mom's still around, though, right? And he has a sister."

"I don't like to talk about people behind their backs." Her gaze shifted to her lap. Liz obviously knew more than she let on.

Bella supposed some families simply didn't get along the way hers did—when they did at all, she thought wryly—but she didn't think that was the case with Kyle. There was more to him than the playboy coach and former Olympic athlete he showed the world. She thought she got him: he had a tough Dad, high expectations of himself, commitment issues...but there was something else going on. He was holding back some part of himself.

She thought about the Bourne-Mortensen fight she'd watched when she'd first come to The Spot, and remembered how Mike Bourne had stayed out of reach. Kyle was kind of like him. In the fight, but keeping himself from engaging, staying at a safe distance, afraid to get personal or messy.

He scanned the room, slowly walking along the bar, presumably trawling for a lonely young lady to sit next to. The bar was sadly empty of college coeds, though. Bella felt a little sorry for him. "Hey, Coach!"

"What are you doing?" Liz whispered.

"You said you don't like talking about people behind their backs. So let's talk to his front." She studied Liz's rapid blinking and said, "I'm sorry. Did I do something wrong?"

"No. Nothing like that." She put on a broad smile as Kyle approached. "Hey, boss."

"Come and join us," Bella invited, patting the seat next to her. "Or are you meeting friends?"

He slid into the booth. "Not tonight. I was…" He trailed off. "Looking for a good seat."

Bella couldn't help thinking about Kyle's behavior in terms of a fight, now. *Dodge. Feint. Keep your feet moving. Stay in motion. Don't give anyone a chance to nail you.*

"I got a call from Reta," Kyle said, once the waitress took his drink order. "Shawnese's doing a lot better. Her hands are going to take a while to heal, but she's doing physical therapy. She's staying with Reta for the holidays." He filled Liz in briefly about their student from Touchstone.

"I don't suppose she's said anything about catching whoever did that to her?" Bella asked.

Maybe she'd given away too much because Kyle's expression darkened. "No. According to Reta, Shawnese insists she fell into a pile of scrap metal."

Of course, Bella understood what Shawnese was facing. Fear of retribution. Fear of being arrested. If she pressed charges, she'd be made to testify in court against her attacker, only to have her testimony put into question. Why should anyone believe a former prostitute and drug addict? It was probably as frustrating for Shawnese as it was for the cops, but what could she do? What could anyone do?

"Well, I'm glad someone's taking care of her." She made a note to call.

"I'm suddenly feeling beat," Liz announced. "Kyle, would you mind driving Bella home?"

He nodded. "Sure. You feeling all right?"

"I think I overdid it today. Shopping's hard work. Bella, if it's okay, I'll just bring your clothes in to work tomorrow."

"Are you sure? I can go with you." A ball of nerves rolled around in her gut. Was Liz plotting to leave her alone with Kyle? Surely the receptionist didn't think they were an item. She hadn't told her about the kiss 'n' grope in the car.

The chemistry between her and Kyle wasn't *that* obvious, was it?

"I'll be fine," Liz insisted. "You two enjoy."

She left. Kyle and Bella sat alone in suddenly awkward silence. The screens showed a rerun of Dominic Payette's most recent UFF fight, defending his belt for the fourth time since winning the championship title. Bella searched for something to say.

Kyle spoke up first. "Are you going home for Christmas?"

Bella set her teeth. Fulvio had made it clear he wouldn't welcome her home unless she intended to stay. While she hated to miss the holidays with her family, she couldn't let them drag her back to play the obedient daughter, nor would she sour the celebrations by ruffling feathers. Her temper was too much like Fulvio's to keep the peace for long. "I plan to stay here," she said. She didn't want Kyle pitying her. "I've always wanted to see what a Christmas in the States is like."

"You should go farther north where there's snow. Funny, even though I grew up in California, I've always felt like there should be snow at Christmas. I blame TV."

"I had enough snowy days while I was in college in Canada, thanks. I think it'll be nice right here. The warm weather will make it feel like home." Just not with any of the people who mattered to her the most.

"Will you be going to the UFF charity ball?"

Bella had almost forgotten about the event she and Ryan had been dress shopping for. She hadn't been keen on going before, but realized Ryan had been right: she needed to network with more people in the industry, especially after her fiasco at the exhibition. She had to get out there and show the world she wasn't beat. "I would if I could. But Ryan was the one with the invitation and the tickets."

"Well, that's no problem. You'll come with me. I've got my invitation. You can be my plus one."

"You mean, your date?"

His lips twitched. "Sure, if you want to call it that." He took a long pull of his beer and fixed his attention on the screen.

A thrill raced through her, and she struggled not to smile too widely or even acknowledge the happiness wending through her. She shouldn't think this meant anything more than a great opportunity to get her name out there and meet some MMA stars, but her mind was stuck firmly on the event now. And the dress she'd bought today would be perfect for the evening.

Oh, my God. I'm going on a date with Kyle Peters. The thought struck her between the eyes. As awkward as things were, she really liked Kyle. More than she should, really. He wasn't worth the drama and the complications, she told herself. She'd seen him in action, seen him go home with innumerable women. If anything were to happen between them... Well, she wasn't about to expect more than one night.

Kyle took her home after finishing his one beer. She'd insisted she could walk, but he refused to let her leave on her own. "I promised Liz I'd drive you home. She'd be pissed if I broke that promise."

"And you're scared of her?"

"She makes my coffee every morning. I have to keep her happy."

The silence in the car wasn't exactly uncomfortable, but she remained ultra-self-aware. She was reminded of the other time he'd driven her home. After the big rainstorm, when he'd come up and ordered takeout. Things had felt easier then somehow. There'd been no pressure, only tension. *And* he hadn't seen the worst of her back then.

Then there was the night after that mind-blowing kiss…. She closed her eyes. This was stupid. Any other guy and she'd have him at heel all the way up to her bedroom with the snap of her fingers. But here she was, paralyzed by her own uncertainty.

He pulled up next to the curb and killed the engine. She didn't move.

"What are you going to do now?" she asked, stalling. "It's still early."

"Probably go home, maybe read."

"You want to come up for a drink?" It was a crazy offer, but she couldn't handle this weirdness between them anymore. She felt as though she was straddling an ever-moving line, and she had to keep dancing to avoid landing too firmly on one side or the other. The problem was she hadn't yet decided which side she should be on.

You're in the fight or you're not.

He stared at her. Her heart bumped, and she lowered her gaze to his lips.

"I shouldn't," he managed in an almost strangled voice.

"That's not a no."

She knew what she wanted. She wouldn't be coy about it anymore. They'd danced around each other long enough.

A gust of wind made the convertible's canopy ripple. He echoed his frustration with a blown-out breath. "We can't."

"Kyle—"

"I can't do this, Bella. I'm your coach and your boss."

Something inside her tweaked at the hard line he'd drawn. She sat up straighter. "I'll be gone in four months. And we wouldn't be the first people to step outside of an employer-employee *or* coach-trainee relationship."

He ran his palms over his face. "Look, it's not you. I think you're great—"

"Well, don't lay it on too thick, Coach."

"—but I can't put either of us in a compromising position. It wouldn't be good for your career or mine."

"What we do outside of work is no one's business." She softened her voice. "This tension between us isn't nothing, Kyle. I'm not saying we should go and get married. All I want is a chance for us to make sure it's *just* tension."

His jaw jutted, the muscles in his cheekbones flexing as he stared out the windshield. She sensed the inner struggle radiating off him.

"Is this because of what happened with Karla?" she ventured. His whole body stiffened.

"That's none of your business."

She sighed. "Okay." She popped her seat belt. "Look, Kyle. I'll admit it. I like you a lot. Even though I probably shouldn't. Even though it goes against my better judgment and everyone else's advice. But at least I'm not afraid of my attraction to you. Can you say the same about me?"

He didn't respond, which was all the answer she needed.

She got out of the car and slammed the door shut.

CHAPTER TWELVE

HADRIAN STARED. He couldn't begin to describe the jaw-droppingly horrendous turn of luck his fighters were experiencing. *Craptapulously efftacular* was the closest he could come.

Burton had decided to bow out of his fight. The man had said he wanted to spend more time with his family, but Hadrian had a feeling Burton couldn't handle the pressure of being featured as the main event. His wife, who was also his manager, had already complained that her husband wasn't being paid enough to risk brain damage, but Burton wasn't exactly a superstar the way Dominic Payette was. And he'd proved it by backing out of his match.

People were expecting something big for the anniversary event—heavy hitters and title matches. But Dom had absolutely refused to fight because his wife, Fiona, was pregnant with twins and due that week. Others were avoiding the card outright, turning him down for one reason or another. People were calling the event cursed.

Hadrian looked at the calendar. Christ. It was less than three weeks to Christmas, and only ten weeks to the anniversary fight. He had enough problems worrying about the monthly cards to promote.

"If you're thinking of breaking something else I'll have to replace, think again, Hadrian," Mrs. Hutzenbiler warned sharply as she entered his office. His P.A. had used that same tone back when he was eight years old and she was his babysitter warning him not to jump off furniture.

"What am I going to do, Mrs. H.?" He rested his chin on the blotter and clasped his hands over the top of his head. "If I cancel the anniversary card, what does that say about me? About this sport?"

"It's not your fault. Things happen. Besides, you won't cancel. You're too stubborn to give up. You'll find a way to fill the card."

"With who? At this rate, I'll be forced to put amateurs on stage. It'll become a freakin' sideshow."

"You never know what'll come out of disasters," Mrs. Hutzenbiler said brusquely. "Remember that young basketball player everyone fell in love with? The one that became really popular when his team was doing so poorly? They put him in out of desperation."

"I've already used up all my subs, Mrs. H. Besides, that was a one-in-a-million shot."

"And you're in a sport where a million different things can happen." She sat primly in the visitor's chair. "Let me tell you a story…."

Hadrian groaned. "I really don't have time—"

"Hadrian Alexander Blackwell, you will make time to listen to your elders and learn from them."

He winced. He still hated it when she yelled at him.

She settled in her seat, her color subsiding. "Back when I was a girl, my younger sister and I wanted to bake a cake for our mother's birthday. We had a recipe, but as we started making it, we realized we were missing ingredients. We used only one egg instead of two. We didn't have vanilla or cream of tartar. We accidentally poured in baking soda instead of baking powder. Our frosting was made with granulated sugar instead of powdered sugar. It was an awful mess."

"Let me guess. Your mother loved it anyhow."

"Goodness' sakes, no. She spit it out, rinsed her mouth and threw the whole thing away."

"This isn't making me feel better."

She glared down her nose at him. "I'm not here to make you feel better. Stop interrupting my story."

He waved at her to continue.

"My mother asked us what we did to the cake recipe that it turned out so wrong. We told her, and she laughed at us. She asked, 'Why didn't you make me a pie instead? We had enough ingredients for that.' On top of which, she'd shown us how to make pie crust before, which was easy. But we were so focused on that birthday cake, we didn't even consider our limitations. We'd never even baked a cake before."

"So you're saying I should make pie," Hadrian concluded.

"I'm saying you should work with what you have and consider some alternatives." She got up. "Cake isn't the answer to everything."

With that, Mrs. Hutzenbiler left him alone to stare at his computer. His email was open so he skimmed the dozens of messages. None from Quinn. She hadn't been in his bed for nearly two weeks. This latest round of fighter cancellations was probably keeping her occupied at work. She'd barely needed to interview him—the fighters' camps were being quite candid about the "cursed" UFF anniversary card.

He opened a message from one of his directors of marketing who was trying to console him about the latest news. He'd added a link to a YouTube video at the end with the note, "Hang in there. We can turn this around."

The video was of the reigning GRRL Fights featherweight champion, Ayumi Kamino. She was trapped in a painful-looking armbar, one that would have ended most other fights. Her opponent twisted and twisted. Hadrian cringed. Kamino's shoulder looked like it was about to pop out of its socket. The referee hovered, ready to call the match. But a look of sheer determination was carved on the champ's face.

Finally, something gave and in a sudden burst of power, Kamino rolled to her side, snaked her legs around her opponent, flipped her over and reversed their positions. The challenger tapped out, and Kamino stood triumphant to the roar of her fans.

Hadrian wanted to cheer with them. Mixed martial arts was all about surprises like this. A fight could turn on a moment's notice....

And that's when he decided he was going to change the UFF forever. "Mrs. H.!"

His P.A. walked calmly back into the room, an expectant look on her face. "You bellowed?"

"Get me the number for Ayumi Kamino's people. Then I need a list of all the female fighters who fight in her weight class."

KYLE'S STRONG ARMS wrapped tight around Bella's middle and squeezed. She pushed out all of the sensations racing across her skin and said to the class, "It's important not to panic. Your attacker will have the element of surprise, of course, and your instinct will be to pull away, but then he'll have the advantage."

The young women giggled as Kyle picked her up off her feet. She kicked uselessly at the air, blandly saying, "Help. Help." She grinned at the class. "If this happens, what do we do?"

The girls emitted an ear-piercing shriek that filled the room and reverberated through her bones. Nice and loud and uninhibited. Getting the girls to vocalize their distress when attacked was an important lesson in self-defense.

"Good. And if you can turn and scream right in your attacker's ear, maybe bite it off, you go for it. Don't let him drag you off. Don't wait to fight. Raise hell and get away."

"I'm going to need an aspirin after this," Kyle groused quietly as he put her back on her feet. She smirked and continued, enjoying his undivided attention. Normally, Wayne played the part of attacker, but he'd come down with a migraine, so Kyle had filled in for him in this new women's self-defense class, much to the students' delight.

One young college-aged woman put up her hand. "What if he has your arms locked up?"

Bella slipped her arms to her sides and let Kyle clasp them tight. She said, "Go," and they reenacted a real struggle as he dragged her backward into an imaginary alley.

Reaching behind her between Kyle's legs, she pinched the flesh of his inner thigh tight and twisted. Kyle yelped and jumped away, and she swung around in a defensive position.

The ladies all sat stunned, then broke out in laughter and applause as Kyle glowered. "You wouldn't have done that to Wayne," he complained.

"Only because Wayne's ticklish. You're much better at this. Now go put on the suit."

He grumbled as he went to don the padded suit Wayne wore for the end of the class, when the students got to throw their hardest kick or punch at a fully armored opponent. But before he got halfway across the room, one girl shouted, "I wanna see you two spar!"

"Yeah!" two younger ladies chimed in. "Fight! Fight! Fight!"

Bella put her hands up. "You know the rules. No horseplay."

Kyle cocked an eyebrow. "Don't tell me you're afraid."

"Ooh," the girls taunted.

Bella planted her hands on her hips as the class chanted, *"Fight, fight, fight,"* until she silenced them with one raised finger.

"If I spar with Kyle, I'm making you all do twenty extra burpees next week."

"Do it, do it, do it!"

She shrugged and started to limber up. Kyle called Tito in to officiate. The class moved back, giving the pair extra room to maneuver.

"This is only a demonstration," Bella warned. "There'd be a lot more danger if we let loose, which is why Tito's here. Everyone understand? Don't try this at home."

"Get on with it!" Tito cajoled with a laugh.

"You ready?" Kyle asked, cracking his neck and stretching his forearms.

She didn't answer, sending him a wide, toothy

smile. Tito inserted himself between them. "I want a nice clean match. And try not to kill each other."

"Do or do not," Kyle said in a perfect imitation of Master Yoda, "there is no try."

He must have planned to make her laugh, because she wasn't ready as he crouched and sprang for her the moment Tito shouted, "Fight!"

She caught him barely in time to put a guard on him, but he was already halfway to cutting the corner, and he was a lot stronger than she was.

She slipped beneath his arm, cinching it between her breasts and keeping him snug against her so he'd have no way to back off. Then she threw her legs around his waist and wrenched all her weight to one side, throwing him off balance. But because his center of gravity was already quite low, her scissor takedown only made him stagger.

Now they were awkwardly posed, with her legs wrapped around his waist, clinging to his one arm, while his other remained locked beneath her thigh. Neither was willing to let go and give the other the advantage. Kyle's strength would eventually wear out, but Bella couldn't hang on forever, either.

She jerked her weight back and forth, trying to make Kyle lose his footing. If they brought it to the ground, they risked a scramble that would end with the most likely victor on top. Despite his strength and size, though, Bella had skills enough to handle him. And though she was intrigued by the idea of being topped by Kyle, this was neither the time nor the place to be experimenting.

Just then, Liz ran up and shouted, "Bella, you have a phone call."

"Kind of busy here, Liz," Tito said.

"It's Hadrian Blackwell. He says it's important."

Her heart stopped. She met Kyle's wide eyes. His muscles bunched and slackened beneath her. He crouched to the ground, and she slid off. The girls groaned, unsatisfied the match hadn't been finished. Bella knew how they felt.

She left Kyle and Tito to wrap up while she ran downstairs to take the call in Kyle's office. She allowed herself a moment to breathe deep before picking up. "Bella Fiore speaking."

"Bella, it's Hadrian Blackwell. How're you doing?" Hadrian's cheerfully gruff voice boomed. "Everyone treating you well? Are you enjoying your time at Payette's?"

"Yes, sir, thank you very much." It didn't sound like he was gearing up to fire her. Maybe he was going to encourage her to go back to São Paulo. Some part of her still believed others would try to carry out her grandfather's dictates and force her home. Who better than the president of the UFF? "I've enjoyed working here. Payette's is like a second home to me." Okay, now she sounded like a suck-up. She clamped her lips shut.

"Excellent. I hope Kyle Peters has been treating you well."

She hedged, but said, "Yes. He's been very good."

"Good. I mean, I saw the footage of that little Fury Fights match. That wasn't exactly your best fight ever."

"No shit." She bit her lip, mortified she'd said that out loud. "I mean—"

Hadrian laughed. "It's fine, Bella. I've probably said worse things to my grandmother."

She wiped at the sweat beading on her upper lip. "I was having an off day," she explained. "My attention slipped. Not that I'm making excuses. It was embarrassing for everyone."

"You don't have to tell me," he replied casually. "Did you ever see my last fight before I got into the promotion business? I think I looked off to one side for half a second, and it was because there was this beautiful woman in the crowd…" He trailed off. "Anyhow, the next thing I knew, I woke up lying on the mat. Stupid mistake, you know. But we all make them."

"Mr. Blackwell, may I ask why you're calling?" she asked slowly. He couldn't be calling just to make her feel better.

"Straight to business. I like that. Bella, I'm calling because I want you to come and fight on the UFF's tenth anniversary card."

Bella put her hand over her mouth and leaned on the edge of Kyle's desk. "You're serious."

"Absolutely. I'll be frank—you've probably heard how we're having a hard time filling the card. Well,

I think now's the perfect time to sign some ladies on with the UFF and see where women's MMA goes. I've heard great things about you. And the fact that so many of your family members have fought or trained my fighters is an added bonus."

Bella thought she might actually faint. She fell onto Kyle's big executive chair and sank into the leather. "This is a real honor...."

"Yeah, it is," Hadrian said. "So what do you say? Third Saturday in February, here in Las Vegas at the MGM Grand."

Be cool. Don't jump on this without asking questions. "Who's my opponent?"

"Ayumi Kamino. Maybe you've heard of her?"

"The GRRL Fights featherweight champ?" Her mouth went dry. "The one they call 'Kamikaze'?"

"That's her." She could hear the grin in his voice. "What do you think?"

She bit her lip. "She's in the 145-pound class. I fight at 155."

"I know. Listen, I'm not about to tell you how to run your life, but I think if you dropped to 145, your career will be that much better. There simply aren't that many women in your weight class."

Bella knew this, of course. But she'd never compromised when it came to her body. She was a healthy weight, and she liked how she looked and operated at 155 pounds. She hadn't fought below that since she was in her teens.

But this was the big leagues—a once-in-a-lifetime opportunity. She chewed on the inside of her cheek.

"Ten weeks, ten pounds. That's perfectly doable and healthy," he added. "I can even send a specialist down to help you."

"I don't need help losing weight," she said testily, but dialed it back. "I mean, I appreciate it. But what happens if I don't make weight?"

"You will." He said it with confidence. "You're a Fiore. You've done things no other fighter has ever done, and I think you've got what it takes to be a star." He paused. "Did I mention the prize money?"

He carefully enunciated the amount she'd win if she KO'd her opponent, submitted her or won by decision. "That's not including the fight bonuses or the title belt," he added. "Not to mention this will be UFF history."

"You're giving the women a belt?"

"Whoever wins this match, absolutely. Big, shiny, gold thing. I'll even find a matching purse and shoes if you like."

A UFF belt. The prize money. Everything she'd always dreamed of. She breathed deep. How could she turn him down? "I'll do it. I accept."

"Excellent. I'll have my people send the paperwork, call you with all the travel details. You're not still repped by Ryan Holbrooke, are you?"

She scoffed. "No. We…had a falling-out."

"You're better off on your own, darling. Ryan's good at wheeling and dealing, and he's found some real great fighters, but frankly, the guy's a muppet." He was so blasé about it, Bella couldn't help but laugh. "Anyhow, congratulations. This is going to be historic. You're coming to the big Starlight fund-raiser gala next week, right? I'll send a private jet for you."

"I—" Everything was happening so fast, she barely had time to sputter, "Thank you, but I said I'd go as Kyle's plus one."

"Plus one? You're going to be a guest of honor, darling. And you'll need to stick around awhile, too. We'll have business to take care of. Media stuff."

They hung up shortly after that. Bella sat there grinning like an idiot, heart soaring and pumping hard at the same time. Had that just happened?

Kyle appeared at the office door, two lines between his eyebrows. Bella grinned at him and leaped out of his chair.

"Are you—" He didn't have time to finish his sentence as she grabbed his face and planted a big, smacking kiss on his lips.

CHAPTER THIRTEEN

KYLE THOUGHT HE should jerk out of Bella's hold, but he stayed stooped over her, frozen in shock.

So much for fight or flight, huh? A third *F* word was floating through his thoughts now, and he closed his hands into fists to keep from grabbing her waist and drawing her closer.

Think about Bree, he told himself stoutly, but it didn't help.

Bella's eyes shone brilliantly as she pulled away. "I'm going to fight in the UFF."

He blinked. "What?"

"Hadrian Blackwell wants to sign me on as the league's first female fighter!" She let go of his face and danced around. "He wants me to fight Ayumi Kamino in February."

"Kamikaze?" Kyle backed away. "You said yes?"

She paused, her smile fading. "Of course I did. Why wouldn't I have?"

"And exactly what weight class are you two fighting in?"

"Featherweight. Don't look at me like that. It's ten weeks away. I can lose the weight. You'll help me."

Kyle pressed his palms together in front of his face and closed his eyes. "I wish you'd talked to me about it first."

Her smile dimmed. "Why? You're not my manager."

"No, but I am your principal trainer." Which sounded like a joke, considering how much time he'd actually spent with her. He blew out a breath. "I could've told you that whatever Hadrian promised you, he can take it away like that." He snapped his fingers. "You shouldn't trust everything he says."

She scowled. "I don't know why you're being so paranoid. I haven't signed anything yet."

"But you will. And when you do, you'll become *his*. A part of his stable of fighters—*if* he even chooses to keep you once your contract's up."

"What do you mean by that?" She propped her fists on her hips.

"C'mon, Bella. You think it's a coincidence that he's finally allowing women into the UFF when his anniversary show is falling apart? This is a desperation move."

"I know that. He said as much when we talked." But her discomfort told him she hadn't fully grasped the situation. "This is exactly the opportunity female fighters like me have wanted for years. How could I turn it down?"

"Bella, the 145-pound division has a lot of female fighters. Why do you think he picked you? Why do you think he's asking you to drop ten pounds rather than get someone like Dana Grimaldi or Shona Sequiera to fight Ayumi Kamino? They're at the top of their division. Don't you think he would've asked *them* first?"

She folded her arms across her chest. "I thought you believed in me."

He did. And he knew he was hurting her by being so cynical, questioning Hadrian's motives. But he couldn't help being suspicious of the UFF president and his motives. "Let's say for the sake of argument that you win. Are you going to stay at 145?"

"Of course not. This is a one-off. A foot in the door."

"Did he promise you a belt? Because he'll take it away from you if you move up a class. Don't you see? If he really wanted you to fight, he would've called *you* first and found *you* an opponent. How many fighters do you think he can find in your class? None, that's the answer."

Her face suffused with dark color. "Are you saying I'm not worth it?"

"I'm saying it's not a sustainable business plan, and Hadrian only makes business decisions."

She crossed and uncrossed her arms, pacing in a tight line in front of his desk. "So, what? You think I should call him back and tell him no because one chance to fight isn't enough?" She threw her hands in the air. "Kyle, my whole career is going to be like this. I'm always going to have a hard time finding fights. I'm always going to be making sacrifices. I can't turn down every opportunity because it isn't perfect. It'll never be perfect. Not for me."

Kyle didn't want to tell her what he really thought. Ten pounds in ten weeks would be difficult. Not impossible, but not easy. "I'm only looking out for you, Bella."

"Well, guess what? I don't need everyone telling me what I should do, or what they think is best for me. My family's been doing that all my life. And I definitely don't need you to tell me this fight's going to be dangerous. They're all dangerous."

Kyle gave up. Nothing he could say would change her mind. In fact, he'd be the exact same way if their positions were reversed. "Do me a favor and have someone read over your contract before you sign. Okay?"

She glowered. "I might be reckless, but I'm not stupid."

He was sure she wasn't. But that didn't keep him from worrying.

WHEN SHE ANNOUNCED to the rest of the gym that she'd be fighting in the UFF, Orville picked Bella up and swung her around in a circle. Tito gave her a crushing hug and they bumped chests and punched each other playfully. Liz was nearly in tears, she was so happy. Bella would be the first woman featured in an internationally broadcast pay-per-view match in one of the biggest MMA franchises in the world.

They celebrated at The Spot, where Neal the bartender brought them a round on the house. Bella decided she could have one drink—her diet would start tomorrow. The trainers immediately began discussing training regimens, planning her weight-loss program and scheduling who would coach her when.

"The pride of Payette's will be on your shoulders," Orville said.

Nerves fluttered in her gut. The pressure, she realized, would only get worse.

She made the decision then and there not to call her family until she'd signed her contract. No sense in riling them up before it was a sure thing. She felt bad for keeping her mother and Marco out of the loop, though. They would be happy for her. Her other brothers and cousins would be, too, she supposed, but they probably wouldn't show it. Mostly in deference to Fulvio.

A sudden burst of homesickness dimmed her mood. It wasn't right to not share this moment with the people who'd helped get her here. She'd celebrated all her milestones with her family. It'd only been when she'd expressed her desire to become a pro fighter that they'd shut her down. Remembering that refueled her assertion she was doing the right thing.

What would it be like to come home a champion? Would her grandfather accept that she was worthwhile then? Would he stop treating the women in the family like nothing more than breeders and caretakers for more sons? She already felt she knew the answer, and it saddened her.

Yes, the only way she could move on as a fighter and carry on the family tradition would be to open her own gym. Ever since Ryan had planted the seed, she'd been thinking about it. Maybe it could be a women's-only MMA gym. She could get teachers from all around the world to come and do clinics. She had the connections. Female fighters would flock to her one-of-a-kind facility. Welcoming and training new talent was the key to bulking up each division. More fighters, more fights. It was that simple.

If she won this match, the prize would be perfect seed money for that project. Her mind exploded with ideas, and the excitement built up inside her. She would win this match, even if it was the only fight she ever got.

Her mind was reeling by the time Kyle entered the bar. He scanned the room the way he always did, as if in search of someone.

When their eyes met, something in her chest kicked. Okay, so she'd kissed him in his office without thinking. But he hadn't seemed too rattled—he'd barely seemed to register it. Was that good or bad? "Hey, Coach," she called, "come join us. We're celebrating."

"Don't bother, Bella." Tito shook his head. "Kyle's a lone wolf. He can't hunt with the rest of the pack."

"I think I can give up one night to drink with

you hyenas." To everyone's surprise, Kyle slid into the booth, his hip bumping up against Bella's. Liz's gaze canted to her, and she sipped her beer quietly.

Orville toasted Kyle as he raised his own glass. "You keeping a closer eye on us now that we have a famous UFF fighter in our midst?"

He lifted one broad shoulder. "Nah, I figured I should find out what kind of rumors you've been telling Bella about me."

"You mean like the harem of Playboy bunnies who live in your hall closet?" Tito said.

"Or your webbed toes?" Orville added.

"I thought the one about being sent to Earth from a dying alien planet was pretty good," Liz chimed in.

Kyle pointed to each in turn. "True, false, and I decline to comment."

They laughed and drank. Bella wondered why Kyle had ever disengaged from the group. They seemed at ease with each other.

The second round came, and Bella bowed out. In solidarity, Kyle announced that as her principal trainer, he would follow Bella's one-drink limit.

"You don't have to do that," she said as the others happily took up the celebratory libations in their honor.

"Hey, I've got to watch my girlish figure, too."

She cocked an eyebrow. "If I had half your *girlish figure,* I'd be a shoo-in to win."

His chuckle sent warmth coursing through her. He threw an arm around the back of her seat and yelled over his shoulder, "Neal, two of your finest, girliest, nonalcoholic, nonfattening drinks, if you please." He left his arm resting behind her. Bella settled back, unable to keep the smile from her face. She felt his fingertips lightly delve into her hair and scrape her scalp. She wanted to rub up against him and purr, and when she glanced at him surreptitiously, she saw him watching her through lowered lids, the vaguest smile on his lips.

A minute later, Neal put a fancy bottle of designer water and two glasses in front of them with a flourish.

Kyle cracked the bottle open and poured with all the finesse of a man serving the finest champagne. "A toast to you, Bella." He handed her a glass.

"To us," she amended. Kyle's eyes darkened and stayed fixed on her. She smiled. "To a winning combination."

"To winning," he said, and sipped.

THE UFF CONTRACT came by courier two days later. It was nearly fifty pages of microscopic legalese. Bella tried to sit down to read through it, but it quickly became clear she'd need an agent.

The Fiores had specialists who helped negotiate these kinds of documents, but she couldn't use them if she wanted to keep this deal quiet until she signed. So she asked Kyle for help, and he contacted Joel Khalib, Dominic Payette's agent and manager.

She liked Joel immediately. He was a compact

guy with a big smile who talked a mile a minute and wore a fedora with his T-shirt and trousers. Something about him reminded Bella of her uncle Thiago. The moment he sat down with her, she knew he'd work out well. He didn't talk down to her and didn't call her sweetheart. He didn't have a fancy suit or expensive business cards, but he was a professional through and through. She decided to put her career in his hands and signed her contract.

Within three days, Joel had confirmed the date of the press conference in Vegas to announce the fight. He lined her up to do interviews and photo shoots with all the major news outlets. Since the Starlight charity ball was coming up on Saturday, she'd stay there for the week.

There was no putting off the phone call home now. Back in her apartment, she dialed the number for the main studio and waited. Her insides quivered.

"Olá, Ginásio Fiore."

"Papai?" She hadn't expected her father to answer. Her mother usually handled reception. "It's Bella."

"Querida, it's been so long since you've talked to me." She could hear his sullen pout. "I was beginning to think you'd forgotten about your poor father and run away with some handsome man."

She smirked. "Nothing like that, *Papai.*"

"How are you? How are things in the States?"

"They're..." The words jammed her throat, and she coughed. "They're going very well. In fact,

I have some wonderful news I want to share. Is *Mamãe* around?"

"Oh! Let me find her. She went to the bathroom. Ana!" He said something over his shoulder, and then the sound over the phone hollowed out with a tinny echo. She could hear the rhythmic punching of the heavy bags and the squeak of the padded rubber mats. *Home,* she thought wistfully.

"You're on speaker now, Bella," her mother's voice came from some distance away. "Marco and Luca are here, too."

"Hey, Bella," Luca said. "What's wrong? Did you get knocked up—? Ow!"

"Don't mind your idiot brother, Bella," her father said, then paused. "You're not pregnant, right?"

"For God's sake, no."

"It's a man, right? She's met someone?" This from her mother, spoken barely above a whisper. Bella cringed. They were still expecting her to find a man to settle her down. She fixed her jaw and asked, "Is Fulvio there?"

"No, he's at an appointment," Marco said. "Stop keeping us in suspense. What's the news? Are things working out with Kyle?"

"He's great," she said, and held her tongue. No need to expand on his virtues. "I'm going to fight in the UFF in February."

For a moment, she felt as if she were at the top of a roller coaster, holding her breath before the plunge. Instead of waiting for their reactions, she plowed on and told them all about Hadrian's call, the contract, and all the pertinent details. They stayed silent as she explained everything, her excitement growing.

"I can't believe it," her mother said quietly. Bella had no idea if she meant it in mourning or in joy, and her lungs felt as though they were being crushed by her ribs.

"This…this is phenomenal," her father said, clearly in shock. "I've always thought Hadrian Blackwell was against women fighting in the UFF."

"Congratulations," Marco said warmly. "You're gonna be great, Bella."

"You're kidding, right? You're trying to give us all heart attacks?"

"No, Luca. For real. They're making the announcement in Las Vegas on Thursday. I'll be at the press conference with Ayumi Kamino."

"Merda…"

"Luca!" her mother exclaimed. Bella heard the distinct sound of her mother slapping her brother's arm. "Watch your tongue!"

"Do you have any idea what Fulvio is going to say about this? Bella, he's going to flip out."

"Be happy for your sister," her father warned. "This is a wonderful opportunity."

"Yeah, don't be jealous, Luca," Marco said.

"I'm not jealous." Luca sniffed. "I think it's great. But she's not the one who has to live with Fulvio's moods and ranting. If you think I'm going to tell the old man, forget it."

"I'll tell him myself," she said. "He should hear it from me."

"No," her father cut in. "I'll tell him. He's still mad from the last time you talked. You need to stay positive and focus on training."

So Fulvio still held that grudge. Her happiness dimmed and she sighed. "Thank you, *Papai*."

"I'm a phone call away if you need me to go there," Marco said.

"We all will," he father added staunchly. "All you have to do is ask."

Bella's heart warmed so quickly it almost cracked. She'd thought the family had been against her all this time—after everything that had happened between her and Antonio, then her and Fulvio, she thought they'd dismissed her, turned their backs on her. But they were happy for her. They were supporting her in their own way. Maybe the story would've been different if Fulvio had been there, but for now, she knew. She swallowed thickly. "Thanks. But…I have the whole team here at Payette's helping me out. The next few weeks are going to be hard, but I'll manage."

"We're family, Bella. No matter what happens, we're here if you need us."

Tears burned the backs of her eyes. "I'll let you know."

"We'll tell the others and tune in to your press conference," her mother said. "But we'll let you go for now. Take care of yourself, Bella."

"Stop riding your bike," her father commanded.

"Drink lots of water." Marco's advice was always practical.

"And don't get knocked up!"

"Luca, one of these days…"

"We love you, *querida*," he father interrupted, "and we're proud of you. Do your best."

After she hung up, Bella got into the shower and let her tears fall. She had her family's support…so why did she still feel so alone?

CHAPTER FOURTEEN

KYLE WATCHED AS Bella repeatedly tugged the hem of her blouse and rubbed the tops of her high-heeled shoes against the back of her calves. It was Thursday afternoon in Las Vegas, the day of the press conference. All around them, people rushed to and fro. Bella danced out of everyone's way, trying to make herself small in this bustling environment. Kyle kept her close, one hand floating near her shoulder or waist to keep her from drifting too far away. She looked as if she were about to bolt.

"Nervous?" he asked.

She looked at him with wide eyes, her lips pursed so tightly they disappeared against her pale face in spite of her makeup. Gently, he squeezed her taut shoulders. "Hey. Relax. I'm right here, and Joel's on the other side. Worse comes to worst, we'll tackle any reporter who asks you a stupid question."

She nodded and blew out a breath. "Thanks for coming here with me."

"I would've been here tomorrow anyhow." He didn't want it to be a big deal. He'd promised to make up for his inadequate training. Being there when she needed him was a part of that.

"Kinda stupid, isn't it?" She grimaced down at her heels. "I've been in front of bigger crowds in less clothing, but I'm sweating like balls right now."

He chuckled. "I used to feel the same way at these big press things. Just relax and be yourself. They'll love you for it."

She scoffed. "They barely know me."

"Hey, *I* barely know you, but I'm rooting for you." He cleared his throat and clapped her on the shoulder. "You'll do fine."

When the conference started, the balding stage manager brusquely ushered Bella out. There was a vacant, wild quality about her forced grin, and she'd started plucking at her blouse again. *Breathe,* Kyle silently told her, taking a deep breath himself.

She met his eye, a panicked look clear on her face. *Help.*

He winked and made a cross-eyed kissy face, and she burst out laughing. *Ah, there she is.*

Camera flashes bathed her in blinding light as the UFF president drew her in for a half hug and a peck on the cheek.

Something inside Kyle pinched, and he folded his arms over his chest with a frown.

"You keep doing that and people will start thinking you're jealous."

He jumped as his sister, Jessica, sidled up next to him. "Jess." Standing a good three inches taller than Kyle and wearing a sequined top, hot-pink tights and electric-blue stilettos, he wondered how she'd been able to sneak up on him so easily. "What are you doing here?"

"'Nice to see you, Jess. It's been so long, oh, and sorry for blowing you off in New Orleans.'" She tossed her bleached-blond bangs out of her eyes. "I'm working. I'm freelancing with a cosmetics company who's sponsoring the Starlight gala thing. A few clients asked me to come down to get them gussied up, too. Maybe you haven't heard, but I'm kind of a big deal." She sighed as her gaze cut across the stage. "I was hoping I'd get to do Bella Fiore's hair. That mane looks like a waterfall of sex and dark chocolate. She's your client, right?"

Kyle wiped a hand across his mouth. "So you just happened to take this job when I was coming down to Vegas?"

"You make it sound like I'm only here to stalk you."

He eyed her suspiciously. "Are you?"

She gave him a withering look. "You think I took a job just to see my little brother? Puh-leez." At Kyle's rigid look, she gave a dramatic sigh. "Of course I want to see you, Kyle. You're family. But you've made your feelings about me pretty clear."

He looked away. "That's not fair. And you know I didn't mean it like that."

The gap of silence between them widened as Ayumi Kamino ascended the stage. The room got quieter. She shook hands with Hadrian and clasped hands with Bella perfunctorily before everyone took their seats. As Hadrian made the official announcement and provided the press with the details of the UFF's first female fight, Ayumi surveyed the crowd as if every reporter in the room were her opponent. Bella's smile had relaxed a little more. She didn't look quite so hunted.

"Okay, so I'll admit, I took this gig 'cause I was curious about what you do," Jess said quietly. Kyle cast her a sidelong glance, a little surprised. Since when did his sister take an interest in anything he did? "But I didn't even realize that client you were talking about was the chick who'd be fighting."

"That 'chick' has a near perfect win-loss record. She's good." He didn't know why he was being so defensive. But Bella was more than some chick. "She'll take the belt home. You watch."

"Speaking of home, Mom's wondering why you haven't called."

"You've been talking to Mom?"

"She called me, said you didn't go home for Thanksgiving. And you still haven't made plans to visit over Christmas. She's still miffed you missed last year."

"She could've called me."

"You could've called her. You *should've* called her."

He turned away sharply. "Excuse me, I need to concentrate on what Bella's saying."

Jess grabbed his arm. "Look, whatever's been going on, I get that you don't want to talk about it.

Dad didn't raise us to put our problems on other people. I sure as hell had stuff to work out, even though I could've used a little support." Her nostrils flared. "But when you don't call home for months and months and Mom resorts to calling me for info…" She blew her bangs out of her eyes and shook her head. "I'm worried about you, squirt. Everyone is."

Kyle's tone was as tight as the fist around his heart. "Tell Mom I'm sorry. I can't make it down this year. Bella's got less than ten weeks to train for this fight and I need to be with her."

"Kyle, it's Christmas."

"There'll be other Christmases."

"And a *bah humbug* to you, too." Jessica huffed. "At least call her yourself."

He conceded with a short nod and tuned back in to the press conference.

Hadrian took questions from the reporters. They were fairly easy—how do you feel about being the first women to fight in the UFF? What do your families think about you fighting?—but then Quinn Bourdain stepped forward. The redheaded reporter in her burgundy suit stood out against the field of mostly male reporters.

"Bella, you're going to drop to the 145-pound division, but you've previously said you would never compromise yourself to pander to the business. What's changed?"

Bella sat still a moment, then leaned toward the mic in front of her. "I don't recall ever saying that."

"You said it to me in early November for a feature I did on you. Quote, 'I won't lose weight to please people.'"

Bella sent a brittle smile toward the reporter. "I think you misunderstood me, Quinn. That was in the context of body image, not business. This is a once-in-a-lifetime chance for me to show the world what I can do, and I'm very honored that Hadrian asked me to sign on with the UFF. That said, I will do whatever necessary so that I will be ready to take on my opponent. I admire Ayumi very much and look forward to meeting her in the cage."

Quinn looked like she was about to ask a follow-up question, but Hadrian moved them on and pointed at another reporter who had his hand up.

"Bella, you're coming off a notoriously bad defeat in New Orleans against Betty Heimer," he said a touch snidely. "Critics have said your performance there wasn't worthy of a spot on a UFF card. How will public opinion affect your game?"

She drummed her fingers on the tabletop, though she looked as though she'd rather drum her knuckles on the guy's skull. "People will always doubt me, same way they doubt any fighter. Every fighter has bad days, and that was a very bad day. But I learn from my mistakes. I know I'll bring my A game in February."

The reporter added, "Ayumi, do you have anything you'd like to say about Bella's performance in New Orleans?"

The woman sat forward, her eyes sharp. "It's true, fighters have bad days. They make mistakes. But if she makes the same mistakes in our fight, I'll be very disappointed. I want to *fight* her and I want her to know my full strength by the end."

Bella tilted her head and smiled. "Bring it on, Ayumi."

The audience chuckled and started giving catcalls. Hadrian, ever the ringmaster, cut off the questions and had the women pose toe to toe, fists raised. Ayumi's stony glower clashed up against Bella's more laid-back half smile. It was pretty clear who the darling of this show was.

"Way to go," Joel said when they met backstage after the photo ops. "You were terrific. The cameras loved you."

Bella nodded, and her gaze canted toward Kyle. She lifted an eyebrow. "Aren't you going to introduce us?"

He hadn't even realized Jess had followed him. "Oh. Uh, Joel, Bella, this is…my *sister,* Jessica."

He watched for that moment in Bella's eyes. That slight widening when she realized Jess hadn't been born a woman. With her surgically enhanced body and flamboyant style, he could understand how some people might miss the little details, but there were some things surgery couldn't erase. Bella's smile widened as she shook Jessica's long-fingered hands, but there was no discernible tic that gave away her surprise.

"So, is Kyle giving it to you hard?" Jess asked.

Kyle's jaw nearly fell to the floor. Bella startled. Joel laughed.

"I mean, has he been training you hard?" Jess corrected with a violent shake of her head, then laughed. "Woo, where is my brain today? Not connected to my tongue, that's for sure." She gave another loud guffaw and slapped Kyle's shoulder so hard it stung.

"Kyle's a good coach," Bella said. "Did you ever get into the family trade?"

"Dad tried, but...well..." She shrugged. "It didn't stick. I was too busy designing outfits for Kyle's G.I. Joes."

Kyle glared, but Jess went on. "Listen, I've been trying to get him to have dinner with me to catch up—maybe you can convince him to break bread with his poor, lonely big sister."

Bella turned to Kyle. "Have dinner with your big sister," she commanded firmly.

"Ha! I like her," Jess declared. "Look, I gotta go. Bella, I'll see you at the gala tomorrow, right? Here, Kyle, take my card, in case...well, you know." Her lips curved. "Good to see you, Joel. And very nice to meet you, Bella—hopefully we'll see each other again soon. Good luck with the fight." She sauntered off, wading through the crowd like a tall ship on heels.

Joel turned to them. "I have some people I need to talk to. Bella, I'll see you back at the hotel. Your first interview starts at two o'clock—don't be late."

"I am so sorry," Kyle said the moment they started toward his rental car. "Jess is…well, Jess."

"I thought your sister was cool."

He hesitated. "You realize she's…"

She laughed. "I was fairly certain. You forget I'm from Brazil—*Carnivale* brings out all the drag queens. You're not embarrassed by her, are you?"

"It's not like that." He struggled to explain. "Things have been awkward between us for a while. Jess—back when he was my brother, Jesse—left home when I was fourteen. My parents weren't very accepting of her…choices. They had a big fight, and then she was dead to my parents. I only talked to her a couple of times before and after the surgeries, but she never came home. Not until Dad's funeral." A bitter taste filled his mouth.

"I'm sorry that happened," Bella said. "It probably wasn't easy for any of you. But I think your sister's amazing. It takes a lot of guts to stand up to your family and the rest of the world to be the person you're meant to be and follow your dreams."

His chest tightened. "I just wish she and Dad could've met in the middle. It would've made life a lot easier." For Mom, who missed her eldest. For Dad, whose whole world had been thrown off its axis. And for Kyle, who'd been caught in the middle and forged by his father's unyielding will into the manliest of men.

He wasn't angry about becoming that man—he was proud of what he'd accomplished. He wasn't even angry that Jess had left. Who could blame her, considering Dad's reaction?

Mostly, he was angry because he was still angry. Jess reminded him of all the lessons their father had beaten into him, all the things a man was supposed to be. All the things he'd failed at....

"Sometimes," Bella said soberly, "there's no room for compromise."

His morose thoughts were interrupted by someone shouting Bella's name. They both halted. Quinn Bourdain ran up to them. "Bella, I'm sorry. I want to make sure you didn't take my question personally," she said.

Bella shrugged, but she was a touch cool. "You were doing your job. But I thought you, of all people, would've understood my comment in context."

"I did. And I do. But you're about to go under a ton of scrutiny, and that article is going to show up again and again. I thought I might head off any misunderstanding if I asked the question."

"So you were doing me a favor by pointing out my weight disadvantage?" Bella gave her a skeptical once-over and started to turn away.

"Ryan Holbrooke's in Vegas as we speak," Quinn said. Kyle jarred to a stop as Bella swung back around. The reporter had his attention, and she stood poised with her notebook. "The last time I talked to him, he told me something that disturbed me, and I wanted to get your comment."

"Okay, Quinn, so tell us what he said."

The reporter flipped to a page. "He said, Bella, that you were, and I quote, 'a second-rate Fiore with no drive to succeed.' He also accused you of making sexual advances toward him in order to gain his attention and firing him when he didn't give you said attention. He called you 'a supercilious diva' and said anyone who took you on as a client would get what they deserved." Her lips twisted distastefully.

Kyle's blood boiled. "You tell that pompous asshat—"

"No comment." Bella pushed Kyle forward, one strong hand pressed against the small of his back. She paused and gave a short humorless laugh. "I really thought you were better than this, Quinn."

The redhead gave a dry smile. "I probably am. But if you want to survive in this business, you do what you have to. I'm just asking the questions. If you want to revise your counterstatement, give me a call."

"I'm going to find Ryan and strangle him with his own tie," Kyle said once they got to the rental car, slamming the door behind him. "You know, I found out that the Star Gym in NOLA banned him. Apparently, the guy was harassing a woman there. I can't believe that jackoff is taking his shit out on you now."

"Are you going to drive angry? Because my contract clearly says I'm not allowed to do anything dangerous before a fight."

He fumed as he pulled out of the parking spot.

"We should release a statement, nip this in the bud. I don't want Quinn or anyone else spreading these lies."

"Joel says the best statement you can make is to say nothing at all. Don't feed the trolls, remember?"

"I'm not sure I believe that anymore." Though as a PR policy, Kyle knew she was right.

Bella placed a hand over his forearm. His skin tingled. "Forget him, Kyle. I already have. He doesn't matter."

For a moment, he was caught by the softness in her gaze. The heat of anger inside him morphed into something else, and he forcefully shook it away. "Sorry. You're right, of course. You should be focusing on training and the fight."

I'll handle Ryan, he promised silently.

THE REST OF the day went by in a whirl. Joel had stacked interview after interview with all the major media outlets, then Bella was invited to dinner and drinks with the head honchos at the UFF. By the time she was free of obligations, she was too tired to do anything more than fall into bed and sleep. Her plans to get in some training time and then explore the Strip had been wiped out.

Early the following morning, Bella attended a photo shoot in the official UFF headquarters training facility—an enormous fitness complex complete with a running track and Olympic-size swimming pool. Both Bella and Ayumi took separate photos against a backdrop, before posing for a few together. Ayumi didn't smile much. She had a purposeful look about her, and whenever she met Bella's eyes, her mouth compressed.

Kamikaze Kamino was known for her fierce determination and muscle-wrenching contortion acts, and seemed to go into every fight as though it'd be her last. Bella couldn't imagine she'd made many friends among her sparring partners.

Joel stood by, checking his BlackBerry frequently and giving her the occasional thumbs-up. As both fighters were changing into yet another official UFF-branded outfit, Ayumi's manager came out and loudly declared those were all the photos the fighter was willing to do today. The small entourage strode out, surrounding Ayumi, who didn't even utter a goodbye or thank-you. The on-site marketing manager chased after them, begging for two or three more pictures.

"Huh. Talk about diva complex. Well, more camera time for you, right?" Joel said.

Inwardly, Bella sighed. She was getting a little tired of this, but she kept pushing.

A few minutes later, Hadrian made a surprise appearance, giving Bella another half hug and peck on the cheek. She wished he'd stop doing that. She'd caught the murderous look on Kyle's face. "I wanted to check on my ladies, see how things are going," Hadrian said, glancing around. "Where's Ayumi?"

"She left."

He seemed unfazed. "She probably needs her beauty sleep. But the photogs are here for another couple of hours, so make the most of it and have fun." He winked and sauntered off, but not before saying, "I'm counting on you, Bella."

She went to the change room for the next outfit. Taking the hanger, a sense of déjà vu struck her. The tiny boy shorts and UFF-branded bra top were the same as the ones the ring girls wore, and would barely cover her.

The UFF logo stared her in the face. "It's not as bad as the shoelace bathing suit," she told herself sternly. With grim determination, she tugged the outfit on.

She stared at herself in the mirror. The bra top didn't have any padding, and it outlined the curves of her breasts perfectly. To her horror, her nipples jutted forth like frozen peas. She rubbed her bare arms and jumped around, trying to get her circulation going.

"Bella? Everything okay in there?"

That was Kyle's voice.

"Um, could you get me a couple of Band-Aids?" she called.

"Why? Are you hurt?"

"No, but I need…something for these shoes." She was sure the wardrobe folks would have some kind of sticker bra or something, but the instructions had been clear about not wearing a bra under the clothing so that they could get a nice, smooth line. They'd probably airbrush and edit out any imperfections.

Or maybe they wouldn't.

"Here you go." Kyle's hand appeared around the edge of the curtained change room. She took the bandages and applied them quickly, smooshing her boobs until she was certain they were behaving.

Kyle's eyes widened as she stepped out, but he didn't say anything.

"What?" She folded her arms over her chest, checking her breasts surreptitiously. "Not a good look?"

He gestured wildly. "I thought…" He couldn't stop staring at her midriff. The intensity of his stare was starting to null the bandages' effectiveness.

"Take a picture, it'll last longer," she quipped, but didn't feel the joke too keenly.

Kyle pulled off his zip-up hoodie and draped it around her shoulders. "You're cold."

The lingering body heat in the sweater wrapped around her senses. She could smell his deodorant and soap in the heavy cotton. "Is it that obvious?" she asked, cheeks flaming. His eyes flicked to her face and back down to her chest. Sensation sparked on the tips of her breasts, and she shivered. So much for the Band-Aids.

"You know, all you have to do is tell Joel that you don't want to do this," he said.

She bit her lip and shook her head. "Ayumi walked out, Kyle. I can't walk out, too."

"It's degrading. Remember that other photo shoot?" He squeezed her shoulder and lowered his voice. "You don't have to do this."

"Yeah, I do. This is business." Ryan had wanted to sell her body, exploit her to build her career. At least here with the UFF, she was being recognized as a fighter first. That's what she told herself, anyhow.

This was part of being a star in the big leagues. Sure, she knew some of these photos would be on the skanky side, and that she'd be judged, criticized, mocked. She'd already faced a lifetime of ridicule.

"I'm doing this, Kyle," she said staunchly, shrugging off his hoodie. "I have to."

He didn't stop her. Which was for the best, really.

She got into the cage and shut the gate.

KYLE DIDN'T SEE Bella all Saturday. They'd been scheduled to train, but then Joel had dragged her away at the last minute for a television interview. She had a hair-and-makeup appointment after that to prepare herself for the charity gala, so he wouldn't see her until that evening.

He'd spent the morning meeting with other gym managers at a UFF breakfast. They'd talked business, and had congratulated Kyle on the quickly growing number of new clients signing up at Payette's. He didn't feel he deserved the praise. The most popular classes were the ones Bella taught. He knew she was responsible for their membership increase, especially among female clients.

Then, when one of the managers had made a joke about selling tickets to watch Bella do jumping jacks, Kyle had nearly taken the guy's head off, but almost immediately felt like a hypocrite. Two years ago, he would've been the one making that joke. And he knew he would've argued that his comments were meant to be more complimentary than offensive. But something had changed. Maybe he was more sensitive after all the things he'd been through.

He'd been extra protective of Bella since the photo shoot, too. The poses hadn't been too provocative, and she'd been firm about what she would and wouldn't do. When the photographer tried to bully her into showing more skin, Kyle had backed up Joel as the pit bull agent told the man that his client would walk if he didn't show more respect.

Respect. That's what this was all about. Even if a deeper feeling persisted, Kyle knew that the core of what he felt for Bella was respect.

On Jess's insistence, he met with his sister for a quick lunch before she had to rush off to her various clients to help them prep for the gala that evening. As they sat down for sandwiches in the hotel lobby café, he realized they hadn't shared a meal since their father's wake.

"So what are you wearing tonight?" she asked, sipping a tall glass of water.

"I've got a suit."

"Let me guess. The charcoal-gray one you wore to Dad's funeral."

"It's the nicest one I own," he groused. "And it's practically new."

"It's a funeral suit. You can wear it when you go for your next job interview. Or to the wedding of a friend you don't particularly like. But not tonight. You're going to be with the guest of honor, after all. You could at least *try* to look like arm candy."

"You know, before this fight took over her life, she was going to be *my* arm candy."

"Really?" Jess arched one well-plucked eyebrow. Her lips spread into a wide smile. "So you *do* like her."

He kept his face straight. "Professionally, sure."

"Uh-huh." Her lips curved. Kyle hated that knowing look.

Jess was probably right about his attire, though. There was something macabre about wearing a funeral suit to the gala, and it was a little too business formal.

Once he said his goodbyes to his sister, he went straight to a tuxedo rental shop inside the hotel's vast boutique mall and within the hour had a tux ready for the evening. Maybe it was a little over-the-top, but it made him look good. And he wanted to be at his best for Bella's sake.

He went back to his hotel room, showered and changed for the gala. Bella had said she'd call him when she was ready to leave. He checked his watch—he'd expected to hear from her by now. She must've run late at the interviews. He went to her hotel room three floors up and knocked. "Bella? It's Kyle. Are you ready yet?"

A pause. "No!"

"Well, can you let me in at least? I need to use the can."

Real classy, Peters. He was overcompensating for the tux. He tugged at his collar, pacing. His hands felt strangely empty. Maybe he should've brought her flowers.

He blew out a breath. He was escorting her to a UFF event, not taking her to prom.

He waited, swinging his arms restlessly, then hopped from one foot to the other to get his blood moving. If he stood outside of Bella's room any longer, he really was going to need to use the bathroom. "Bella, the limo's going to be here any minute. Let me in."

The door unlocked. "Don't laugh."

"Why, what—" His jaw snapped shut as he took in the dress she'd squeezed into. He'd heard the term *sausage casing,* but she actually looked like a chain of bratwurst squeezed into a hideous peach-colored thing made of some kind of shiny material.

"Hadrian sent it over," she moaned. "He said it was a gift from a sponsor—some big Paris fashion house. I can't even pull the zipper all the way up, and I'm wearing two pairs of Spanx."

No amount of shoehorning would get her into that thing, but he wasn't about to say it out loud. Besides that, even Kyle knew the color and shape of the dress didn't suit her. Apparently Hadrian had zero taste. "Don't you have anything else?"

"I brought a dress with me that I'd bought on Black Friday, but I just noticed a huge stain on it. I guess that's why it was on sale." She chewed on her thumbnail. "I mentioned the stain to Hadrian, so he sent this thing. I can't show up to the gala in jeans. Especially with you dressed like that." She gave him a weak smile. "You look great, by the way."

He was too concerned about her state to preen. "What size are you?"

"Excuse me?"

"Your dimensions. Write them down for me. And your shoe size." He pulled out his cell phone and the business card he'd tucked into his wallet.

She grabbed a notepad off the desk and scribbled some numbers down. "Who're you calling?"

He put up a quelling hand. "Hi, Jess? It's me. Listen, I have a big emergency...."

Within the hour, his sister swept in with an armload of dresses. With the gravitas of a seasoned referee, Jess gave Bella a judicious once-over and held out two hangers. "Pretty sure these will be the best ones, but try them all on."

Kyle frowned. "We don't have time. The party's starting in fifteen minutes and the limo—"

"Oh, please. She's the guest of honor. She can't fly in half-dressed and looking like she actually cares about being on time. That's the definition of *fashion-*

ably late." She beamed at Bella. "You've got plenty of time. Choose wisely," she pronounced.

"Where'd you get all those dresses?" Kyle asked as Bella hurried into the bedroom.

"Borrowed them. All I had to say was, 'I need dresses for Bella Fiore,' and three guys appeared, like, out of nowhere. They're all sponsors. I'm shocked they didn't try dressing her before this."

"Hadrian did." He picked up the peach monstrosity and tossed it to Jess. She held it up and her eyes bulged.

"Oh, barf. The man must be blind to think this would go with her complexion."

"Yeah, well, there are a few things beyond Hadrian's fashion sense that I have a problem with. For one, he shouldn't be showing his preference to fighters like this," Kyle said. "Did you know this is the UFF's guest suite they keep on reserve here? He booked it for her and made sure she didn't pay for it. I don't think Kamino's getting the same treatment."

"I say, take the perks where you can get 'em. It's his company and she's going to be a star. You realize she's going to go through a lot more than training, right? All the media stuff she's done in the past couple of days is just the tip of the iceberg."

Jess was right. There would undoubtedly be interest from all the major media outlets. Kyle made a mental note to talk with Joel and make sure Bella didn't burn out. They'd already skipped too many training sessions.

Expecting a long wait, Kyle parked himself on the white leather couch and looked around the suite. Jess went to the kitchenette and started rooting through the fridge. The strip glittered below, casting everything in a rainbow of gaudy, flickering lights. His knee bounced as he waited for Bella to emerge from the bedroom.

"Nervous?" Jessica asked, helping herself to the complimentary wine.

"No." Not for Bella. Well, maybe a little—he hated it when things didn't go according to plan.

"Sure you're not." She watched him, running the edge of her wineglass against her lip. "Nice tux, by the way. I'm glad you listened...and that you trusted me enough with this to call me. You could've gone shopping down in the mall for a dress."

He blinked. "That would've taken too long. Besides, you make your living doing this kind of thing. I trust your judgment more than mine."

"Dad never believed I could do it. He thought I was...tacky."

That was the least of what their father had thought of Jess, and Kyle could see she knew it, too. He wiped a hand over his mouth. "I'm sorry I haven't been around. That I didn't call more often."

Jess sighed. "We have our own lives to live. I'm sorry I didn't stay. I know Dad was hard on you."

"I didn't need you to protect me."

"No. But you needed me to be in your corner, same way I needed you."

"Okay, here's the red." Bella walked out, still barefoot. Kyle swallowed thickly. Red was definitely a better color on her than peach. He couldn't tear his eyes away from her plumped-up cleavage, mounds of golden-hued pillowy flesh that he wanted to bury his face in.

Jess made a noise like a cat bringing up a hairball. "You look like a harlot. Try the green."

"You didn't happen to bring a little black dress, did you?" Bella asked hopefully. "Black is classic. Black is slimming. And I have black shoes to match."

"Black? Snore." Jess turned her nose up. "Don't you worry. I brought you sandals to go with all these outfits." She held up flashy gold stilettos, and Bella groaned. "Now, try the green. Go on."

"I thought the red looked fine," Kyle mumbled, sitting back.

"Yeah, but you're biased toward boobs." She challenged him with an arch look, and he didn't argue. "*You're* not the stylist here. My reputation's at stake, you know."

"Does anyone even know you're here?"

She pooh-poohed him. "Whatever. Just leave this to us ladies, will you?"

Twenty minutes later, they settled on a one-shouldered dove-gray chiffon dress with gold trim. Once the stiletto sandals had been strapped on, Bella instantly reminded Kyle of Diana, the Greek goddess of the hunt. The outfit wasn't nearly as revealing as the red dress, but Kyle decided that was just as well. She was already tempting enough.

"Perfect." Jess primped Bella's loose-flowing hair, tucking a pearl-and-gold laurel barrette against her temple. She slid on a pair of gold cuff bangles and crossed Bella's wrists up in front of her. *"Wonder Wo-man!"*

Kyle chuckled. Bella was absolutely stunning. He felt like the luckiest guy in the world. "You look fantastic," he said, getting to his feet. His knee creaked and pulled, and he stumbled forward.

In a flash, Bella was there, practically catching him before he fell to his knees. "You okay?" She helped him into a standing position, strong arms wrapped around him. The warmth and softness of her skin had him inhaling sharply. The scent of cinnamon and vanilla tickled his nose and made his mouth water.

He winced as his knee reminded him of where he was. "I've been sitting too long. I probably won't be dancing much tonight."

"Like I can? Look at these things." She turned her deadly looking heels this way and that. He couldn't help but notice she hadn't had any trouble hurrying to help him, though. "C'mon. We can hold each other up." She slipped her arm beneath his. Together, they straightened, finding their balance.

"Careful. Those are four-inchers." Jess nodded at her heels. "You'll need to hang on to Kyle if you want to go anywhere with speed. I don't want to be the one responsible if you twist an ankle."

Bella took a tentative few steps forward, leaning on Kyle for support. He got the sense she was doing it for show to make him feel better. He said, "I thought your contract said you weren't allowed to do anything dangerous before the fight."

"If that were true, I wouldn't be on the arm of Double-O-Handsome here." She batted her thickly mascaraed lashes. "If looks could kill…"

"That's not what that saying means."

She rolled her eyes. "Just take a compliment where you can get it, Coach."

CHAPTER FIFTEEN

THE STARLIGHT FOUNDATION charity ball was held annually to raise money for underprivileged inner city children. Hadrian had come from a family with very little money, and he'd only gotten into mixed martial arts when a Jeet Kun Do teacher had taken him under his wing. Aside from being one of the foundation's biggest supporters, Hadrian also sat on the board. He hosted the event, which counted on well-to-do folks willing to pay thousands of dollars to rub elbows with the world's greatest athletes, celebrities and socialites.

Kyle had told Bella all this on the ride to the event, but she had no idea what a big deal the ball was. Part of her had expected a stuffy hotel ballroom filled with monocle-wearing seniors.

But this was no cartoon snob society event. It was an outdoor dance party, complete with a big-name DJ, sponsored open bar and lots of muscly security guys who could've passed for heavyweight fighters themselves.

Jess had hitched a ride with Bella and Kyle in the limo. She explained she would be adjusting people's hair, makeup and wardrobe throughout the night in a special VIP salon. She peeled away as soon as the car stopped in front of the entrance, waving her fingers. "You two have a good time. Don't do anything I wouldn't do."

"Thanks again, Jess," Kyle called after her, genuine warmth behind his gratitude. Bella stepped onto the red carpet and was met by a blinding explosion of light. The media and paparazzi were gathered at the entrance, snapping photos and footage of the guests as they arrived. She squinted and shaded her eyes, trying to remember Joel's advice. *Smile. Wave. Let the crowd love you.*

Kind of hard to do when her armpits were suddenly drenched. Panic struck when she couldn't recall whether she'd applied deodorant.

"C'mon." Kyle took her arm and gently guided her forward. People shouted her name, asking about her outfit. She parroted what Jess had told her—glad that Kyle's sister had been so specific and had drilled her on the car ride to make sure she gave the designer's name correctly. Apparently, sister and brother shared that compulsion for perfection.

After posing and studiously ignoring the questions thrown her way, Kyle escorted her into the party proper.

She wiped her brow. "Remind me to thank Jess. I don't know what I'd have done if it weren't for her. Good thing you bumped into her at the press conference."

"Sheer dumb luck," Kyle agreed lightly, a thoughtful look flitting across his face.

They made their way through the horde of dancers. It seemed every horizontal surface had been transformed into a dance floor. She spotted one barefoot girl gyrating between two guys perched on the rim of a planter. None of the security guys seemed inclined to stop them.

Joel and some of the fighters were clustered together on a dais at the other end of the party. As they got closer, they saw why it wasn't so crowded around them: a ring of security guards two deep kept the regular party folk away from the beautiful people who'd found refuge on the raised island.

"Bella," Hadrian exclaimed, pushing out of his deep red couch throne. He gestured at the bouncers to let her and Kyle past the velvet ropes, grinning as he swept Bella head to toe with his glittering gaze. "We were starting to wonder where you were. You look gorgeous. But what happened to the dress I sent over?"

She smiled politely. "I spilled a glass of *Hellno* on it."

"Is that some kind of Brazilian wine?"

She bit the inside of her cheek. "Yeah. Stains like a bitch. Sorry."

Kyle shuddered with suppressed laughter and he coughed discreetly. Hadrian didn't even blink. "Don't sweat it. They won't ask for it back—perks of having sponsors with deep pockets, as you'll soon discover. Your man Joel has them climbing all over each other to slap a logo on your ass."

Kyle's muscles jumped beneath her palm at Hadrian's suggestive tone. The UFF president scooped up two champagne flutes from a passing waiter and offered one to each of them.

Bella shook her head. "I can't. I'm training."

"Little secret. It's not champagne, it's seltzer water and coloring. Cristal would be a waste on these guys. They're all watching their figures." Hadrian nodded to the fighters behind him. "I can get you something else, if you like. Vitamin water? Herbal tea?"

"This'll be fine." She accepted the flute and took a sip. True to his word, the drink fizzed, but there was no sugar, no alcohol. It was purely for aesthetics. Somehow, she felt a little cheated.

"Good to see you, Kyle." Hadrian's smile didn't quite reach his eyes as they shook hands. "Been behaving yourself?"

"Like a dog on a leash," he said through bared teeth.

"I saw some of the other board members over there." Hadrian waved vaguely toward the swimming pool. "You can go and catch up with them while Bella and I talk business."

"Kyle's not going anywhere," Bella said firmly, squeezing his arm. She didn't want to be left alone with Hadrian. He was relatively harmless, he'd just been a little too casual with his hands, and while she could take care of herself, punching the president of the UFF in the face might not be the best way to start her career. "I need him to keep me upright."

Hadrian's smile took on a steely quality. "Well, I'd be happy to act as your crutch."

"I wouldn't be able to forgive myself if I kept you from your job, mingling with all these people. So thank you for the offer, but Kyle's the only one I need."

And she meant it. That sudden insight had her looking at her coach in a totally new, totally weird light. There'd been attraction. There'd been tension. There'd been camaraderie. But she hadn't realized there'd been trust, too. Somehow, despite the fights and disappointments, she knew that he was there for her—as her trainer, friend...

Kyle gave a small, reassuring smile and squeezed her arm. And just like that, something clicked, as if all the pieces of a puzzle they'd been mashing together suddenly snapped into place. A pleasant fuzzy, squiggly feeling crawled through her insides.

"Where's Ayumi?" she asked to change the subject.

"She and her camp went back to Ohio after lunch." He shrugged. "See, that's the difference between a star and a diva. A star does whatever is necessary to get what she wants. A diva does whatever she wants. Honestly, I thought she'd be easier to deal with."

Hadrian was about to introduce her to the other fighters aboard the mother ship when a commotion interrupted him. The crowd thickened at the base of the dais as Dominic Payette arrived on the arm of a pregnant blonde. Payette was one of the most popular and well-recognized fighters in the UFF, his clean-shaven head, winsome smile and distinct dimples having appeared on almost every magazine, newspaper and TV station. He cut a striking figure in a light gray-blue suit that matched his eyes. The woman, who Bella assumed was his wife, gracefully ascended the steps in a sequined black dress.

Payette and Kyle clasped each other in a brief, back-slapping hug and Kyle dragged him over. "Dom, meet Bella Fiore. She's training with us in New Orleans."

"I'm a big fan of your grandfather's teachings," the welterweight champion enthused, pumping Bella's hand vigorously. "I've trained under Thiago— your uncle, right? It's a real honor to meet you." He looped an arm around the blonde's waist. "This is my wife, Fiona."

"Nice to meet you. Congratulations to you both," Bella said, shaking the woman's hand. "How far along are you?"

"Six months," Fiona replied as Hadrian brought her a chair and insisted she sit. She plopped down as Dom asked a waiter to bring her water. "Sorry, hope you don't mind. These two have been going at it all day." She rubbed her belly. "They seemed to enjoy the flight."

"Twins?" Kyle's eyes bulged, and he punched Dom

in the arm. "Mazel tov! Must be boys to be fighting so early. Those would be Dom's kids all right."

"We're leaving the sexes a mystery for now," he said. "Besides, I wouldn't mind a couple of nice, quiet girls. I've got my hands full with Sean right now—we're training to get his purple belt."

"Sean is Fiona's son from her first marriage," Kyle explained to Bella. "What is he now, twelve?"

"Fourteen, man. And a big fourteen. Kid had a crazy growth spurt. He'll be taller than me pretty soon."

Kyle wiped away an imaginary tear. "They grow up so fast."

"Don't wish too hard for girls," Bella chimed in. "We can be just as nasty, you know."

"Of course, of course. And congratulations to you, too. You're exactly what the sport needs right now. I don't think Hadrian could've picked better to debut the women's league."

She grinned. Bella decided she really liked Dominic Payette. The welterweight champ clapped Kyle on the shoulder. "This guy was a big help when I was training for the title bout. He's a good man to have in your corner."

"Aw, shucks." Kyle feigned bashfulness. "If you really want to show your gratitude, dude, you should come and do a clinic at the gym."

"No can do. I'm a family man now. With the babies coming, it's harder and harder for me to travel for training the way I used to. I'm lucky so many people are willing to come to Salmon River to work with me." He smiled down at his wife and wrapped an arm around her shoulders. "Totally worth it, though."

Bella smiled warmly. The two of them were obviously deeply in love. She glanced down again at Fiona's round belly and wondered about the day she'd give up fighting for a baby. Of course, lots of fighters eventually went back to the cage after giving birth, the way Betty Heimer had. But she had a hard time imagining the climb back to fitness.

They chatted some more with Dom before circulating the room with Hadrian, who insisted on dragging them here and there to meet celebrities and important officials. When Joel finally got off his BlackBerry, he towed them in the opposite direction to meet sponsors and other fighters.

Throughout it all, Kyle stayed by her side. She signed autographs for fans, and he stayed with her. He didn't try to steer her or handle her, though he did gently maneuver them away when someone became too intense. Kyle's presence went a long way to keeping the jerks and crazies at bay. It was comforting to know he was there if she needed a way out.

"Hey, hey!" The harsh voice made her scalp tighten and her spine go rigid. She whipped around to see Ryan Holbrooke pushing through the throng and heading straight for her. Her stomach torqued at the sight of his too-crisp shirt and suit. She thought the bouncers would stop him, but he flashed the passes on his lanyard, and they let him climb the steps. "There's my girl." Sarcasm dripped from his words as he opened his arms for a hug that sure as hell would never come.

Kyle stepped between them, his broad chest like a shield. "Hello, Ryan." The menace vibrating from him startled Bella.

"Peters, didn't think you'd be here." The agent's gaze bounced between them and he leered. "Or maybe I should've guessed."

"Why don't you get yourself a drink and then jump into the pool to cool off? We don't need a scene here."

"Calling the kettle black, are we?" Ryan snickered. "You always were a drama queen. That's what Karla told me, anyhow."

The wrestler's face grew dark, and his feet shifted apart as if readying to lunge.

"He's trying to goad you, Kyle," Bella said, gripping his arm. She shot Ryan a daggered look. "He's not worth it."

"*I'm* not worth it?" His face tinted purple. "Listen here, you ungrateful bitch. You're here because of *me*. I was the one who got your name out there. Without me, the only way you'd ever have made it here would've been on your knees." He advanced toward her. "You should be groveling at my feet. You owe me—" Ryan reached for her, his hatred blinding him to the fact that he was trying to grab her through Kyle.

Bella was ready to break that hand off, but then Kyle planted a big palm on Ryan's chest and shoved. The agent lost his balance and toppled down the steps, skidding backward on his ass all the way to the bottom.

Kyle turned to her with a look of fierce concern. "You okay?"

She wasn't, but she would be soon. She glared down at her ex-manager, heart pounding in her throat as those horrible feelings from that shocking day returned. Her fury intensified as all the things she should've said to him bubbled up. She pointed at Ryan with an accusing finger. "I don't owe you squat. And I should've called the cops when you tried to take advantage of me. If you *ever* touch me again—if I even see you within smacking distance of me—I *will* press charges."

The heavy base throbbed on, underscoring the blood pounding through her skull. All chatter around them had ceased—and that's when she realized everyone was watching and taking phone camera pictures and video.

Her cheeks flared hot.

"And here I would've threatened to rip his arms out." Hadrian appeared next to Bella. He stared down at Ryan Holbrooke with an almost bored expression, then jerked his chin at the ring of bouncers closing in. "Guys. Take this asshole out back, will you? And make sure he doesn't come back. Ever."

Ryan's eyes widened. "Hadrian, you can't do that. I have fighters you—"

"Don't worry about *my* fighters. I'll make sure they're taken care of." His voice had gone very soft. Three bouncers scooped Ryan up and frog-marched him out kicking and screaming. The cameras followed.

The tension seeped from Bella's bones. Kyle clutched her close, rubbing her arms but not saying anything.

"Great. Just freakin' great. That's gonna be all over YouTube tonight, isn't it?" She grabbed a flute of champagne and downed it, grimacing when she realized it was just colored fizzy water. "I signed a contract with him. Is it possible he'll sue for breach of contract?"

"Not if I have anything to say about it," Hadrian interjected. "Joel and I will work it out. Don't you worry yourself about this. I'll take care of everything, darling." He strode off.

Kyle led her to the shelter of the tent away from the public eye. Bella ran a hand through her hair, unable to hide her trembling. "Kyle?"

He glanced down, dark eyes hard. "Yeah?"

She exhaled sharply. "I don't want to sound like a wuss, but I'm kind of freaked-out."

Thank God, he knew exactly what she was asking for without having to say it. Wordlessly, he gathered her close and wrapped his arms tight around her. She closed her eyes and absorbed his strength.

KYLE DIDN'T WANT to pull away. He kept his arms around Bella's waist, hand resting against the small of her back. She was breathing deeply, as if she'd just sprinted a hundred meters. Probably the comedown from the adrenaline kick, he thought. He knew that feeling well—he was experiencing it himself. He'd been ready to follow the bouncers out and make sure Ryan never bothered her again. But Bella needed him more. And he wanted to be here for her.

He started to run his palms over her back, but stilled. It would've been a soothing gesture, nothing more, but the old Kyle was rearing his head. Those thoughts brought on others, making things stir that didn't need stirring.

Bella leaned into him and burrowed into his shoulder with a sigh, making disentanglement impossible. If he stayed like this much longer, he was going to embarrass himself again.

Luckily, Dom saved him from that. "You need someone's knees broken?" he asked in a low growl. Kyle kept one arm around Bella's waist as she eased away. "I know that guy. He was Bruno DiMartino's manager when we had our big match a few years back. He didn't even visit the guy when he was in the hospital."

"Thanks, but I can break my own knees," Bella said.

Dom nodded. "So what happened? What's his deal?"

Haltingly, she related the sordid tale, and a few of

the other fighters closed around her to listen. Kyle envied how brave she was, telling this story to a bunch of big, macho guys. He'd expected them to dismiss Ryan's behavior. But they listened, and they didn't interrogate her or try to make excuses for Ryan. She didn't gloss over any details, either—she told them the story in minute detail, right down to the horrendous bathing suit he'd tried to make her wear. They laughed the way people did at stories that were only funny in hindsight, but there was anger and disbelief there, too. Their faces twisted in shock when she got to the attack he'd witnessed.

"Motherf— What a douche."

"I'll tell all my students and teachers about this guy—make sure none of them sign on with him."

"If he'd done that to my sister or my daughter…"

Now Kyle wished he *had* decked Ryan. The guy was a criminal, but Kyle had a feeling Bella still wasn't going to press charges. Then again, the way things were going, Ryan Holbrooke would be blacklisted for the rest of his life. The MMA community was a close one, and despite the rivalries that developed, no one ever wanted to see a fighter get stuck with bad representation.

Bonded by this horror, the guys did whatever they could to make Bella feel better, making jokes and telling their own stories, acting like goofs—anything to wash away the moment that had marred the evening's festivities.

As close as Kyle stayed, he was eventually pushed to the sidelines when Bella was dragged onto the dance floor. He watched the group hop around wildly, swinging her this way and that. She laughed and stumbled and eventually stopped to take off her sandals.

Kyle brooded. *He* should be the one down there with her. He should be the one to make her feel better. He downed a mouthful of champagne—the real stuff, not Hadrian's colored water—and made his way across the dance floor where she was grooving with the UFF's current featherweight champion. Her killer stilettos nearly took his eye out as she swung them around on one hooked finger. He grabbed her waist and spun her to face him.

"Hi," she said breathlessly, cheeks rosy. She quirked an eyebrow. "I thought your knee wasn't letting you dance tonight."

"Screw the knee." He narrowed his eyes at the featherweight, who raised his hands, mouthed a smiling *sorry* and backed away.

Bella wrapped her arms around his shoulders and laughed. She had a terrific laugh, full and rich. Kyle wanted to swim in the sound of it. "Feeling better?" he asked.

"Much."

He locked his arms around her and cinched her closer. He couldn't stop smiling. Considering how the night had gone so far—first with the dress emergency, then arriving late, the encounter with Ryan, and fending off Hadrian and the other men—he shouldn't have been so pleased, but he was.

He didn't pull away and try to hide his arousal. Until now he hadn't allowed himself to feel the full force of his attraction to Bella. He'd been suppressing it since the day she'd come barreling toward him on her bike. And now, he had her pressed against him, soft and warm and practically purring. Maybe it wasn't professional in the strictest sense, but frankly he didn't care. All he knew was that it felt right, even if it was miles from safe or smart. Maybe tonight was the night they'd explore this thing between them further, continue where they'd left off after that explosive kiss.

"Do you want to get out of here?" she asked, threading her fingers through the hair at his temple as if reading his mind. A shiver of pleasure made him stiffen further.

Yes rested on his tongue, melted there. But he couldn't say it without first making sure she wouldn't regret tonight. Maybe he was really asking for himself. "You're the guest of honor. Wouldn't you be missed?"

She didn't say anything in response as she towed him toward the exit. He spotted Jess by the bar, nursing a martini, and she craned her neck. "Hey! Where're you two going?"

"We've got training to do," Bella said with a mischievous grin.

Jess's gaze moved to Kyle. She grinned and toasted him as they ducked out.

BELLA'S BODY BUZZED. She wondered if she'd accidentally sipped some real champagne. In the limo, she and Kyle only held hands, but it was the most erotic hand-holding she'd ever experienced. He traced circles over the top of her skin, dragging his fingertips down to the Vs between each of her digits before turning her palm up and massaging the center with his thumb.

Maybe he knew some magical pressure point, because she swore she nearly came right there.

The limo pulled up to the hotel and they got out. The walk across the lobby took forever. They got on the elevator with an old man and woman who smiled at them as they rode up. They must have been in their seventies, and they were holding hands. What an adorable couple. Bella caught Kyle's eye and bit on her lower lip to keep from giggling.

The elderly couple got off on the fifth floor. The old man said, "You two have a good night," and chuckled as if it were the funniest thing ever.

The moment the elevator door closed, Kyle grabbed her around the waist and kissed her deeply, backing her up until she leaned against the cool, mirrored wall.

"I think that old man knew we were up to something," Bella said, fingers delving beneath his tuxedo jacket. His flesh was hard and hot under the fine shirt.

"The list of *somethings* I want to be up to with you goes on forever." He buried his nose against her neck and inhaled as he drove his hips against her.

Bella gasped as the hard length of him hit her dead center. She was shivering on the edge, holding back, but Kyle was relentless. He hitched one thigh up and pressed her against the wall as he bit down on her exposed shoulder and gently ground his hips in delicious figure eights.

He didn't even need to be inside her. Her climax spiraled and rushed through her limbs. The elevator reached her floor with a loud *ding!*

Her heart fluttered and her head spun as she languished in what she was sure would be the first of many orgasms that night. The elevator doors slid open. Together, they fumbled with the key card and entered the suite. Kyle half carried her into the living room, kicking off his shoes as he went. She dropped her sandals on the floor and climbed her way down his body until she was cinched against his erection once more, his hands supporting her thighs. They groaned together as she gyrated.

He breathed deep. "Better not do that too much or it'll be over before we get to the real fun."

"Tap out if you want to stop," she teased, letting herself slide the rest of the way to her feet. She pulled at his bow tie. "You're wearing too much clothing."

He quickly divested himself of his jacket and tie. Bella undid the top buttons of his shirt, their lips dipping and tasting as he backed her toward the couch. She got his shirt undone all the way to the navel, exposing his firm, rippling abs. She needed him touching her, surrounding her, buried inside her.... She shoved him hard. He toppled back onto the couch, his eyes wide.

"Sorry, Coach, too rough?" She straddled his lap, fingers playing through the light smattering of hair on his chest and stomach. His eyes softened when she guided his hands up to her breasts, then grew intense as he gently kneaded, thumbs caressing her nipples. Slowly, he drew down the single strap of her dress and deftly unhooked the strapless bra.

Cool air hit her, and she broke out in all-over goose bumps. Kyle's body heat dispelled the chill quickly. He kissed first one breast, almost chastely, then the other, before applying himself to the task more ardently.

Bella's eyes rolled back. Of course Kyle would be good at this. He'd had so much practice with all those girls....

Don't think about that, she scolded, trying to dive back into the moment...the feel of Kyle's tongue and lips, the way he was thrusting slowly against her.

She reached between them and unsnapped his pants, scooting back so she could gain access. Kyle tried to slow her down, but she wanted him in her hand, wanted to make him crazy and drive him to the edge.

"Bed," he bit out, scooping her up under the knees and carrying her into the bedroom. She squealed, distantly thinking how not even Antonio had made her squeal. Kyle dropped her onto the mattress, pulled off his shirt and quickly shucked his pants, underwear and socks.

Bella had seen a lot of nearly naked men. Symmetrical abs and ridged obliques with well-formed but not overly pronounced pecs declared Kyle an ideal specimen of man. Her gaze drifted lower to where other muscles twitched to get her attention.

Make that a perfect and virile specimen.

And how many college coeds have thought that exact same thing?

She yanked off her dress hastily, hoping he hadn't detected her flash of reservation. Kyle was going to be the best bang of her life. She needed this. She deserved it. She'd earned it, dammit. She made to take off her panties, but he caught her wrist and stopped her. "Let me."

He crawled onto the bed, kissing her toes, her ankles, calves, thighs, hips, waist, breast…up, up, up he climbed until their lips molded together. The moment bare skin met bare skin, she melted. She couldn't stop thinking how good he was at this, how completely in touch he was with her body, knowing when to touch her, when to slip his fingers through her slick folds and plumb her depths. She wriggled beneath him, arching for more. She was used to being in charge of her own pleasure, and here he was taking her right to the brink again….

No. She wouldn't come again, not until he was deep inside her, panting her name.

She wanted him begging. She wanted him helpless and squirming and unable to say anything but "yes," "please" and "oh, God, Bella."

She turned over abruptly and pushed him flat onto his back, pinning him as she straddled his hips. His eyes went huge. "What are you doing?"

"Just lie back and enjoy yourself." She pinned his wrists to either side of his head and started to climb down the length of him.

Every muscle in his body tensed, snapping her out of her lustful haze.

"Get off, get off!" He swore as he bucked, nearly kneeing her in the face. He scrambled to the edge of the bed, his back to her, breaths rasping harshly through his lungs.

CHAPTER SIXTEEN

BELLA STARED AT the stranger at the other end of the bed. The rank smell of fear lay thick in her nostrils. Her skin cooled, and though she felt every sensation clearly, her head was fogged. "Kyle…did I hurt you?"

It took him a long moment to reply. "No."

She reached for him, but the moment her fingers made contact, he leaped off the mattress. "Don't touch me."

She flinched. Slowly, she drew the comforter around her. "Did I do something wrong?"

He didn't respond. Instead, he pushed off the bed and hurried into the en suite bathroom, slamming the door.

Bella ran a hand over her hair, finding the gold-and-pearl barrette still tangled in the mess. She heard the sink running at full blast, followed by the sounds of Kyle rinsing his mouth and splashing his face. She heard his deep, gasping breaths and wondered if he was on the brink of throwing up. Had he had too much to drink? Was he feeling sick?

She replayed the evening in her head, hunting for clues to what had gone wrong. They'd been getting along fine. They'd been having fun. Kyle had finally given in to his attraction to her. He hadn't been shy about it, either. She'd assumed he'd simply wanted a night of steamy sex to get all that tension and frustration out—that'd been what she'd wanted.

He finally came out, eyes cast down. He gathered up his clothes, bunching them up around his semierect penis.

"Talk to me, Kyle." Her voice came out soft, even though she was trying to show him that his rejection couldn't hurt her. Not that she'd ever admit she was feeling insecure. She cleared her throat and tried for a smile. "At least tell me it wasn't food poisoning from the canapés. If it is…"

"It's not." He stepped into his boxer briefs. He hadn't even stopped to check that they were inside out. He started to pull his pants on, and Bella sensed him already on his way out the door. Running from her. Running from his problems, whatever they were.

"Please don't walk out on me. It's killing me to think I hurt you. I didn't mean to. Please. Tell me what I did wrong." She sounded as though she were asking for help with her wrestling techniques. "Whatever it is, I'm right here for you, Kyle. Right here."

He froze and sat heavily on the corner of the bed, his back still to her. "I'm sorry. It's…it's not you."

Maybe it was selfish to be relieved by that statement, whether or not it was true. It was a while before he continued.

"About a year and a half ago, I had a…*relationship* with a trainer at Payette's named Karla. You've probably heard about it. It wasn't supposed to be anything serious. My dad had passed away a few months earlier, and she'd been really nice to me…"

"And when you broke it off with her, she didn't like it."

"So the guys did tell you about it, then." He blew out a harsh breath. "There were phone calls in the middle of the night. Emails. Letters. Packages. I had to change my phone number, but that didn't stop her.… I had no choice but to fire her."

He linked his hands behind his head, and the muscles on his bare back bunched as he wrung the tension from them.

"A few weeks after her termination, she called and told me she wanted to bury the hatchet. Said she wanted to apologize. I gave her that chance. I guess I didn't think too hard about it at the time—I just wanted it over with. So I met her at a bar. We talked, and she said she was going to Ireland or something. She was leaving the country for good to work at another gym, and she didn't want her crazy behavior to reflect badly on her. Wanted a letter of recommendation. I was happy to give it. I wished her good luck and we had some drinks to celebrate.…" He jammed his thumbs into the base of his skull. "Then I started feeling crappy, so I went home. I can't remember much more. They say that's what happens.…" His voice grew hoarse. "I woke up and she was there. On top of me. And…I was inside her."

Bella's insides turned to ice. She didn't dare breathe for fear of the wrong words coming out. Or worse, laughter. Because that's what she wanted to do—laugh. Not because this was funny, but because she simply had no other response for it.

Nothing about this was funny.

"She'd dropped something in my drink—at least, that's what I'm guessing. Maybe I wasn't handling my beer well that night. I didn't eat much that day. Just a hot dog."

Strange detail to remember, she thought distantly, but then, bad memories did that. He turned his head, but his eyes didn't meet hers over his shoulder. "I guess she'd taken me home and put me in bed. I…" He scrubbed his hands over his face. "She told me I should go with it, that it was one last night before she went away for good. I thought it was a dream. I told myself I enjoyed it…" His hands fell limply to his sides. "She was gone in the morning."

Bella felt ill. Karla had never left Kyle—she was still here, haunting him. He'd been powerless to stop her….

Hadn't he? Bella surveyed all that muscle and those big, strong hands. Of course he could've stopped her. He'd picked Bella up like she weighed nothing. She'd seen him bench-press his own weight.

But did that mean anything? If he'd been drunk or drugged…

"I found out later from Hadrian that she'd gone to the UFF and threatened to expose me, bring a scandal to the whole organization. Their solution was to find her a swank job in another country and pay her off. Then Hadrian called me, told me he knew everything. He chewed me out. The fact that I had proof of her insane behavior… It was the only thing that saved my job."

She chewed on her lip, found herself struggling to believe him, and it made her sick. Why wouldn't he defend himself more ardently against Karla's allegations?

She thought of Shawnese suddenly, lying in that hospital bed, afraid to speak the truth, embarrassed by it, helpless and stewing in her own anger and mistrust.

Bella opened her mouth, but no words came. What was she supposed to do? Apologize for her gender? She tried to imagine what other men might say. Make jokes, maybe. Tell him they wished they could wake up every night to a woman riding them.

Bella didn't know what to say. She wasn't accustomed to being this useless. How was she supposed to make him feel better? Dragging him back into bed and trying to make him forget all his worries with sex seemed insensitive to say the least.

"You must think I'm the worst," Kyle said finally, letting out a wry laugh that sent shards of guilt stabbing through her, "telling you all this when I've never told anyone."

"Not even your family? What about the police?"

"You think they'd believe me?" He shook his head.

"But if you were drugged…and you've got a bum knee." She winced. Wrong thing to say. Definitely the wrong thing to say.

He gave a snort. "Yeah. 'Cause they'll really go for that story. My dad didn't even believe I had an injury. He thought I was faking it right up to the day he died—kept insisting I try all these radical therapies to make my knee better, but he didn't get that all I wanted was to stop…."

Meu Deus. All Bella could think to say was, "I'm sorry." It was the only platitude she had to offer. Weak. Insincere sounding.

"No, I'm sorry. This wasn't the way this night was supposed to go," Kyle said casually, almost by rote. He scoffed. "I might as well tell you you're not the first girl I've left in this state. They all thought I was just a doped-up loser who couldn't get it up."

Jokes. That was his shield. He used humor to hide his suffering. And all those pretty young things he went around with, all of them petite and nonthreatening and easy to abandon—they were all part of the facade. The playboy still playing his game as if nothing was wrong.

Part of her still couldn't believe big, bad Kyle had gone through this trauma. She was still expecting him to turn around and say, "Gotcha!" It seemed like a Kyle thing to do. He'd fought with her, got in her space, avoided her, played her white knight, shied away from her. They'd never been able to get out of each other's way—it'd only been a matter of time before they'd crashed headlong into one another. And now here they were, naked and unfulfilled and completely exposed.

"This is why you don't sleep well, isn't it?"

He exhaled, his whole body sagging. "It's hard to fall asleep when every creak sounds like someone in your house."

HADRIAN STUDIED THE final photos of Bella Fiore for the special edition *UFF Brawl* magazine and hummed in approval, her smoky, sexy eyes beckoning the reader to *Buy me!* It wouldn't hurt sales if she showed a little more skin, though—maybe he could get the art team to make her shorts smaller.

Mrs. H. knocked on the door frame. "Quinn called again," she said, handing him a message slip. "She really wants to talk to you."

"Not now." He'd been giving her a taste of her own medicine since the last time she'd ditched their plans to chase a story. Quinn hadn't even come to the gala after everything he'd done to get her on the VIP guest list. He'd even booked a limo and a personal stylist to help her get ready. But she'd blown him off to cover some press conference about a retiring baseball player in New York.

His P.A. frowned. "You can't keep putting her off."

"Of course I can. I'm busy with work, too, you

know." He spotted another slip clutched in her hands. "What's that?"

"He won't stop calling," The uncharacteristic worry in Mrs. Hutzenbiler's voice made Hadrian sit up tall. "He insists on talking to you."

"He, who? A lot of people want to talk to me."

"Fulvio Fiore."

Oh. Him. He stalled. "I'm surprised, Mrs. H. I've heard you yell at heavyweight fighters without blinking. Fulvio Fiore's in his seventies. Don't tell me an old man is scaring you."

She gave him a narrowed look. "He threatened to come and speak to you in person if you don't take his call."

Hadrian sighed. Fiores didn't bluff.

He picked up the phone and hit the line. "Fulvio, how are you?"

"Don't you ask me how I am! How could you do this to my family?"

Hadrian swung around in his chair to face the window as Mrs. H. departed and quietly shut the door behind her. "If you mean sign Bella on with the UFF—"

"Caralho!" On the other end of the line, something slammed down hard. "She is not capable and not ready."

"Now, hold up a minute. I think you underestimate her." He didn't appreciate being yelled at by anyone, not when it came to his business. "I've seen her fight and she's good. Better than good. She's star material." He picked up the photo again. Definitely a good choice.

"Only because you can't find anyone better. I know you called three other women before you called Bella. How stupid do you think I am?"

He closed his eyes. Of course. Fiore-trained BJJ teachers were scattered across the globe. Some of them would have dutifully reported Hadrian's call to their old master. In the world of MMA, everyone talked. You couldn't stub a toe without someone on the other side of the world hearing about it. "Bella wasn't my fourth pick. She's my first. They all were. I'd sign them all on if they came to me now. The others simply didn't want to step into the cage with such short notice."

"No, they don't want to fight Kamikaze Kamino, you bastard. How can you put my granddaughter up against that maniac?"

"Ayumi's not a monster, Fulvio—her methods are just a bit unorthodox. Anyway, this is business. Bella's signed. She wants to fight. You can't stop her."

As the terse silence on the other end of the line stretched on, Hadrian pictured them standing in an arena, Fulvio dressed as a bull, while he waved a red cape at him. "You leave me no choice. If you don't cancel this fight, I will cancel Fiore sponsorship of all UFF events."

He ground his teeth. The Fiore BJJ School provided a good chunk of cash to the organization and the Starlight Foundation. *But* all kinds of sponsors had recently been stepping up to get their logos on the first ever UFF women's match.

It was only money, he thought.

Hadrian hated antagonizing the head of one of the most influential MMA families around, but as far as he was concerned, Fulvio was an old man whose hold on his family was slipping. He was an aging lion unwilling to turn his pride over to the younger generation.

"I'm not canceling this match," Hadrian said firmly. "The show is sold out. The media loves Bella, and the world will, too. She's going to make history. Why can't you accept that?"

"Women do not belong in the cage. You said so yourself."

"Yeah, well, I changed my mind."

Silence, and then Fulvio said, "You will regret this."

Hadrian smiled at the photo of Bella. "I don't think I will." And he hung up.

BELLA STOOPED OVER the sewer grate and vomited up her breakfast smoothie, gasping for breath, heart pounding.

"You have to stop." Kyle stood by, watching impassively. "Let's walk it off back to the gym."

"I'm good," she insisted as she rinsed her mouth and spit. She wiped her lips with the back of her hand. "Let's keep going."

"No." His firm tone told her he would not be

argued with. "You've been pushing yourself too hard ever since we got back from Vegas. That's the second time you've thrown up in four days. You're going to hurt yourself. You've got to know your limits."

"I know my limits. I haven't reached them yet," she snapped irritably. "I ate too much is all."

He frowned. "You sticking to your diet?"

"Of course." It was that or subsist on the dozens of vitamin pills and powdered drinks the dietician had recommended. She couldn't stand the thought of not eating real food. Though currently, most of her meals consisted of water and raw fruit and vegetables, much of it in smoothie form mixed with numerous supplements.

"C'mon. We're going to walk, and then you're going to rest."

Sullenly, Bella followed. She knew part of her bad mood was simply the sugar withdrawal talking. She was used to having carbs and lots of meat, and they'd been cut out. The other part of her mood was because of the man who plodded ahead of her.

They hadn't talked about that night at the hotel. She'd lain awake after he'd gone back to his room, trying to figure out what it was she was supposed to do and what she wanted. They'd boarded the plane together the next day and remained silent the whole flight. Maybe it was for the best. Bella had had no idea what to say. She couldn't afford to get tangled up with his issues and distract herself from the fight. But she couldn't ignore what she'd learned, either,

because she now saw his pain in every little inter-
action, every breath he took.

When their eyes met, she saw the shame and vul-
nerability beneath his lopsided smiles. She noticed
the way he tensed when women approached him.
His arm's-length relationships with the rest of the
Payette's crew suddenly made a lot more sense, too.
They didn't know the truth. He didn't want them to
know—didn't want them to get close enough to realize Karla had changed him. She couldn't blame
him. She could picture the guys' reactions—ridicule,
disbelief, disgust. Some of them actually believed
he'd invited trouble with his womanizing. Hadn't she
thought the same in the back of her mind?

It made her all the more adamant to help him. Of
course, she had her own reasons—and she knew it
was selfish of her to still want Kyle in her bed. But
it was less about sex now than it was about comfort and reassurance. She wanted him to heal. She
wanted him to stop being afraid. She wanted to be
the one to help him.

She wanted to be worthy of helping him.

She glanced at him as they walked. He looked lost
in thought. She could practically see the flashes of
darkness in his eyes. Her gaze slid past him, and she
noticed the sign on the building across the street. The
adobe facade was painted dark orange, but much of
the plaster was chipping. A few young men and a
couple of girls stood outside, propping up the wall

and smoking. One of the boys in a dark hoodie hollered, "Kyle!" and waved.

"I didn't realize the Touchstone youth center was here. Isn't that one of our students?"

"Yeah." Kyle seemed to hesitate at first, but then they crossed the street together.

"Hey, man, how's it going?" the young man greeted.

"Jerome. It's been a while." They shook hands and clapped each other on the back, surprising Bella. Jerome was one of the guys who came in for the self-defense class. He'd shown a lot of promise. After introducing his friends, he acknowledged Bella with a bob of his head. "Miss Bella. I hear you're going to be fighting in the UFF. Congratulations."

"Thanks. Have you heard from Shawnese at all?" She felt bad that she hadn't made time to visit the young woman, though they'd talked on the phone. Last she'd heard, she was still staying with Reta.

"Shawnese? Nah, she left a couple of weeks back. I'm not sure where to." He grimaced. "It's a shame, but you know how it is. Things are tough. She's gotta figure them out on her own."

Bella's consternation grew. Where would she go? What if Andre found her again? What if she went back to her old habits?

"Won't be so tough for her now though, eh?" One of the other guys snickered. "Jerome told us all about you, Mr. Peters."

"Badass," another chimed in with a respectful nod.

Kyle smiled grimly, rubbing the back of his neck. Bella stared. Slowly, she asked, "What did you do?"

"He didn't tell you?" Jerome's eyes widened, and he laughed. "This *upstanding gentleman* waited around out here for days to see if Andre would show up. When he finally did, Kyle told him to step off and leave Shawnese alone. Andre got up in his business and makes to, like, pull a knife or something. Then this monster—" he pointed at Kyle "—grabs the guy and tosses him to the ground, like, three times."

The guys laughed as Jerome mimed the scene. "Boom! On his side. Boom! On his back. Third time, this guy's bored, and Andre's still trying to get his knife out, stumbling around like a drunk. So Kyle grabs his wrist, twists him around, and I swear to God, flips him over onto his knee and spanks his ass, then drops him on his face and says, 'Stay.'"

The rest of the guys howled with laughter while Kyle shuffled his feet, abashed.

"He deserved it, man," Jerome said, wiping tears away as he shook Kyle's hand and gave him a fist bump. "This guy's okay."

"Kyle, that's assault!" Bella hissed.

"That's justice, ma'am," one of Jerome's friends said somberly. "Andre won't show his face around here again. Guy was nothing but a punk. He's too chicken shit to take on someone his own size."

"You guys have plans for the holidays?" Kyle asked, eager to change the subject.

"Plans? You mean Christmas trees and presents?" Jerome's grin dimmed. "We'll probably be here." He cocked his head at the building. "They do turkey dinner. We get some stockings. It's all right."

Kyle nodded. "Well, I'll be in town. If you need a place to go, give me a call and come down to the gym." He handed Jerome a business card. "I appreciate you letting me hang with you guys."

"Hey, it was worth seeing Andre schooled." Jerome waved as they departed.

"And exactly when did this all happen?" Bella asked him as soon as they were out of earshot.

Kyle kept his gaze straight ahead. "I went after work and on weekends. I was there for less than two weeks. I just hung around outside—nothing illegal about that. Reta told me Andre comes in sometimes and that she couldn't legally do anything about it if he didn't bother anyone." He lifted a shoulder carelessly. "I figured I'd wait him out, make sure he understood what the deal was. Let him know Shawnese has friends."

"Kyle, do you have any idea how stupid and dangerous that was?" Her chest hurt, but she wasn't sure if it was because she was mad, sad or exhilarated. Maybe this was his way of dealing with his own pain—by helping others who couldn't help themselves. Even so, she couldn't condone this macho behavior. "Did you think you were being noble or something? What if he'd had a gun? Or friends?"

"I took all the proper precautions. I told Jerome

and his boys not to get involved except to call the cops if things went south. Anyhow, Jerome's one of the best students in the self-defense class. He doesn't lose his head. He's a really good guy. I trusted him to watch my back, and he did."

"You shouldn't have involved him at all. You both could've been seriously hurt. What if Andre comes after you looking for revenge? What if he presses charges?"

"C'mon, Bella. You think a known pimp is going to go to the cops? You and I both know Shawnese will never press charges. And Andre won't leave her alone unless he knows she's got someone on her side. Guys like him prey on vulnerable women. He had to learn she wasn't his punching bag anymore. If you'd heard the way he talked about her, trust me, you would've done the same thing."

"No, I wouldn't, because I don't take the law into my own hands. He could've stabbed you."

"Ain't nothin' but a thang," he said in an affected accent.

She halted midstride. "Are you seriously making a joke about this? Stop pretending that you're invincible, like you have to prove to the world you're a freaking superman. You aren't, okay? And there's nothing wrong with that. You don't have to go around rescuing damsels in distress and waving your fists around to prove you're a man." Tears rushed to her eyes and she dashed them away angrily.

Kyle's cheekbones stood out like blades, and a

vein pulsed at his temple. "You think *I'm* trying to prove something? What about you? You've been running yourself sick and working yourself into exhaustion when I've explicitly told you not to. You've fought me every step of the way since I met you, Bella. What do *you* have to prove?"

She should have shouted it, but it barely came out a whisper. "Everything." She was suddenly bone tired. She sagged and leaned against a post. "That's what you don't get. I have everything to prove because people out there are always going to judge me. You? You had your moment—you got three of them. But that time's over now, Kyle. You have to let go. You're human like the rest of us. The things that have happened to you since—"

He turned and walked away from her, from her words. She bolted after him. "That messed up everything for you—I know," she yelled, and he quickened his pace to a jog. "You think being a man means keeping all your pain and problems to yourself, but it doesn't. You think you can control everything in your life? You can't."

He slowed as they reached a small park. He stumbled and doubled over, gasping as he clutched his bad knee. Bella's breath sawed in and out of her lungs and her blood pumped hard through her temples, but it wasn't from running. "That's why you went after Andre, isn't it? You're trying to redeem yourself or something."

He straightened and started walking. His limp was

much more pronounced now. He paced back toward her in a tight circle, his features set like concrete.

"I helped Shawnese because she needed help. Because I could. Because no one else was going to step up for her." Despite the angry lines wreathing his face, all she wanted to do was brush her hand along his jaw and soothe his fury.

"Tell me something, Kyle. You like helping defenseless young women. Are you man enough to let them help you back?" She was sick of being kept at arm's length. They were more than friends. More than coach and trainee. Dammit, she was going to help him whether he wanted her help or not.

Kyle stared at the sky and let out a breath. "I should never have said anything to you."

"I'm glad you did."

"You would say that. You'd probably thank me for a punch in the mouth." He gave a humorless chuckle.

She smacked him in the arm. "Only because I'd learn how to duck it and punch you right back."

"Yeah." He rubbed the hollows of his eyes. "Look, I can't talk about this stuff, Bella. I don't even know why I told you. All this touchy-feely crap…it's not who I am."

"If you can't talk to me about it, we can find someone—"

"I'm not going to a shrink."

"A counselor, then. I bet Reta could recommend someone."

"I don't think so. Leave it alone."

"Kyle, you can't sleep in your own home. You have intimacy issues, and you're averse to physical contact with strong women. I'm no psychologist, but I'd say you have things you need to work out, preferably with a professional."

"I *am* working them out," he snapped.

Bella wanted to shake sense into him. But arguing wasn't going to solve anything. The harder she pushed, the more stubborn he'd become.

Unstoppable force, meet unmovable object.

She couldn't be the aggressor. She couldn't tackle his problems head-on and pin them down the way she usually did with any challenge she was presented with.

It was time to try something new. Something unexpected.

CHAPTER SEVENTEEN

CHRISTMAS SUCKED.

And not just because Kyle was alone in his house, but because he'd insisted on being left alone to wallow in his misery.

After his morning run, he'd spent the day reading a thriller—doing paperwork for the gym felt a little too Ebenezer Scrooge even for him. He watched a couple of Christmas specials on TV, then called his mother and sister to wish them a happy holidays.

"I really wish you'd come home," Holly Peters said. "We could've had a real turkey with all the trimmings, the way we used to. Your father always loved Christmas dinner...." She sighed. "What are you having, dear?"

He glanced at the box of spring mix garden salad he'd bought. "Oh, you know. Ham and mashed potatoes and gravy. Crawfish and corn. An authentic Big Easy Christmas."

Thinking about it made his mouth water, but he'd committed to eating a little healthier—he'd been having takeout way too often, and it was beginning to show.

"He's probably having a Hungry Man while he watches the *Charlie Brown Christmas* special," Jess said on the other line. "You're missing out, squirt. Organic Cornish game hens are all the rage in L.A."

"Thanks, but I think I'll survive." Truth was, he'd stayed in town because he didn't want to face his family.

Since telling Bella his darkest secret, he'd been moody—and he was pretty sure he didn't have the patience for his mom and sister right now. He could predict exactly what would've happened if he'd gone home. Jess would ask after Bella, speculating about their relationship, and when he got snippy, his mother and sister would only interrogate him further. He'd end up storming off and ruining Christmas. It was best not to expose anyone to that.

After hanging up, he sat down to dinner in front of his TV. He took one look at his wilting salad and set it aside. Why had he turned down all those invitations to join people for Christmas? What was he trying to prove?

Bella's words from earlier that week rang in his ears. Apparently, he was trying to prove he was an unfriendly, brooding asshole.

He pushed up off the couch. There were a dozen different ways he could be spreading good cheer, doing things people normally did over the holidays. He wouldn't sit and sulk the way Dad used to when he didn't get his way. He grabbed his jacket and keys and headed out.

He drove the mostly deserted streets—apparently even the most hard core partygoers stayed home on Christmas. A couple of bars and restaurants were still open, though, catering to tourists and guys like him who couldn't get home for the holidays. He was lucky enough to have family, friends…but he'd pushed them all away. And for what? To show everyone he could take care of himself?

He found himself parked outside the Touchstone youth center. Muscle memory had guided him here, apparently. The lights were on inside, and he remembered that the center was hosting Christmas dinner.

He felt like a heel for being so petulant.

During those long nights waiting for Andre with Jerome and his crew, he'd learned a lot about where these young people came from. Life had treated them rough. Some had come from horrible home situations and had had to do some awful things in order to survive. Yet the staff didn't judge them. They gave them the help they needed and fostered their dreams of the future in any way they could.

Harsh as his father had been, Kyle couldn't compare his upbringing to theirs. He didn't even like to think that any of his problems measured up to the everyday challenges kids like Shawnese faced. It was hard to remember why he'd been so hesitant to host the self-defense class in the first place. Maybe he hadn't wanted to relate to their plight.

Kyle released a breath as he finally admitted the

truth to himself. Bella was right about the way he'd helped Shawnese—he was compensating for something.

He walked into the center and followed the delicious smells wafting down the institutional-looking hallways to a big room bustling with activity.

He scanned the room and was taken aback when he met Bella's wide green eyes.

"What are you doing here?" His heart tumbled strangely seeing her in a bright red boat-necked top and black dress pants. Large gold hoop earrings dangled from her ears. Her hair hung down and had been straightened. His lips inched up in an involuntary smile. "I thought you were spending Christmas at Liz's," he said.

"I was." She set down a large bowl of salad and tugged at his sleeve and pointed. "Look who gave me a call."

Behind her at a table with several other people sat Shawnese, smiling and laughing as they ate soup and salad appetizers.

"She called to say Merry Christmas," Bella said. "We talked for an hour. She's doing much better."

Shawnese looked up and caught his eye. Her smile widened and she greeted him with a lift of her chin.

"Aren't you giving up your Christmas dinner?" He looked at his watch and was surprised to find it was still early. Had he really sat down to his sad salad dinner before six?

"Liz and I were baking all day, and by the end, we

had all these pies and only five people to eat them. I can't even have any." She pouted. "As soon as I heard Shawnese was here, I wanted to see her. Liz drove me out and her parents insisted we bring what we could to share, so here we are." She pointed with her tongs. Liz stood in the serving line, dishing out pieces of pumpkin pie.

"She's a saint," Reta said as she flitted by with a tray of drinks. "Merry Christmas, Kyle. Won't you join us?"

Kyle shucked his jacket. "Actually, if you don't mind, I'd like to help."

Reta's face lit up. "Aprons and hairnets are behind the counter. We've got mashed potatoes in a big pot on the stove that will need to be served."

Kyle's spirits picked up as he helped the other volunteers with the heavy lifting. Jerome and his friends showed up, and after they'd all had a helping of turkey and stuffing, potatoes, string beans, rolls and more pie, they played board games, shared a few laughs and had some good conversation.

Kyle discovered his melancholy had evaporated. He really had been a jerk. He'd call his mom again tonight and apologize for his behavior. He promised himself, too, that he'd go and visit her as soon as he could.

"You're in a good mood." Bella handed him a cup of eggnog. She drank herbal tea, he noticed. What a sucky time to go on a diet. She hadn't eaten much more than a bowl of salad and a tiny portion of dry-looking breast meat for dinner.

"The day started out kind of awful for me, I admit. But it got better the minute I stepped foot in here and saw you."

Her lips pursed into a bashful smile. She squeezed his thigh, and a tingle went through him. If there'd been a bunch of mistletoe hanging somewhere, he would've had the perfect excuse to kiss her. And then he realized he really *did* want to kiss her.

"Kyle?" Shawnese approached them timidly. The bruises and swelling in her face were gone, but her hands remained hidden beneath fingerless gloves. "It's so great to see you two. I was going to leave these with Ms. Reta, but now I can give them to both of you." She pulled out a couple of packages from a plastic shopping bag. "It's nothing fancy. I mean, I made them. Part of my rehab." She flexed her stiff fingers.

"You didn't have to do that," Kyle said, but took the little drawstring pouch from her. He opened it and drew out a small carved wood cross on a leather thong. The word HERO was burned across the lintel.

His eyes stung, and his throat worked hard over a lump.

"I heard…well, maybe I didn't hear nothin' about it at all, but I want to say thank-you for what you did."

"Thank *you*. This is…more than I deserve." Kyle got up and hugged Shawnese.

The young woman turned to Bella and handed her a gift bag. "I made something for you, too."

It was an adorable hand-sewn voodoo doll with a big bobble head. It made Bella laugh, and she cuddled it against her cheek. Kyle couldn't help but smile...and feel a little jealous of the doll.

"I thought you could name her Ayumi," Shawnese said with a grin. "Treat her rough, but not too rough."

"I love it. Thank you, Shawnese."

They left shortly after that. Liz invited Kyle back to her parents'. With both Liz and Bella insisting, he couldn't refuse. At the house, Mrs. Gonçalves fussed over her daughter's boss, heaping his plate full even though he'd already eaten, primly informing him that it was his duty to make up for Bella's uneaten portion. After coffee and dessert, they said goodnight and Kyle volunteered to drive Bella home.

"That was really nice," he said sincerely, cruising along the quiet streets. To think he'd been prepared to spend the whole evening alone.

"I'm glad you came out. I was worried you'd be at home moping."

"I was." He gave her a sidelong glance. "I'm glad I got to see you tonight."

He pulled up outside of her place and shut off the engine. A beat of silence passed between them before she cleared her throat.

"I have a gift for you," she said. "It's upstairs. Do you want to come up?"

Kyle's chest lurched. He wanted to go up there.

He really did. But he couldn't bear another humiliating moment like he'd had in Vegas.

"Just for a moment. And just for the gift. I promise." She said it as though she were coaxing a scared animal from a cage.

He relaxed his white-knuckled grip from around the steering wheel. He was being ridiculous. It was Christmas. Bella wasn't going to hurt him.

That's when it hit him. *Bella wasn't going to hurt him.*

He got out of the car, forcing one foot ahead of the other as he followed her up the stairs. "I only found it late on Christmas Eve," she explained. "And then I wasn't sure I should give it to you."

"You didn't need to get me anything." He hadn't done more than write cards for his staff. He'd been adamant that they save their money for gifts for their families, or else donate to charity.

"I know, but I wanted to." She unlocked the door and let him in. His arm brushed against her chest as he passed, sending a thrill up his spine. "Can I offer you a cup of tea? Coffee?"

"Thanks, no." Though the idea of sticking around did appeal to him. Maybe he should accept something so he'd have an excuse to linger.

Before he could change his mind, she grabbed a plastic bag off the dining table and brought it to him. "Sorry. I didn't wrap it."

He reached in and pulled out a scroll tied with twine. He untied it and unrolled the thick paper.

"'*Kishi Kaisei,*'" he read the *kanji* aloud.

"You can read Japanese?"

"I studied in Kyoto for a year," he explained. "This phrase was on a banner posted in the dojo I trained in."

"The sales guy told me it means 'Wake from death and return to life.' He told me it's really about getting out of desperate situations in one sudden burst. I thought it might be appropriate for your office."

He grinned. "This is great. Thank you, Bella." He leaned down to give her a peck on the cheek, but he changed his mind at the last minute and aimed for her lips.

It probably wasn't professional, but damn, it felt good. And he was tired of doing what he thought was right. That hadn't always been him. Her hands slid up around his shoulders as the kiss deepened. But along with the surge of lust came a longing that seemed to climb through him from deep down.

She broke the kiss first and stepped back, smiling hugely. "That was nice," she said.

Kyle was at once insulted and abashed. Most women he'd kissed usually begged for more. They didn't say it had been *nice*.

He wanted to show her he was more than *nice*.

"It's getting late." She glanced pointedly at the clock. "I need to call my family before I go to bed."

"Of course. Thank you for this." He held the scroll close to his chest. Held her hand. Willed her to ask him to stay. The invitation hung between them, but she didn't ask.

Instead, she led him to the door, held it open.

"Merry Christmas." He leaned in again. He just wanted a peck. A friendly touch of her lips.

She pulled back before it became more, desire smoldering in her eyes. "Good night, Kyle."

He stepped out, and she closed the door after him.

Damn. He hadn't thought he could desire her after what they'd been through. Clomping back down to his car, though, he realized Bella was the only thing he'd really wanted for Christmas.

BELLA LOVED THE first Monday in January after the holidays. It felt like newness to her. A sense of being reborn. She didn't make resolutions, but she had a lot to look forward to, and had a lot of hard work ahead of her to get there.

Well, there was one resolution she'd made. She glanced at Kyle and sighed. He still hadn't made a move. *The* move.

After Christmas, they'd seen each other at a New Year's party at The Spot, but hadn't talked much with all the loud music and dancing. She'd purpose-fully kept her distance. She knew that whatever she felt for him—whether it was lust or something more—she couldn't act on it. *He* had to come to *her*. And for someone who was used to actively pursuing her men, it made her crazy to stand by and watch him flounder.

They were attracted to each other—that went without a doubt. That kiss in her apartment, chaste as it was, had nearly set her pants on fire. And she could see he'd wanted more, but after she'd gently broken away, he hadn't reached for her, hadn't wrapped her up in his arms, hadn't even asked to stay. Maybe he was waiting for her to make the next move, but she couldn't. Not in this case.

She laughed at herself bitterly. She felt about as flighty as she had in her senior year of high school, with prom and graduation on the horizon and a complete inability to focus on one or the other. The fight was six weeks away, and Bella had only dropped three pounds. Kyle drove her hard, and the rest of the trainers made sure she went home exhausted every day. But she still had seven more pounds to go.

Wayne was especially attentive whenever he was around—which she really appreciated. But she'd noticed the boxing coach had been sick a lot. The others joked that he was a big baby, but watching him move stiffly around, she wondered how no one else saw that Wayne was in a lot of pain.

"It's nothing you need to worry about," he said with a shake of his head. "I'm just getting old."

"Have you seen a doctor about the migraines?" It was his most frequent complaint.

"Dozens of them. I have prescriptions for everything—painkillers, acupuncture, massage, chiropractic and naturopathic medicine. Anything they can think of to manage the pain short of doping me up. I don't want to take anything I don't have to." He rubbed his temple. "I've had all kinds of tests, too— CAT scans, MRIs. Everyone's worried I'm going to have a stroke or something. All those years fighting, I got beat around the noggin a lot. They haven't found anything injury related, though." He chuckled. "Even if I'd known this would happen, I wouldn't have given any of it up. That's the price of glory. *This*—" he indicated his worn-out body "—is just a thing that happens. Not much I can do about it."

"There has to be something."

He gave her a compassionate look. "Kid, some hurts you gotta live with. Most people don't understand that kind of pain. They don't understand till it happens to them."

KYLE BRACED HIMSELF behind the large rectangular striking pad, absorbing Bella's blows, but her strikes barely connected.

"C'mon, Bella, you can hit harder," Wayne said. "Kyle's not that big a guy. Look at him. A stiff breeze could knock him over."

She repeated the striking pattern. Kyle shrank further behind the pad, expecting the jabs to shake his bones. They barely made him shudder.

"Hit him like he's done you wrong," the boxing coach shouted. "Hit him like he deserves it. C'mon, do you think Kamikaze Kamino's gonna go easy on you?"

The halfhearted one-two had Kyle slackening his grip.

"Stop, stop, stop." Wayne frowned sharply. "Kyle, was she hitting hard enough?"

"Barely." Somehow, it felt like it was his fault.

Wayne took the pad from him. "Okay, I don't like doing this, but you leave me no choice." He faced her with the pad. "You hit like a girl." He quickly ducked behind the pad.

Bella scoffed, grinning lopsidedly. "Really? That's your plan? Insult me till I get mad enough to hit you?"

He peeked up. "Your hair looks stupid and your clothes aren't fashionable!" He ducked again, and Bella laughed. "C'mon! Hit me!"

"Try insulting my mother," Bella suggested casually.

"Oh, hell, no. I'm not insulting the mother of five Fiores."

Kyle grimaced. Her future was on the line. He needed her to quit goofing off and focus. "You wanna lose, Bella? Are you trying to sabotage yourself?"

"I'm not trying anything." Her teeth ground together as she jabbed, right, left, right.

"Yeah, you're not trying at all. The fight's in six weeks, you amateur. Pick up your pace. Is this a joke to you?"

Wayne grunted, bracing himself as Bella scowled

at the pads. "No, but your insults are," she muttered, throwing a hard jab.

He was starting to get to her. Good. "You want to show your grandfather what kind of fighter you are? Then give this your all. I want to see 110 percent."

She stood down abruptly. "I have to pee." She went to the change room, leaving Kyle and Wayne alone.

The boxer tossed the pad aside. "Maybe she's having an off day."

Kyle wished he could agree with Wayne, but he didn't think it was just an off day. Bella had been restrained lately. He'd seen it when she'd grappled with him, too. Her fire had been banked. She was nothing like the warrior woman who'd charged him on her bike the first time they'd met.

"Kyle." Liz hurried over, her brow pleated. "Where's Bella?"

"Bathroom. Why?"

She grabbed him by the arm and led him to his office, then opened his internet browser on his laptop and entered in a web address for a popular sports magazine. "Read."

CHAPTER EIGHTEEN

THE WEBPAGE LIZ brought up displayed a feature titled Girl Fight: Will Women's MMA Be the Death of Feminism? by Quinn Bourdain. He scanned the first few paragraphs. It was a diatribe about whether women's MMA was sustainable, and mentioned Bella and Ayumi's match repeatedly.

His stomach pitched when he spotted Ryan Holbrooke's name.

Fiore's former agent and manager, Ryan Holbrooke, broke ties with Bella in November. He claimed she was "belligerent...a hotheaded diva who's done nothing to earn her chance to fight for the UFF."

"If anything, she'll be the end of WMMA. She thinks she knows everything," the manager who has worked with former UFF contenders such as Bruno DiMartino and Jackson De Sena said. He went on to describe her coaching efforts as "amateur at best, dangerous at worst." "She doesn't know what she's doing. She was training a bunch of street kids how to fight and nearly got one of them killed."

Fiore has been teaching a self-defense class in New Orleans alongside her principal coach, former Olympic medal-winning wrestler Kyle Peters. The students were from the Touchstone youth center, a community outreach program for at-risk youth. Members of the class confirmed that one of the students was hospitalized in November after failing to defend herself from a knife attack.

Kyle's gorge rose. The article went on to suggest that Hadrian Blackwell was putting on an appeasement fight—a sideshow to distract people from a host of issues, including frequent harassment of female UFF employees to unequal pay and the fostering of misogynistic attitudes in fighters and fans. He pushed away from his desk with disgust as he finished reading.

"The article ends with that bit about Touchstone in the online unpaid version," Liz pointed out. "We can read the whole thing because we have a paid subscription to the magazine. But everyone else will read this excerpt and only see—"

"That Bella is incapable of teaching." Kyle hissed out a breath and sat back. "Thanks for bringing this to my attention. Don't show it to Bella."

"Are you sure? I mean, won't Joel…"

"She doesn't need the distraction." He glimpsed

the top five comments on the article and his blood pressure spiked. He shut the laptop firmly. "We need to keep her focused. No internet, no magazines. Hide our subscription. In fact, cancel it." He was mad. Quinn had seemed like an intelligent and responsible journalist. He was surprised she'd written such an inflammatory piece.

"Guys."

Kyle looked up. Bella stood in his office doorway. Her face was pale and strained. She held her cell phone out, her mobile web browser showing the article they'd tried to hide from her.

He shot out of his seat. "How did you—"

"Someone sent it to me anonymously." She glanced at the screen and gave a crooked smile. "Maybe it's the Kamino camp trying to psyche me out."

More likely it was Ryan, Kyle thought—at the Starlight gala he had promised to get back at her.

"Don't think about it, Bella," Liz said encouragingly. "No one will remember any of this after you win that fight. Ryan's a dick and everyone who matters in this business knows it."

Bella gave a slight shrug, but her vivaciousness had dimmed. Kyle got what she was going through. The higher you ranked in the sports world, the more criticism and mockery you got. She'd start to doubt herself, afraid she couldn't live up to the hype. He'd gone through the same thing.

They went back to training. Bella hesitated,

though, and her strikes barely dented the pads. Kyle yelled at her, trying to incite a reaction, but she was working on autopilot. He'd hoped the article might have enraged her, but instead she seemed empty. Not Zen-like, but zombielike. Kyle was worried.

By the end of the day, they were all wrung out. Kyle drove her home.

"Tough day."

Bella didn't reply, her expression pensive. He didn't know whether to scream at her to wake up or pull her into his arms and tell her everything would be all right.

"Look, I know that article was harsh. But Quinn Bourdain doesn't know what she's talking about."

Bella chewed her lower lip. "At least she didn't mention Shawnese by name."

"She shouldn't have mentioned Touchstone at all, considering what the article was supposed to be about. I ought to call her editor and give him a piece of my mind."

Bella didn't respond. She just stared out the window.

"Forget about Quinn and the article. I'm more concerned about you right now. Is your diet giving you trouble? Are you feeling tired? Hungry?"

"I'm fine."

"Then what's wrong?"

"Don't worry about it." Her sad smile did nothing to reassure him.

He watched her walk up to her apartment, feeling

shut out as she closed her door. He stifled the urge to go up there and demand she tell him what was going on. He couldn't help but think her lackluster performance was his fault somehow. If he was any kind of man, he'd figure out a way to fix it, to get her out of her slump and back into fighting form. He had an idea, but he wasn't sure if, as Bella's coach and boss, he had any right getting into her personal business.

Right. Because you're so good at boundaries...

His job was to make sure she fought to win—and that was it. She deserved a coach who was completely dedicated to her training and success.

But the moment they stepped foot off the mat...the moment she threw him that flirty, secretive smile, he couldn't help himself. He wanted things from her that he couldn't begin to list out. And it scared him.

Kyle knew one thing: he was tired of this frustrating dance that he and Bella kept doing.

It's not like she was asking for marriage—she'd made it clear she didn't want anything more than a one-night stand. Well, why not give her what she wanted? They both needed to let off some steam, and she really needed to get her fighting spirit back. He used to always loosen up and wrestle better after getting laid. There'd even been studies that showed sex released testosterone. It was biology, plain and simple.

He chewed on his lower lip. He'd botched their chance in Vegas, but he was certain he could go through with it now. He had to. For her sake.

He stepped too hard on the gas as conviction set its claws in. The engine revved hard.

They could do this *and* still be professional afterward.

If Kyle could get through one night with Bella Fiore—if he could sleep with her without having another freak-out—they'd both be better off.

He just needed to convince her it would be good for her, too.

HADRIAN SWUNG THE bat hard, nearly wrenching his shoulder as the fastball whistled past. The pitching machine whirred and reloaded, waiting to lob another missile at his head.

He actually hated baseball. It'd bored him to tears as a kid, but watching the games on TV had been the only time his father was willing to spend with him. The old man had loved his games more than anything. Hadrian remembered how as a boy, in an effort to win the man's affections, he had tried out for Little League. He was so bad that his father had laughed at him when he'd come home. And he'd continued to mock Hadrian every time his son tried to sit and watch the game with him.

Hadrian was sure a shrink would have a million things to say about why he'd had a batting cage installed in his backyard after he'd made his first million. Nothing got Hadrian worked up more than missing that ball every single time—he'd gotten quite good at swinging hard and hitting nothing. It was humbling and reminded him that no matter how much he tried, there were some things he'd never be able to do.

"Sweetie?" Quinn's voice drifted to him from the back porch door. She walked out onto the deck, her burgundy blazer slung over her shoulder. Her shirt looked a little rumpled, and a mustard stain glowed bright on the collar.

Hadrian carefully replaced the bat and turned off the pitching machine. He didn't greet her as he stripped off his helmet and gloves, and barely made eye contact as she made her way across the grass. "You having a bad day?"

He pressed his lips together. "Mmm-hmm."

"You read the article."

"Oh, yeah." He slammed the cage shut, leaving his hot anger behind and donning his cool business facade. He'd promised himself he wouldn't get angry, but his feelings had been on simmer all day. "You made me sound like a jerk, Quinn."

"I didn't make you sound like anything." She said it so smoothly, oil would've rolled off her tongue. "I told you I'd been working on this piece. I made requests for interviews with you through Mrs. H. instead of ambushing you in bed, and that was only out of respect for what's between us." She dropped her blazer over the back of a patio chair.

What's between us. He snorted and grabbed a beer from the wet bar. He snapped off the cap and took a swig. The cold liquid did little to soothe him.

"'UFF president Hadrian Blackwell has previously sworn never to have women fight in the UFF,'" he quoted, the words seared into his memory. "'His is a world of old boys and closed doors, where jokes about harridan wives and gold digger girlfriends are exchanged freely, where women are hired and fired based on their dimensions. Critics have said inviting the girls to play must be a desperation move on his part to hide these chauvinistic practices.'" He glared at her. "That's all bullshit, Quinn, and poorly written, to boot. If you're going to tell me I'm sexist, why don't you tell me to my face?"

She gazed at him coolly. "I gave you the chance to respond. You didn't."

"You went behind my back." He slammed the beer bottle on the countertop. "You told me this was about the future of MMA."

"It is." She squared her shoulders. "When you announced the Fiore-Kamino fight, it changed the story. Why a women's fight? Why now? You have critics, Hadrian."

"I didn't expect *you* to be one of them." That sounded petulant and accusatory even to his ears, but he stood his ground.

"Well, I *am* one of them. Do you have any idea what kind of world your female employees live in? What I put up with? How about your female fans—do you have the slightest idea what they deal with?"

"Women don't even make up a third of my fan base, Quinn. If we're talking business—"

"See? There you go right there. You've marginalized half the population by reducing this to business. You used to say every fan mattered. Did you even read my article?"

"Several times. Mostly because I couldn't believe the garbage I was reading. All you did was bitch and whine about the lack of women's fights. I'm giving you a goddamned women's fight! What more do you want?"

She shook her head slowly. "You didn't read it at all."

"So I'm the bad guy in all this? I'm doing my job, Quinn. I promote MMA fights. I make money and bring tourism dollars to cities that host them. I make jobs and I make stars."

"And *I'm* doing my job as a reporter and as a woman who is sick and tired of taking misogynistic crap. I gave you every opportunity to sit down with me professionally for an interview, and you put me off."

"I was busy announcing a history-making fight. I thought you understood. You think all those long nights and missed dinners were me at a strip club or something?" He forked his fingers through his hair. "What's this really about? Are you jealous that I've been spending time with Bella Fiore? I couldn't help but notice all the potshots you took at her in your rag."

Quinn's cheeks burned red, and her nostrils flared. "How dare you."

It was three little words, said almost on a whisper, yet Hadrian felt them sink in slowly like knives dropped point first into pound cake.

"I'm a professional, Hadrian. I didn't start this relationship with you because I wanted a *scoop*. I liked you, and I was halfway to falling in love with you. I actually thought you cared—thought you liked me as more than some plaything. And now you…you cheapen me by suggesting I'm playing catty games because I'm jealous of another woman?"

If it had been any other woman in front of him, he would've believed that the tears in Quinn's eyes were from sadness. But he knew Quinn better than that—at least that's what he told himself. He swigged his beer and muttered, "Sounds pretty plausible to me."

She stared at him a moment longer, her calm fracturing. "If that's what you think, then I guess I've been an idiot." She folded her arms across her chest and looked toward the horizon. "The fact I had to write this story should've told you something, Hadrian. You can't throw us a bone and call it a feast. Screw this *baby steps in equality* crap. I've spent twelve years reporting sports, did you know that? Twelve years of letting guys pat my ass and call me honey, all so I could get a good story. And you know what I get for it? An average of 17 percent less pay than the guy five years my junior and a hundred comments a day from jocks who all think they know better than me. Guys who make fun of my clothes and hair and call me a dog and say my tits aren't big enough. Guys who've threatened to rape and kill me if I don't agree with their thoughts on a fighter's technique."

His gut squirmed uneasily, but he wasn't about to apologize for something he didn't do. "It's not my job to police every dickhead's ignorant-ass comments on the internet, Quinn. You can't hold that against me."

"This isn't about you!" she exploded. "And it's not about *one* women's fight, either—it's about *all* of them. And from what I've learned and the way you're acting, we're still losing." She plucked her blazer from the chair. "I'm going now."

A chill descended over him. "Not without leaving your press pass you aren't."

"Excuse me?"

He turned toward her, his heart a cold stone in his chest. "You heard me. Hand over your press pass. You're not welcome in the bullpen anymore. Your access privileges are being revoked."

She paled, her jaw dropping, feeding the vindictive little demon inside Hadrian. But then she snapped her mouth closed and straightened further, if such a thing were possible. "If you do this, I'll write about it."

"I don't like threats."

"And I don't like control freaks." She reached into her blazer pocket and drew out a lanyard with half a dozen pass cards attached. She tossed it onto the table. "Don't worry, I won't write about all the sex we've had. There isn't much to tell." She whirled away. "But if you want to tell the world about us… go ahead. I've heard it all. It'll hurt more coming from you, but I know how to take a little criticism, unlike some people."

Her heels rapped sharply across the flagstones and back through the house. Hadrian didn't move from his spot until he heard her car back noisily out of the driveway. He picked up the beer bottle, drained it in one go and whipped it at the batting cage. It exploded into a million little shards against the chain link fence.

CHAPTER NINETEEN

As BELLA CAME out of the locker room, bag in hand, she noticed Kyle's clothes first—a pair of khakis that outlined his narrow hips and strong thighs, paired with a short-sleeved formfitting gray golf shirt. Instead of his usual running shoes, he wore weekend loafers.

"You have a tee-off time at the links or something?" she asked with a smile.

He chuckled as he approached. She could smell his soap on him. "I was wondering if you have any plans tonight. I'd like to take you out for dinner."

She blinked. "Are you serious?"

"Absolutely."

"What's the occasion?"

"I just thought it'd be nice to celebrate your training progress." He smiled enigmatically. Bella felt all her nerve endings fizzle. Expectation and anticipation licked at her brain. This had to be the signal she was waiting for. The invitation to proceed. She accepted.

She wasn't sure what to expect from a night out with Kyle. She wasn't dressed for anything fancy, but she doubted he was taking her to a greasy spoon, either. He led her to his car and they drove west on St. Charles Avenue. Twenty minutes later, they ended up in a residential neighborhood full of quaint little bungalow houses. "Where are we going, exactly?"

"To a place that serves the best steaks in town." He parked under the carport next to a small gingerbread-colored cottage surrounded by a white picket fence. "Welcome to Casa del Peters."

"Wow. You live here?" She got out of the car, marveling at the picturesque front garden brimming with colorful flowers. "It's so cute. I never pegged you for a gardener."

"My neighbor takes care of them, actually. She has a long-standing arrangement with the landlord. I'm all black thumbs. But what I lack in the garden I make up for on the grill."

This was it. The Move. He'd invited her back to his home. He'd ply her with food and drink and then…dessert?

Her stomach knotted. Had she shaved her legs recently? Did she smell okay? Which pair of panties had she put on?

He unlocked the door, and Bella was enveloped by the scent of him: wood polish, clean sweat, rubber and something like pine. Almost like a new car. The house sported two bedrooms—one of which had been converted into a home office and man cave—a living room and a small kitchen.

Morbidly, she wondered whether this was the

same cozy home Karla had invited herself into. Whether the triple dead bolt locks on the doors had been installed before or after that night. She didn't ask.

After the brief tour, Kyle led her to the kitchen, where he'd laid out a wrought-iron table and cushioned chairs.

"I was going to have dinner outside, but it's a little too cool, so I thought we'd go halfsies—eat inside with the screen door open so you can have a proper American barbecue atmosphere." He gestured at the patio furniture. "Normally, I eat in front of the TV, so I don't have a real kitchen table."

She laughed. "Sounds perfect."

Kyle opened the fridge and took out two marinating steaks. "I consulted a dietician before I set out to make this," he said. "It's perfectly portioned for your diet, so eat hearty." He donned an apron that had Kiss the Cook printed on the front. She imagined an ex-girlfriend had bought that apron for him. Thinking about Kyle with other women reminded her she was not looking for anything beyond one night of sex…even if her heart told her otherwise. His apron might be an invitation, right along with the suggestive cock of his eyebrows and the tilt of his lips, but she wasn't about to jump his bones unless he specifically asked her to. She didn't want to scare him off again.

Kyle didn't make resisting temptation easy. He turned the radio on to some Top 40 hits station. He danced and sang along to a teen sensation's latest as he grilled the steaks on the gas barbecue outside. She laughed as he switched between a girly falsetto and the pubescent male part. She kept herself busy by helping with the salad.

They talked through the sliding screen door about simple things—music, movies, TV. It was on the tip of her tongue to ask if this was a date, but she held back. She didn't need labels on all the moving parts of their increasingly complicated relationship. She had to let go and accept tonight for whatever it was.

Deep down, though, she wasn't entirely sure she could do that. A one-night stand would require only a surface appreciation for who and what Kyle Peters was. If they'd hooked up when she'd first arrived, she would've had no qualms. Hopping into the sack with the Olympic medalist would've been a fantasy come true. But he'd come to mean much more to her. He was a person with layers, flaws, secrets... and she cared about him.

When they were ready to eat, Kyle pulled out her chair for her and whipped off the apron with almost Chippendale-esque flair.

"You're really trying to charm my pants off, aren't you?"

"Is it working?"

She decided not to answer. "This steak is perfect," she said instead, cutting into the butter-soft medium-rare meat.

"Old family recipe. My dad never cooked except

when we barbecued. He was really a control freak when it came to the grill. I learned from him." He chuckled drily. "He'd probably have a fit if he knew I was using propane instead of good old-fashioned charcoal the way a real man would."

"I think anyone who's shameless enough to sing and dance while cooking is man enough for me."

"You like that? 'Cause I'm a karaoke fiend. I can rock me some Backstreet Boys like no one's business." He launched into a throaty version of "I Want It That Way," and Bella had to throw a piece of lettuce at him to make him stop.

When they finished eating, Kyle collected the dishes and insisted she enjoy the evening air while he washed up. She didn't want to be idle, but she was feeling much more relaxed. Good food, fine weather and a handsome man did wonders for a girl's mood.

Of course, there was one thing that would make the night perfect. She peeked over to where Kyle was loading the dishwasher, bent at the waist, his trousers pulled tight against that firm butt. She could've sworn he was wiggling his hips on purpose. Her mouth watered, as if she hadn't already had her share of meat for the day. She fanned herself, feeling a little too hot under her T-shirt. If it were anyone but Kyle, she'd have pulled her top off and made him take her on the kitchen counter.

But she had to play it cool. He'd said stay, so she was staying.

He came back with tea for both of them and sat

back. "I love this time of day. Everything's cooling down, settling in. I feel like the day is just getting comfortable."

"And how do *you* get comfortable?" She kept her tone light.

He slid her a heavy-lidded look, and his slow smile melted her insides. Oh, he was good. "Drink your tea. Then I'll show you."

She sipped her tea, but it did little to soothe the excitement building inside her. She was remembering the way he'd made her come in the elevator and couldn't help but squirm. To calm herself, she cataloged the contents of her gym bag, which Kyle had carried in for her. Lucky thing she kept a toothbrush in there.

You're not staying over, she reminded herself. *If this is going to be a one-off, you should call a cab and go home afterward.*

She swept all those thoughts aside. She was here for dinner. As far as anything else, she was still fully clothed and nowhere near Kyle's bed. *You're not there yet, Bella. Calm down.*

A light breeze brought the sweet scent of flowers and greenery through the doorway. She closed her eyes and breathed deep to slow her heart and let the moment soak in. Anticipation was half the fun. Instead of picturing Kyle in all his panty-wetting glory, she'd meditate on the high of breathtaking hope.

"Hey." The light brush of his fingers on her bare

arm sent electricity zigzagging through her, and her eyes popped open. "You okay? Are you tired?"

"No!" She almost shouted it, because she could predict Kyle's next words—a suggestion that he take her home so she could rest, leaving her to another night alone. "I'm fine. I'm better than fine. I'm good and ready."

Kyle raised an eyebrow. "Ready for what?"

She felt as though the air had been crushed out of her lungs. When he turned on the charm, it was like being tackled by a heavyweight—unsubtle and overwhelming. This was the legendary playboy everyone talked about.

She played it coy, lowering her lashes and tilting her chin to one side, even though she wanted to grab him by the collar and haul him onto the nearest flat surface, preferably with her on top. "It all depends."

"On what?" He leaned toward her.

"On whether you intend to make good on your promise. You said you'd show me how you get comfortable."

He set his mug down. "Come here."

She got up and was surprised at how shaky her knees were. The trembling only increased when he took her hand and stood in one smooth motion—barely an inch separated them.

His fingers skated along her waist and up her arms to her shoulders, then back down. She closed her eyes, holding still. He leaned closer, and she could smell smoke on him. "I thought—" his breath fanned over her "—that we could go into my bedroom—" his lips skimmed over the bare spot between her neck and shoulder, sending pulses of pure pleasure straight through her core "—and play my favorite board game."

The haze evaporated, and she leaned back to look him in the face. He was still seducing her with his eyes, while his mouth formed a wry line that curved at the corners and gave him adorable dimples. "You're serious."

"C'mon. I'll show you." He took her hand and led her to the bedroom.

"I NEED WOOD," Bella declared testily an hour later. "I'll give you a sheep for a wood."

"I don't have wood for your sheep," Kyle quipped, and they both laughed. "I don't care if I sound like I'm five. That never gets old."

"How am I supposed to build anything without wood?" She recrossed her legs on the bed, glaring at her cards. "They make this game impossible."

"Not impossible. You just have to be mercenary about it." Of course, he had an unfair advantage, having played the game hundreds of times. But then, strategy games were good for Bella's psyche. It was training.

Okay, so maybe he'd pulled out the board game because he was still nervous and needed more time to gather his courage. All the old lines had come back easily, but behind the cool exterior, he was anxious. He wished he'd had some wine, but it didn't seem fair to drink when Bella couldn't.

She seemed fine with playing along, though. Her competitive nature wouldn't allow her to do anything but accept his challenge. Besides, he preferred this side of her. That tenacity and readiness to tackle anyone and anything head-on was better than the automaton he'd faced on the mats all week.

Her lower lip jutted out as she studied her cards and the board. He wanted to take that soft lip between his teeth and nibble it.

But he was taking it slow. He was going to take the whole night slow. The last thing he wanted was to blow it in thirty seconds. More than that, though, he wanted Bella leaving his bed fully sated. What he got out of this would be secondary. That's what he told himself, anyway.

He glanced at his handful of wood cards. Lucky for him, he'd managed to monopolize that one resource on the board. Bella's holdings weren't insubstantial, but she hadn't figured out how to bargain with him. She hadn't figured out what he really wanted.

"You're going to make me beg, aren't you?"

"You can't build roads, much less settlements, without wood." He leaned back against the pillows. "So what are you willing to give up for it?"

Challenge lit her bright green eyes. She set her cards down and eased up the hem of her T-shirt to expose the flat, smooth surface of her taut belly.

Kyle's nostrils flared as he drank in the warm, spicy scent of her. "How much wood can I get for this?" She quickly flashed her gray sports bra at him

Kyle licked his lips and tossed her one card. She snatched it up greedily and placed her first road on the board. "Ha! If I'd known you were so easily bought, I would have done that a long time ago."

"Guess I'll have to make you work harder if you want to keep building."

She cocked her chin to one side and grinned. Slowly, she slid from the bed. Kyle's hand of wood cards scattered around him as he watched her draw her shirt up over her head. He'd always admired her body from an athlete's perspective, but right now, he wasn't thinking about sports. Or much of anything.

"Something tells me you want more." Her voice was husky and low. Kyle could barely restrain a groan as she unsnapped the top button of her jeans and tugged them past the curves of her hips.

He wasn't sure what to expect underwear-wise— maybe boy shorts or cotton bikini bottoms. He hadn't anticipated the lacy electric-blue thong. Lust powered through him as unstoppable as a runaway locomotive. His fingers clenched at his thighs, pulling the fabric tight against the already tented crotch.

Bella crawled back onto the king-size bed and sprawled onto her side. "So," she purred, spreading her unbound hair out behind her. "Can I have your wood now?"

Kyle swept the board aside, the cards and pieces

scattering like confetti across his bedroom. He gathered her into his arms, kissing her, drinking from her lips. She was so soft. He broke from her to regain himself. His heart hammered as he knelt above her. She watched him with a predator's smile but didn't reach for him.

I can do this, he told himself. And suddenly, it didn't seem like such a trial. He wanted this. Wanted to lie down with Bella and press his length against her. Wanted to feel her skin and flesh ripple beneath him as he pushed into her—

His vision clouded and he breathed deep. Damn, he was hair-trigger sensitive.

"Kyle?" Bella's worry flickered in those deep green eyes. She lifted a hand but hesitated. He shifted and took her by the wrist, guiding her fingers beneath the hem of his shirt. His abs—and everything else—twitched at her touch.

"Are you sure?" Questions swirled across her soft features. His chest constricted—she'd been so forgiving. So patient. She had no reason to want this with him. He'd tried to drive her away from day one.

But here they were. And neither of them was running away.

He slowly pulled his T-shirt over his head and guided her hands across his chest, settling one palm against his heart. She seemed to know exactly what he needed. In silence, she explored the light sprinkling of hair on his chest and tentatively traced the peaks and valleys of his muscles, her touch becoming bolder with each stroke.

This was right, he thought through a thickening haze of desire. This was exactly what he wanted. It was like slipping back into a warm, wonderful dream where he could fly and make magic happen.

She brushed her lips over his stomach and kissed her way up to his nipples. Her tongue painted lazy circles over them. Kyle breathed through it, experiencing every sensation as if it were new. In a lot of ways, it was.

She needs this as much as you do, he reminded himself sharply. *He* was supposed to be pleasuring *her.* Releasing her tension so she'd be ready to fight. Unfortunately, that tight feeling building at the base of his spine was distracting him from his purpose.

He drew Bella to her knees and kissed her again, pouring every bit of seduction he could into it. He kept his lips soft even though he wanted to dive right in and taste her inside and out, finding all of her secret places. He stroked her back and hair and held her as delicately as a flower, kissing her until she whimpered.

"Please, Kyle." She drew back for a breath, hands seeking. "I need you."

"I'm right here for you." He lowered his mouth. "Right here."

WHEN IT CAME to sex, Bella had always taken what she wanted. Men had appreciated her aggressiveness—even Antonio had let her be the boss in bed. But she couldn't do that with Kyle.

She wasn't being completely passive, though. Maybe it was instinct that had her fingers questing gently, probing and testing rather than grabbing and clutching. The heat was just as intense, but the urgency wasn't there—no frantic tearing of clothing, no crashing of open mouths. He was being careful. They both were. It was frustrating...and achingly seductive.

Wordlessly, he drew her hands down and unzipped his pants. She helped. In seconds, he was naked, fully sprung, reaching for her. He unhooked her bra, and when her breasts were free, she could see in his face fascination and wonderment. She felt...exposed.

They lay down side by side, facing each other. Skin to skin, electricity seemed to skate across her back and breasts. He reached between them and stroked her deftly, precisely, and she gave a soft, surprised moan as pleasure arced through her spine. Her mind drifted as he pressed her onto her back and gave her a slow, drugging kiss that cruised lower, to her chin, her throat, her breasts and stomach and...

Oh.

It was a long time before he came back up, and Bella was so mindless all she could do was lie there and stare. His lustrous gaze drifted over her as he rolled on a condom. He seemed to be taking in every angle the way an artist studied a blank canvas—

planning every stroke, intent on imprinting pleasure onto every inch of her body.

His blunt fingertips glided across her inner thighs. Goose bumps erupted all along her arms. How was he doing this to her? She'd never felt so vulnerable or needy. "Please hurry," she whispered. The plea wasn't faked. None of her feelings were. She knew this because if he walked away now, she was sure she'd burst into tears.

"You," he murmured against her neck, "are a selfish, greedy girl."

"Only because I always get what I—" Her challenge was cut off as he slid home, and her breath left her. Kyle held still, poised above her, trembling. They stayed like that, clinging to each other on the brink of a crumbling cliff.

"Meu Deus." She clutched his shoulders, desperate for more...or less. Hovering on the edge, she couldn't decide whether to relax and subside or throw herself from the precipice. Amazing. For once, she didn't know what she wanted.

"Bella." Kyle's voice came out hoarsely. "I... You're so..." His eyes were rolling up as if he were going to pass out. She caressed his rough cheek, bringing him back.

"I'm yours tonight, Kyle. All yours."

The harsh lines on his face softened. He sank deeper into her, and Bella lay back and let go, absorbing him with every thrust. Feeling nothing but Kyle and his muscles and his hot breath and hands.

Letting him pour his passion into her, letting him take his fill.

His grip tightened. An almost bestial look snarled his face as his pace increased. Bella's insides coiled and she arched into him, trying to get closer, trying to trap him in this pure, wild moment.

Yes. This is what I want.

She flung her arms around him as everything inside her ratcheted tight. Then she shattered, sheer release throbbing through every muscle. Almost simultaneously, Kyle threw his head back and stiffened, mouth open in a silent groan.

He collapsed on top of her, sighing as he planted kisses along her clavicle, tenderly fondling her breast. She was empty of sensation, her pleasure wrung dry. All she could think about apart from the damp weight between her legs and the bonelessness of her limbs was that this was where she wanted to be forever and ever.

"Not bad," Kyle murmured after a while, "for a first go."

She stared at him shell-shocked as he rolled her over and made her straddle him. Her face split in a delighted grin.

"Now," he growled, digging his fingers into her hips, "show me what you can do."

CHAPTER TWENTY

BORN AGAIN. That was the only thing Kyle could compare this feeling to as he woke up the next morning. Every limb felt supple, and his back and chest felt light. It was like he was twenty-one again, rather than thirty-six—energetic, vital, invincible.

Bella slept like a log next to him, her mouth slightly open, and her body still deliciously naked. He watched her as the late-morning light cast a prism of rainbow colors on her thick black hair. He doubted a jet engine could rattle her. . . .

He paused in wonder. It'd been the first time in months since he'd had a full—he glanced at the clock—whoa, ten hours of sleep in his own bed, undisturbed. A sense of accomplishment and pride rushed through him. He'd made it through the night with Bella. He hadn't had any nightmares, hadn't shot up out of his bed at the slightest sound. He'd had sex without embarrassing himself. His body had listened to him. He'd stayed fully in control of himself.

Just like the good old days.

He lay back with a grin. Part of him wanted to jump up and whoop, but he couldn't bring himself to wake Bella. After last night's activities, they both deserved to sleep.

He watched the woman lying next to him, and a funny pang went through him. How had he ever thought she looked like a man when her curves were so damned sexy? Her breasts weren't huge, sure, but anything more than a handful was a waste anyhow.

Classy, Peters. Real classy. He shook the thought away. That was no way to think of this wonderful woman. This paragon. This...

Bella snorted and began snoring loudly. He held back a chuckle and stroked her shoulder, kissing the warm skin there. His lower parts stirred, tapping against the small of her back, and he knew she was awake the moment she stopped snoring and wiggled against him.

"You keep doing that and we'll be here all day," he said.

"That a bad thing?" She cracked one eye open and groaned. "What time is it?"

"Past ten. Don't get up yet." He wrapped his arm around her waist to keep her from turning over. "There are things I want to do to you still."

"Now who's the greedy one?" She kissed him, lips lingering until he was fully awake and ready to go a few more rounds, but then drew back. "I have to pee." She flung the blanket off, rising and stretching fully naked before walking to the bathroom. Kyle enjoyed the view all the way.

As she returned, she stumbled. "Ow! Dammit—

your robber." She held up the board game piece that had lodged in the sole of her foot, then grimaced. "We should clean this up."

"Later." He held his arms open. "C'mere. We can play afterward."

She climbed under the blankets next to him, hugging him around his torso like a koala bear. "Forget the board games. I want to play with something else."

Morning quickly became afternoon, and Kyle would've let it bleed into the evening, too, if Bella hadn't insisted on going home. She wanted a shower, a change of clothes and then a light workout, despite all the exercise they were getting at his place.

He'd never felt so relaxed in his life. He should've been bone tired, but he felt as if he could take on the world.

After she'd left, he stooped to gather up the pieces of the board game off the floor. Sunlight painted the room in pale gold, and he thought how different things in here suddenly felt. Brighter. More open. Bella had consecrated this space. After Karla—after he'd moved—he'd never brought any woman to his home before. He didn't want any of them knowing where he lived—but Bella was different.

He opened the window, letting a cool, damp breeze sweep through. He hadn't realized how claustrophobic the room had felt before. He was forced to admit now that all those sleepless nights hadn't been caused by scratchy sheets or a lumpy mattress.

As he turned from the window, he looked at his shadow on the wall, then tilted his head to one side. Strange, he'd never noticed how thin the paint job in here was. He could see the darker color beneath the streaks of off-white. The color beneath it was a dark maroon, like a bruise.

He shook off a chill as the sunlight suddenly disappeared behind a cloud. He'd make a point of giving the place another coat of paint at some point. Maybe Bella would help him...

A bittersweet pang arrowed through him. Her contract with Payette's would be up in April. And if she won the women's featherweight championship, she'd become a star. Media interviews, sponsorships, charity events, movie roles—Bella would have her hands full. Even if she didn't win the match, she'd probably go back to Brazil. In either case, he didn't have a claim to her. A foreign feeling corkscrewed through his gut.

Bree's coming, he reminded himself. She would be in the States soon, and they could continue where they'd left off without fear.

His future looked wide-open. Which was how he'd always liked it.

FIVE POUNDS. Twenty-five days.

Those were the only things Bella should have been concentrating on, but Kyle's intense gaze and inexorable commands only made her think of the weekend they'd spent together.

"Harder," Kyle demanded. "C'mon, harder!"

Bella ignored the tightening of her insides and threw herself into the punches. Sweat dripped into her eyes. Every precious drop was another fraction of an ounce. Every second brought her closer to her future.

Where did Kyle figure into that future? He didn't, she told herself, even if she had stayed overnight—and longer—against her own advice. So instead, she wondered about how many calories she could burn in bed with Kyle and hoped she got to test her hypothesis.

Her fists throbbed, her arms burned. Wayne said, "Stop," and she hunched, hands on her knees, breathing hard. She winced as the boxing coach glowered down at her.

"Take a rest." He looked angrier than usual, the ruched flesh between his eyebrows ruddy. Maybe he was on the verge of another migraine.

Kyle set the pads aside and sipped from his water bottle, eyes still on her. The corner of his mouth twitched as she toasted him with her own bottle. On Sunday after she'd gone home for her shower and change of clothes, Kyle had convinced her to skip the workout. They'd had a late lunch, gone for a stroll, and managed a quickie before dinner. Despite being on a strict diet and training for the fight of her life, she'd never felt so full and satisfied and pampered.

The suggestive smile in Kyle's eyes told her he

knew it, too. Heat trickled between her thighs, and she danced in place, trying to shake off his intense perusal.

"I said take a break," Wayne barked. "Meaning, slow your goddamned heart down before it explodes."

"Sorry." What was his deal? Wayne stalked toward Kyle and said something she couldn't hear. Kyle frowned.

"We'll stop for now," he told Bella. "Would you do me a favor and ask Liz about the flyers we're handing out at Mardi Gras? I'd like you to have a look at them, read them over, tell me what you think."

"Uh…sure."

She found the flyer on Liz's desk and sat down to read it. Out of the corner of her eye she spotted Wayne entering Kyle's office. The door swung only partially shut behind them. Their voices were low at first, but it was obvious Wayne was upset about something. She could see him gesturing sharply through the blinds. She couldn't make out anything they said, though, and then the phone at reception rang. Since Liz wasn't there, she picked up. "Payette's Gym."

"Hi, I'm looking for Kyle Peters." The voice on the other end of the line was like a Brillo Pad rolled in butter. "Could you tell him it's Bree? I'm an old friend."

"Sure. I'll transfer you. Hang on." She stared at the phone. She'd never forwarded a call before from the front desk, and the letters had long since been worn off the buttons. Ten seconds went by as she tried to find a manual, and she brought the receiver to her ear again. "Sorry, I'm not the normal receptionist and I don't know how to use this phone. Can you wait a minute? I'll call Kyle over."

"Take your time."

Bella put the receiver down and went to Kyle's office. At the door, she halted when she heard Wayne say, "She's not going to survive one round at this rate. You want to be the one responsible when she ends up being carried out on a stretcher?"

"She won't, Wayne. Have some faith." Kyle's voice was hard but even.

"God, Kyle—I thought you'd keep it in your pants, but it's pretty clear to me you two did something."

"What either of us does during our off time is none of your business."

"Bullshit. It's everyone's business. You know why? Because all that freaking crap you went through with Karla scared off nearly half our clients. Before Bella got here, the place was falling apart. Now we've got a chance to bring Payette's back, but she's got to win the belt if you want to make sure we all keep our jobs. Instead, you're screwing Bella—"

Bella knocked loudly and pushed the door open. Wayne towered over Kyle, who sat rigidly behind his desk. Wayne's face turned a bright shade of red. She cleared her throat. "There's a phone call for you, Kyle. A woman named Bree. She said she's an old friend."

Kyle blinked slowly and gave a tight smile. "Can you transfer the call?"

"Sorry, Liz isn't at the desk, and I can't figure out how to…" She made empty gestures.

Kyle got up swiftly. "Wayne, we'll talk later."

"Yeah. Right." The heavyweight lumbered out without meeting Bella's eye.

She followed the boxing coach back toward his corner, where he started wrapping his hands, his movements jerky. She wasn't sure how she should feel about Wayne's lack of confidence in her, or the way he was blaming Kyle. All she knew was they needed to talk. "You have something you want to say to me?" she asked.

"You weren't supposed to hear any of that." He kept the tape tight, frowning hard.

"C'mon, Coach. I'm a big girl. I know I haven't been at my best, but it's got nothing to do with Kyle."

His face bloomed with color again, and he gave a low curse. "I didn't mean for it to sound like it did. The gym's not in that much trouble, but Kyle…" He rubbed a finger beneath his nose. "Well, in any case, you'll kick ass. That's all that matters."

"I know you're just looking out for me. But I can take care of myself. I know what I'm doing."

"You kids think you know everything." He sighed. "Look, Bella. I like you. You remind me of my oldest daughter. Scrappy and tough as nails. I wasn't much of a dad to her, y'know. That's what happens when you travel all over for fights and training and stuff."

Warmth filtered through her. "If you're worried Kyle's distracting me from the fight, he's not."

"I'd hate to see you get hurt is all." He put up a hand. "I respect him, being my boss and all. But he's not the guy I'd want dating *my* kid, y'know?"

She gave a wry smile. "We're not dating." Saying so out loud, though, made something inside her twinge.

His gaze rested on her as heavily as one of his meaty hands. The longer it sat there, the more she felt the weight of her self-delusion. She and Kyle might not be "dating," but what she felt for him was more than friendly affection or lust.

"I see the way you guys look at each other. Don't deny it. I have four kids from three different moms and each relationship started with those googly eyes. I know what that look means. And I've seen that look on his face before."

"You're crazy. There's nothing—"

"Nothing? Really?" He gave a snort and glanced over at where Kyle stood by the reception desk. "Tiger can't change its spots, kid."

"You mean stripes."

"Kyle's a peculiar cat. You know, cuddles up to you one second and then…" He snapped his fingers. "Gone." He wiped a hand over his mouth. "I'm just trying to look out for you, kid."

A sour taste rose in her throat, and Bella's veins

churned with restless energy. She glanced at Kyle again, who smiled and leaned against the counter, looking supremely relaxed…not unlike the way he'd looked the morning after.

Her cheek ticked. Who was this Bree woman he was talking to? Was she really an old friend?

Unable to restrain her curiosity, she hurried to the back of the gym where an interoffice phone hung on the back pillar. She didn't know how to use Liz's big receptionist's phone, but she understood this one—it had the three lines labeled, and she could clearly see only the one at the front desk was occupied. Heart trembling, she picked up the receiver and brought it to her ear, one hand clamped over the mouthpiece, and hit a few buttons.

"I wasn't expecting you so soon. I thought you said you'd be here in February." She could hear Kyle's smile through the phone.

"I came early. I've missed you terribly, Kyle," the husky, buttery voice cooed.

"I've missed you, too."

Bella's heart squeezed. He'd used that same honeyed tone on her not twenty-four hours ago. She leaned heavily against the pillar, her fingers going icy cold as they clutched the receiver.

"You won't be too busy, I hope? I've been dreaming of that Sunday breakfast you promised me."

"Not too busy, no. I have a client I'm working with right now. Her fight's on the third Saturday of the month, but that leaves Mardi Gras and Valentine's

Day wide-open. We could make reservations at the Ritz-Carleton like we did before."

"And order room service all weekend." The woman's rich, sex-drenched laughter sent shards of glass through Bella's blood. She didn't want to hear any more. Her chest felt as though it was caving in. Her eyes watered. No, not because she felt like crying, dammit, but because she was tired. Because she hadn't blinked. The air was dry.

Dammit, she was not crying over a *mulherengo estúpido!*

She put the receiver back onto the cradle and ran for the locker room. She didn't want anyone to see how shocked she was. How could she be surprised? This was Kyle. This was…

She opened her locker and started emptying it as Liz exited the bathroom stall. Liz's eyes widened. "What is it? What's happened?"

"I have to go." She zipped up her gym bag quickly. Her emotions were bloating inside her, pushing against her skin, threatening to burst her open.

"Why?"

Heat seared her cheeks and brow, crawling down her neck and across her chest like a rash. She couldn't admit her foolishness. The receptionist had tried to warn her about Kyle. Everyone had. Not in so many words, but with furtive looks and gentle suggestions, playful jabs and scandalous stories. But Bella hadn't listened to anyone. Kyle was a playboy through and through. She couldn't expect a weekend of sex with him to change that.

And she shouldn't have been so naive to believe her feelings for him weren't deeper than she'd made them out to be.

"Where are you going? Bella…"

"Something's come up. I have to leave. I have to go…" Where did she have to go? All she knew right now was that she couldn't stay there another minute.

Yes, run away, her grandfather's voice mocked her. The parting shot before she'd left São Paulo. *That is why you will fail. Why you will always fail. You have the weak heart of a woman.*

Shame and rage collided inside her chest. She inhaled deeply. She was better than this. Better than that *filho de uma cadela.*

She pushed out of the locker room as Kyle hung up, a sly smile curving those sensuous lips. Lips that had worshipped her. Lips that had whispered soft, sexy words in her ear and trailed across her skin.

"Cachorro!" She flung at him, her cool facade cracking wide-open. She'd never let herself feel anger in the cage. She had a tight rein on her temper when it came to fighting. For a moment she was outside of herself, witnessing the wild, potent jealousy seething from her. But the pot had boiled over, and the gushing of emotions did not subside with the outburst. "Who was that? Who is this Bree, exactly?"

Kyle's smile froze. "She's an old friend."

"'Old friend'? You expect me to believe you'd

invite her for a weekend of…of *breakfast* and hotel stays and—"

"You were listening to my phone call?" His gaze sharpened and flickered over her shoulder. She hadn't realized Wayne and Liz were right behind her, maybe trying to talk her down. But she wasn't about to let them.

"Yeah, I listened. And good thing. What is this to you, huh? This thing between us—"

He pointed. "Office. Now."

Stupidly, she followed him, unable to deny his simple command. What had he turned her into? A hapless, biddable woman? The woman her family expected her to be? Her heart twisted like a feral cat trying to tear its way out of her rib cage.

They marched into the office. He slammed the door shut and whirled on her. "How dare you listen in on my private conversation."

"If I didn't, I wouldn't know what kind of man you really were. What the hell were you planning with that…that woman?" She didn't want specifics—her imagination was fertile enough. What she'd really meant to ask was, *What are you planning to do with me?*

"It's none of your business," he said irately. "Bree is an old friend. We've had a previous relationship, but I don't see why that should bother you."

Her heart tore in half. *Cristo.* She didn't think heartbreak could be such an intense physical hurt. She sank into a chair and breathed through the shock.

Kyle perched against the edge of the desk. He didn't go to her or ask if she was all right. He only sighed. "I'm sorry, but what we did— What we had didn't mean more than what it was." He forked his fingers through his hair. "We had fun, okay?"

"No." She shook her head. "It was not just *fun*. Honestly, Kyle, that's what I wanted it to be at first— tried to convince myself that's all it was. Fun." The word was like mud in her mouth. "But we... we shared something. Not the kind of thing you'd share with casual partners. Don't you see?" Her voice pitched down a notch. "All the women and sleeplessness... I didn't cure you, Kyle. And I'm not a notch on your belt. I wouldn't have slept with you if I thought that's all I would be." And she realized it was the truth. She would never have pursued Kyle while she had a fight to train for. She wouldn't have involved herself if she didn't care. She was so stupid to have believed otherwise. "You can't go chasing women trying to make yourself feel better. You need to talk to someone. You need help."

"Help from who? You?" Deep lines carved his face. "You don't get to hang on to me like some broken toy you can fix. I'm fine, okay? And I appreciate what you helped me through, but it's done now."

Tears burned in the backs of her eyes. "You think I slept with you just to help you?" Maybe that was partially true—and wasn't that what she was telling herself all along?—but she was too hurt to give him that.

"We both know it was a one-off. Anyhow, I don't need *you* to help me." He ran his hands over his face. "Maybe you thought there was something more between us, but there wasn't. I'm sorry, Bella, but I only slept with you because you needed to relax."

A bitter, dusty taste flooded her mouth. *"Excuse me?"*

"You weren't hitting as hard as you normally do. You needed to let loose." The corner of his mouth jerked up. "I was doing you a favor."

Bella's vision dimmed. Her blood pushed up and outward.

She couldn't get another word out. She grabbed the nearest heavy object.

"How dare you."

Her hand rested on the tape dispenser, knuckles white. Kyle's heart hammered in his chest, and he found himself sweating head to toe and backing up into the filing cabinets behind him. She hadn't thrown a punch or even raised her voice, but he was shaking violently.

Because of what she could do. What she would do. What she was capable of.

"I don't need you to do me any favors, you…" She lapsed into a long string of Portuguese, the consonants cutting, spittle flying from her mouth as she gathered steam. Her hand flexed over the tape dispenser, as if she might grind it into the tabletop.

The moment she lifted it, Kyle shot out from behind the shelter of his desk. He was not hiding from her, dammit. In two long strides, he grabbed her by the shoulders. The tape dispenser clattered to the ground. He forced her away from any other heavy objects she might want to lob at him.

"Listen to me." When she flinched, he clung tighter. "Listen to me!" he shouted again.

Bella thrashed in his hold. The more she struggled, the more he tried to contain her, hold her down. Fat tears leaked from her eyes, but she wasn't crying. Not by a long shot.

Bile rose in Kyle's throat. Not in guilt, he told himself. No, the moment Bella had confronted him, tried to make a claim to him...that was the moment he knew he'd made a mistake.

"Let go of me."

Her plea, broken and rusty voiced, undid him. He released her and took two steps back, hands raised, ready to defend himself.

"I'm sorry, Bella." The words spilled from him in harsh gasps. "I never meant to hurt you. This was for your own good. And mine, too. I won't lie and say I didn't do it for my own selfish reasons. When you've calmed down you'll realize it, too." Sweat beaded on his upper lip. Bella balled her fists, and he thought for a blinding moment that she was going to punch herself the way Karla had—smug self-righteousness flashing across her face an instant before the hit connected. A wave of nausea struck him and he leaned heavily to one side.

She watched him, stricken. "You're lying. To me and to yourself." She pushed strands of hair out of her face, smearing the wetness on her cheeks into her hairline.

"I didn't want anything more than what we had. I'm not into you that way." Bella grew very still. Kyle backed away another step. "We had fun."

Every time he said the word *fun,* another needle stabbed his conscience. He was hurting her. He could see it plainly. But he couldn't stop himself. "I made a mistake," he went on ruthlessly. "*We* made a mistake. Obviously."

"Obviously." Her mottled complexion paled. She spun around and wrenched the door open. The windowpanes and the blinds rattled as the door slammed against the thin wall, and she barreled out.

A half-dozen pairs of eyes stared through the open portal. Stiffly, Kyle went to the door and gently shut it again. Carefully, he pulled all the blinds closed.

CHAPTER TWENTY-ONE

HADRIAN'S PERSONAL GYM wasn't much to look at. A few mats, some free weights, a couple of yoga balls and some other cheap equipment made up the majority of his gear. The only concession to the Spartan facility was the heavy bag chained to the reinforced ceiling beam. He had access to all the official UFF facilities, of course, but when it came to his own workout, he preferred to be alone and to use what was at hand. It didn't feel right to him, somehow, to have a fully-equipped home gym when he so rarely used it.

Well, it was paying off now. In the past couple of weeks since he'd kicked Quinn out, he'd worked a deep groove into the heavy bag, and the plaster on the ceiling was starting to crack. He knew he should probably stop and get it fixed before the whole house came crashing down on his head. At the same time, he wasn't sure he'd care if it did.

He sneezed as the plaster dust tickled his nose, then spit to get rid of the chalky texture on his lips.

"If you had someone spotting you and holding that bag, you wouldn't have to worry so much about the ceiling." Mrs. Hutzenbiler's voice echoed through the room as she approached on silent sneakers. Hadrian paused as she rolled up her sleeves and grasped the bottom of the sand-filled sack, then braced her weight against it. "Go ahead."

Hadrian didn't argue with her. She might be closing in on sixty-three, but he had no doubt his P.A. could kick his butt if she wanted to. She could scare osteoporosis away with one mean look.

His fists sank into the leather with a satisfying thud. Mrs. H. didn't even flinch. "I got a call from Joel Khalib," she said in an even tone. "He wanted to update us on a situation regarding Bella Fiore."

His lungs deflated and he stopped. "Dear God. Please don't tell me—"

"Bella's fine. She's still in for the fight, and so is Ayumi."

Thank God. "So, what's the deal?"

"Don't let your heart rate go down," she ordered. Obediently, he resumed his striking rhythm. "Bella left Payette's."

"What?" His punch slipped and his knuckles cracked loudly. He hissed and shook out his hand.

"She had some kind of falling-out with Kyle Peters and left the gym. A lover's spat, apparently. There were quite a few witnesses, but I'm only getting this story fourth or fifth hand."

"Freaking Kyle Peters. I swear that guy trips and ends up dick deep in—" He caught Mrs. H.'s unimpressed look and cut himself off. "This better not end up costing me another settlement."

"Maybe Mr. Peters isn't the man you want representing your gym," she said coolly.

Hadrian chewed the inside of his cheek. Maybe Mrs. H. was right.

He gave the bag another couple of frustrated hits, then stopped. He'd hurt his hand. "So Bella's not at Payette's. Where is she?" He mopped his face with a towel and let out a deep breath.

"Joel's not saying. He said she doesn't want anyone disturbing her while she trains."

"We have more media events lined up. She'd better come to those."

"Give her some time, Hadrian. I'm sure she'll be professional about it, you'll see."

"She never should've gotten involved with Peters in the first place." He took a swig of tepid water from his bottle to wash away the bitter taste in his mouth. "I even warned him off, but I knew the moment I saw them together at the gala, something was going to happen. I'd like to skin him alive."

"I don't think we should be assigning blame when we don't know the whole story."

He lifted an eyebrow. "That's uncharacteristic of you, Mrs. H. I was under the impression you didn't like Peters."

"I don't feel one way or another about him. I just don't like it when people jump to conclusions."

"So you don't believe what Karla Brutsch said about what he did to her?"

"I believe *something* happened. But the facts never came out, and instead of investigating further and getting the authorities involved like you should have, you gave Kyle a pass and swept the girl under a rug."

"With fifty thousand dollars and a new freaking life." Despite that bitter memory, her words made him uncomfortable. "And when did this issue become about me? I didn't give Peters a pass. That guy has a reputation, granted, but you're asking me to believe he punched a girl—an employee—in the face. There were witnesses who saw her do it to herself. And I know the guy. Kyle wouldn't do that."

"So you believe Kyle over Karla."

"That's not what I'm saying." Hadrian blew out a breath. He hated the doubts clouding his judgment. "Look, this isn't about that woman or what's happened. This is about Bella and Kyle. She shouldn't have hooked up with him. The guy's a notorious player. He was never going to commit to anything long-term, and she knew she had a career to look after, so why the hell even bother?"

Mrs. Hutzenbiler studied him silently for a moment. "This isn't about Kyle and Bella at all, is it?"

He tried to skirt around her, but she raised a hand. "Cool down. You're not allowed to leave until your heart rate is back to normal. And judging by the way you're fuming, that'll be a while."

He grumbled and sat on the ground, stretching

his arms, calves and thighs. The muscles around his neck seized. He felt ready to snap.

Mrs. H. saw his pain, knelt and kneaded his shoulders. "You haven't talked to Quinn in a while."

"I kicked that traitor out of here."

"Why's that?" She dug her knuckles in deep, making him inhale sharply.

"She accused me of being a chauvinistic pig. I've donated thousands of dollars to women's shelters and community programs. There are all kinds of equal opportunity hiring programs at the UFF. I'm hosting a goddamned women's fight, which she's been whining about since I met her. She's never shut up about it, you know. Every freaking month, it was 'So when are you going to open the UFF to women?' I finally do and she's on me like I've been cheating on her."

"You never did give her that interview."

"Because I was busy!"

His P.A. stopped her massage and fixed him with a look. "I asked you several times when you wanted to talk to her. I gave you times in your schedule for when it was doable."

"Are you actually taking Quinn's side?"

"That's not the issue, though she's right about a few things. I helped her with the research, after all."

Hadrian felt a stab of betrayal. Would any woman ever take his side? This was almost as bad as when his mom—

No. He wasn't going there. Mom had left him to his own devices, told him she didn't have time to deal with anything except keeping up with the bills because his father sure as hell wasn't helping....

No, this had nothing to do with his mother, or with anyone else. "I don't want you giving her any more information," he declared. "Quinn's not welcome anywhere on my property. If I had any say in it—"

"You'd what? Get a woman fired for doing her job? All because you can't take a little criticism?" She gave a tired sigh and shook her head sharply so her iron-gray curls bounced. "I thought you'd out-grown your pettiness, Hadrian, but then, you always were emotionally immature. Some days I just want to slap some sense into your stupid face."

He sat back, stunned and a little afraid she might do just that.

"You're not angry because of the article or about the issues she brought up. This isn't about how you treat women. This is about how you treat Quinn."

He snorted. "You don't know what you're talk-ing about."

"When was the last time you had a long-term relationship with a woman?"

"I don't have time for—"

"I'll tell you. You spent five months three years ago with a cage girl—Valerie Francis. That ended when she turned twenty-four and she got that mod-eling gig."

"Never happier to see the back of her. And I'd seen a lot of it."

Mrs. H.'s steep frown shut him up. "Before Valerie, there was that actress. Odious little thing with that awful sex tape. And before her, it was that coed student who wanted to be a cage girl."

He smirked. "The one with the mole. I remember."

His P.A. pointed at him accusingly. "Don't you see? None of these girls were your equal. None of them challenged you the way Quinn does. She made you happy. She made you want to be with her, and that scared you, didn't it?"

"Leave me alone." He made to get up, but she clamped her steellike grip around his ankle and punched him in the back of the knee hard enough that he fell back on his ass.

"Are you looking to get fired?" he exclaimed, rubbing his tailbone.

"You can try. But I think you'll find I'm a lot harder to get rid of than any reporter." Her expression softened. "I know there wasn't a lot of room for love while you were growing up—your mother did what she had to, God rest her soul, even if you don't feel the same way. But that's no excuse for the way you've treated Quinn. You have feelings for that woman. The moment you realized she had the power to hurt you, you put as much distance between you as you could."

"I asked her to move in with me half a dozen times," he countered bitterly. "I offered her everything, and she still turned me down."

"You offered to keep her like a pet." Hadrian opened his mouth to retort but found himself unable to refute the claim. She went on, "You wanted to buy her love and loyalty. You wanted to keep her here where she couldn't fight you."

"I don't see what's wrong with that."

"Because she's smarter than that, you idiot." Mrs. H. sat back, exasperated. "When she published that feature and you saw how she could hurt you, you decided it would be safer to dump her. Am I right?"

He glowered and muttered a reply that had her glaring right back.

"I'll expect an apology for that remark after you've sulked for a while and figured out what it is you really want from Quinn." She climbed to her feet. "Destroying her career isn't going to get you anything." She paused before exiting. "You might want to start by thinking about what she *has* done for you and maybe appreciate what she's had to put up with."

KYLE STARED AT his calendar, the days of the week blurring into a continuous stretch terminating with the big, bold words BELLA'S UFF FIGHT!!!!

He tried to see the other significant scheduled dates, but his gaze kept drifting back to Saturday's event. He remembered the pride mixed with excitement and trepidation that he'd felt as he'd marked it on the calendar. Remembered how clearly the immediate future had looked in terms of what he and Bella had needed to accomplish.

Right now, nothing seemed clear. Even with tonight's plans.

Carefully, he added his date with Bree to the calendar. The writing was small and faint. He scratched harder, trying to make the ink flow, but the pen petered out entirely. He tossed it aside in defeat.

"Boss." Liz stood in the doorway. "There's someone here to see you."

"Bella?" His cheeks heated. He hadn't meant to blurt it out loud or sound quite so desperate. The receptionist kept her expression fixed. He'd quizzed her about Bella's whereabouts since she'd stormed out of Payette's, but Liz knew nothing. He'd gone by Bella's apartment a few times, but she hadn't been home, and the store owner downstairs had said he hadn't seen her lately.

Was it possible she'd gone home to Brazil?

"I think she's one of the girls from the Touchstone youth center. She's waiting at the front desk."

He hurried out. Shawnese leaned against the counter, chatting amiably with Tito. She smiled wide at his approach. "Hey, Kyle. I was actually looking for Bella."

The look Tito gave him wasn't quite a stink eye, but it definitely bordered on hostile. A lot of guys had been avoiding him since Bella's departure.

"She…she's off training with a specialist," he answered. "She's on lockdown for the fight. No one can reach her."

"Oh." Shawnese's smiled faded, and she studied him closely, eyes wide and watchful. It was almost as if she were reading his thoughts, his fears, the lines on his face forming a map of guilt. She rubbed her neck. "Well, I thought I'd swing by, let you guys know where I'm working now."

"You got a job? That's great. Congrats."

"Yeah. I'm doing some admin work at a real estate office downtown. Pay's pretty good. I'll get to rent my own place soon. Once I've got first month's rent, I'm gonna come back here and take more lessons with Bella."

Kyle's jaw clenched so tight he saw spots. "That's…that's great." Would she still join if Bella wasn't here? He was certain he'd driven her off for good. "Has anyone been giving you grief? Andre been around?" he asked instead.

"I haven't seen him. Jerome told me he's going to another center on the east side of town now." She lifted a shoulder. "Still, I'd feel safer if I knew I could take care of myself. You know, the way you and Bella can."

Every mention of Bella twisted the knife.

Her gaze flicked over him critically. "You're not wearing my necklace."

"Huh?" He suddenly remembered her Christmas gift. "Oh. It's hanging up in my office." On the same nail that Bella's scroll hung from, in fact. He amended quickly, "It's not that I don't like it—"

"Hey, don't worry. No jewelry, I remember the rules." She waved him off. "Anyhow, when you see Bella next, tell her hi for me."

"I will." He had no idea if he'd ever see Bella

again, though. And if he did, he had a feeling she wouldn't want to see *him*.

"WATCH MY LEG, Bella," Marco said, lifting his knee. "You see that opening? You reach around fast and grab it, and—"

Bella did as he instructed, giving his ankle a twist and a pull. Put off balance, he tipped to the side and fell over. She scrambled on top of him for the cross mount and then hopped off.

"Very good," her father said. "Remember, watch out for Kamino's legs. She'd give up her guard if she thought she could surprise you."

"Anticipate the unknown?" Bella chuckled as she shook out her limbs.

"Just watch out for surprises."

"Advice like that, and she'll start wondering why we even came," Marco said as he rolled to his feet. "C'mon, *Papai,* we need to step up her game, not baby her with the basics. Fulvio would never let us get away with this kind of beginners stuff for any of his advanced students." He made a sour expression. "Not that he'd be crazy about us being here in the first place."

"Don't worry about what your grandfather thinks." Carlos Fiore ground his jaw. "I've listened to him for too long. I should've been here for Bella all this time, shown everyone the family's behind her. She's been through enough on her own." He clapped his daughter's shoulder. "The basics will get you as far as any advanced technique, Bella. Kamino will be expecting something showy."

"And so will Hadrian Blackwell, so we'd better work on your stand-up. If you take it to the ground too early, you'll risk boring everyone."

"This isn't a show, Marco."

"Of course it is, *Papai*. This is the UFF. You think people pay hundreds of dollars to watch two women grappling on the mat for five rounds?" He shook his head. "We need to cleanse your brain of everything Kyle taught you. I never should've trusted him." He said that last part almost to himself. "We'll focus on your BJJ and stand-up. Those are your strong points anyhow."

She was about to argue that what Kyle had taught her—apart from the fact that she should never have trusted her heart *not* to get involved—had been valuable, but then Bella caught sight of a familiar figure watching her from across the room. She bristled as the redhead approached.

"Bella." Quinn Bourdain gave a tentative smile. "I've been looking everywhere for you."

She snatched her towel off the bench and mopped her brow. She was still cross about the article the reporter had written. Quinn was only doing her job, but in Bella's opinion, it'd been a shitty job. "How'd you find me?"

"I waited outside your apartment almost half a day and found out from the guy in the shop below you hadn't been home. Said he hadn't seen your bike, either."

"I've been staying with my father and brother. We have early mornings and late nights, so there's no point riding all the way home." She didn't explain that she hadn't wanted to risk a confrontation with Kyle at her apartment.

"I had eyes and ears at practically every gym in New Orleans. It was only by chance that a friend of a friend recognized you coming out of here a couple of days ago. I thought you'd head to the Star Gym for sure. They have all the equipment and trainers—"

"I don't need anything fancy to train. Not with my dad and Marco here."

"Yes, I can see that." Quinn glanced over to where the two men were giving her flat, suspicious looks. "I didn't even know this studio existed."

"Fiore trade secret." The family had contacts all over the world who let them use their facilities when they were traveling. In this case, her father and Marco had managed to secure the whole upper studio for themselves in exchange for a week's worth of private tutelage.

"Does this mean you're still in the fight?"

"Someone saying otherwise?" Bella countered.

"Your sudden departure from Payette's has people wondering if you're committed to the card." Her gazed sharpened. "Are you?"

"Hey, Bella." Marco strolled up next to her, dark green eyes fixed on Quinn. "Is there a problem here?"

"Quinn Bourdain, *Las Vegas Sun News*." The redhead stuck out her hand. "Marco Fiore, right? I've been following your family a long time."

Marco shook her hand automatically. "I've read your work," he said, wiping his palm against his shorts. "If you have business with Bella, Ms. Bourdain, it'll have to wait until after the fight. We're on a tight schedule."

"I was hoping to do an interview—"

"You'll have to talk to her agent, then. Bella's on lockdown."

Bella started to turn away. Then Quinn said, "I wanted to talk to you about Kyle Peters."

She whirled around and shot the reporter a warning look. She hadn't told Marco or her father the details of her departure from Payette's, though they obviously had their theories. All she'd said over the phone was that she needed their help and they were on a plane the next day, no questions asked.

"Bella," Marco called.

"Give us a minute." She directed Quinn to the stairwell, away from her family. The door shut behind them. "Whatever it is you think you have on me or Kyle, I'm telling you right now, it's wrong. And I want you to know that piece you wrote about me and women in MMA was hurtful and just plain *bad*. What was the point of quoting Ryan? Why did you even mention that stuff about Shawnese? You were there, Quinn. She was in trouble, and you used it. You used her and me both." Her pent-up anger came to a boil. "I don't appreciate cheap innuendo, either. All that stuff you put in about how I was getting special treatment from Hadrian was unnecessary." The hurt intensified as she remembered how the article reduced Bella's role to token female fighter. "I thought I could trust you. I thought you were a professional."

Quinn crossed her arms. "Look, I'm sorry I offended you, but I was reporting a fact. Hadrian *was* giving you special treatment, and I think you and I both know why." Bella didn't respond, and Quinn continued, "Maybe I let my feelings fuel my writing too much, but the reality is that that story probably would've been buried in the back pages if I hadn't written it the way I did. Being edgy and interesting—that's how magazines and papers sell these days. My profile at the paper has been hit and miss, and with all the cuts and layoffs…"

Quinn glanced down and sighed. "Shit, I'm screwing this up." She pinched the flesh between her eyes. "Look I did have a real point to make with that feature, but I realize that some of the things I left in were way off the mark. I'm sorry, Bella."

Weirdly, Bella understood where the redhead was coming from—having to do whatever it took to make her career. Even if it meant not always making the best judgment calls. "Why are you here, Quinn?" she asked.

"I want to do another article on you—right some of the wrongs from my first piece. If women's MMA is going to stand a chance, we need champions. I want to properly showcase the women of MMA and highlight all the challenges you face as both fighters and women. I want to make things right."

"How can I trust you? How do I know you're not here for another sensational story?"

Quinn's jaw set and she raised her eyes. "I can't promise it'll be a fluff piece. But it will be truthful. I ask hard questions—that's how I built my reputation. And not asking them is what got me into the mess in the first place."

Bella regarded her a moment longer, making sure the reporter sweated a little. "Are you going to ask me about my relationship with Kyle?"

"I'll ask. But I can only report what you tell me."

"And if I decline to comment?"

"Then I'll report that. But I can't promise I won't repeat what others have been saying."

Heat flooded her face. "What are people saying?"

"That you had a big fight with Kyle about another woman. You've probably heard he has a reputation for this kind of thing. He had an instructor at Payette's—"

"I've heard." She didn't want to gossip about Kyle with the reporter. "It really isn't anyone's business what happened between us."

"All right." Quinn folded her hands. "So will you do the interview?"

Bella sighed. It was probably more prudent if she talked to Joel first. Or Marco or her father. Or even

Kyle. But she'd never before needed anyone else's opinion to know what the right thing to do was. "Yeah. Let's do this."

CHAPTER TWENTY-TWO

KYLE GLANCED BETWEEN the recycling bin brimming with crumpled sheets of paper and the clock. The note he'd been trying to write all afternoon wasn't great, but it was a start. He supposed he could have done it on the computer and saved his hand from cramping, but he felt as if it would've been too impersonal.

It had been a weird day, anticipating his date with Bree while thinking about another woman. After work, Kyle went home and showered, then got dressed. He changed his tie-and-shirt combo three times before opting for a polo top instead. Business-casual was overrated.

He made a detour on the drive to Bree's hotel. He parked under the tree next to the convenience store below Bella's apartment. Letter in hand, he started up the steps.

"She ain't home, man," the store owner said from his stool on the porch. "I've been keeping my eye out." It sounded like a warning.

"I thought I'd leave her a note. Would that be okay?"

The man shrugged and puffed his cigarette. "You leave what you gotta."

Staring at the tiny envelope, Kyle hoped the note said all the right things—how sorry he was, how he wished things had turned out differently. But he wasn't a poet. All he could be was honest with her.... He pushed the note through the mail slot, letting his hopes for the best disappear through that dark slit in the door. Who knew whether she'd even get it?

He drove to the hotel. Bree stood beneath the carport in jeans, a light blue sweater and high-top running shoes. Even in plain street clothes, her tall, thin frame and radiant complexion made her effortlessly gorgeous. She pushed her blond bangs out of her eyes and waved, grinning toothily.

"Hey, you." They exchanged kisses on the cheek, and she hugged him briefly. She felt like a small bird against him.

They drove down to the Garden District. Bree watched him steadily, and he became self-conscious. "You've changed."

"Gained or lost weight?" he joked.

"Not weight. You seem…different."

He deflected by asking about her flight. Her hotel. Her last job and the next one. Bree gave perfunctory responses, and he answered her questions about the gym and his family. He should've felt exhilarated to be out with one of the world's most beautiful women. Hell, he'd been expecting to have to hide his lap under a jacket all evening. Instead, he felt antsy. The last time they'd been together, they could barely keep their hands off each other. Now it felt as if he were going out to dinner with his sister, only Jess would've inspired more interesting conversation.

He scanned the street for parking. Bree pointed out a spot, but he zoomed right by it. It didn't look roomy enough to fit the convertible. At least, he didn't think it did. The truth was, he wanted to park a little farther from the restaurant. He felt as though he needed a longer walk. If he could make it through the meal and then get Bree back to her hotel...

Right. That was all he needed.

"You're awfully quiet," she commented on the walk. "Everything okay?"

He tried for a smile. "I'm fine. Things have just been...busy."

"Worrying about your client?"

He tensed up and glanced at her. Her lips were compressed into a thin line. "No. It's fine. She's fine."

Eventually, they arrived at the restaurant, got a table, ordered and ate. He could see Bree watching him from beneath her lashes, but she didn't say much beyond the cursory comment about her meal.

"Do you want dessert?" she asked as the waiter took their plates away. "Coffee?"

He suddenly remembered Bella's invitations into her apartment. Compared to tonight's awkwardness, those moments had seemed like a breeze. "No thanks."

"We can get a drink back at the hotel," she said.

Right. A drink. He could use one.

At the hotel, Kyle handed his keys to the valet and followed Bree up to her room. His palms grew damp and his steps faltered. She was opening the door to her room when she looked over her shoulder. He was standing ten steps behind her in the middle of the hallway. "Kyle? Are you okay?"

"I…" His eyes dodged to her door. The look on her face asked the same question he was shouting at himself: *What is your problem?*

"I have gas."

Mentally, he facepalmed himself.

Bree made a face. "Ew. Well, don't trail it in with you." She darted in.

He followed her a moment later. She dropped her purse on the side table, toed off her shoes and went to the fridge in the kitchenette, pulling out a bottle of white wine. She poured two glasses and handed him one. He took it, but too late—she noticed his shaking hands.

"Seriously, Kyle, I'm starting to worry here." She made him sit on the couch. "You've been looking kind of sick all night. You barely touched your food."

He tried for a smile, but a close, clammy feeling swamped his chest. She touched his chin. "Look at me, Kyle."

He met her soft blue eyes reluctantly. "Hmm." Her fingers delved through his hair. She sat on his lap. He stifled the urge to dump her from her seat. "I'm going to try something. Don't move." She leaned in and kissed him.

Kyle closed his eyes, forced himself not to turn his head, not to get up and walk out that door. He tried to sink into her softness, the gentle swipe of her tongue against the seam of his tightly clamped lips. Her touch drifted down to his neck and across his shoulders, and his muscles jumped. He made himself slide a hand across her thigh. Finally, she broke the kiss and looked him in the eyes.

"I see." She got off his lap, then picked up her glass and sat in a chair opposite him. Kyle released a held breath. "Tell me about her."

"About who?"

"The woman you're in love with. The one you've been thinking about."

"I haven't been thinking about anyone but you."

"C'mon, Kyle. I know you, and I know when a man is thinking about someone other than the woman he's with. Henri was like that a lot...." She shook her head. "Your shoulders were hard as rock, too. And that was about the only thing that *was* hard."

He gulped his wine. It burned the back of his throat. "I'm sorry. It's not you, really. I don't mean that as a line, either. I mean, who wouldn't want to sleep with you? You're a freaking supermodel."

"And here I thought it was my personality you liked."

He opened his mouth, flustered. "Well, of course—"

She interrupted him with a wave and sighed. "It's okay. I've got enough self-respect not to settle for being second in a man's thoughts." She looked him over. "Something's changed since we were last together. You're more…serious."

He stared intently into his glass. "People change."

She didn't say anything at first. She simply sat back and gazed out the window. "Well, whatever you've changed into, I hope it's for the better. I care about you, Kyle. I hope you know that."

"I should get going." He put his half-empty glass down, feeling stupid and humiliated. "I'm sorry. I thought I could do this."

She gave him a quick peck on the cheek and told him to call her if he changed his mind or simply wanted to talk.

If the guys ever found out about this, they would kick his ass. A beautiful, sensual, willing woman who he knew could blow his mind had offered him everything, and he was walking away.

Not out of fear, though. He inhaled the sweet night air, and the knot inside him eased. The valet brought his car, and he got in, driving aimlessly. He'd been nervous, certainly. Uncomfortable. But it'd had more to do with the fact that he was with a woman who wasn't Bella than the fact he was with a woman.

He didn't want to think his feelings for Bella were that strong. It was residual guilt, he was certain.

But if that were the case, why was he parked in front of her apartment once again, hoping and waiting for a miracle?

HADRIAN WATCHED THE crews set up the cage at the MGM Grand Garden Arena. The place buzzed with activity, but no one noticed him up in the stands, leaned up against the railing, reveling in his memories. The first really big UFF event had taken place here, with over eight thousand fans in attendance. That'd been the day he'd known that his business would take off.

"I remember when I first met you," a familiar voice said. "It was right here, and I was a junior reporter at the *Sun*. You took pity on me and gave me an exclusive interview."

"I gave you an interview because I was trying to get into your pants," he replied. He didn't turn to look at Quinn. He was still mad at her, but not as angry as he'd been before Mrs. H. had given him that talking-to. Before he'd thought about what Quinn had done for the UFF and MMA. And for him.

"If that's what you want to tell yourself. I happen to know you're a lot nicer than you let on." She leaned against the railing and looked down at the arena as the cage walls were slid into place and bolted down.

"How'd you get in here? I thought I took your press pass away."

"A good reporter knows other ways in."

He felt her eyes boring into the side of his head, but still, he wouldn't look at her, even though all he wanted to do was grab on to her and never let go.

"Listen, Hadrian. I came to apologize. The feature was unfair to you and a lot of other people."

A part of him wanted to be petulant and hold that grudge. He didn't forgive easily. But as with everything else in his life, he had to treat this like a business decision. He'd already realized Quinn was too smart and too talented to kick to the curb. "I accept your apology."

"I'm also sorry about what I said about us and... you know."

"That the sex wasn't worth talking about?" Silence met him. He did look at her now, and boy, was it ever hard to keep his hands to himself. She was wearing a brand-new tailored gray pantsuit with a cream-colored blouse. Her silky reddish hair was piled into a loose bun. He cleared his throat. "I accept your apology for that, too. Though to be fair, I knew you were lying about that." He smirked.

Her mouth crimped wryly. "And?"

"And..." He mustered his strength. Mrs. H. had said he would have a hard time doing this—she knew he was a stubborn goat. He wanted to prove her wrong. "I'm sorry I said all those things about you being jealous of Bella."

She nodded but didn't say anything to acknowledge how hard it'd been for him to admit wrongdoing.

"I've just flown in from New Orleans," she said. "I went to see Bella Fiore."

"You found her? Her agent wouldn't even tell me where she was."

"I went to bury the hatchet. We reached an understanding." She didn't elaborate. Quinn played her cards close to her chest. It'd always been a struggle getting things out of her without giving up something in return.

He didn't want to play that game anymore. He missed her.

"You have passes for Saturday?" he asked, changing the subject.

"I do."

"But not the VIP media pass."

"No."

He turned to her. "I'll fix that. You'll get it all back, Quinn. Your UFF credentials, access to the green room, everything. I shouldn't have pulled them from you in the first place."

"Thank you."

Those two simple words released the tight band around his lungs. He hadn't realized how much she'd needed to hear that simple admission. "We should celebrate. You can tell me all about your interview with Bella over dinner."

She sucked in her lower lip. "Hadrian, we have to talk about this…*thing* between us. I can't have this with you anymore. I've been using you, thinking I could make this constant compromise because you were good for my career. We both deserve better than that. It's not fair to us. To what we could have."

He smiled crookedly, feeling his happiness quickly slipping away. "I don't mind."

"But I do. There's been too much accounting. Too much quid pro quo. I don't want us forever scratching each other's backs because we feel obliged to and not talking about the things that *should* matter to a couple."

"I want to do more than scratch your back, Quinn," he said with a grin, but silently admitted that that was exactly what he'd been doing—tallying up all her rebuffs when she'd refused his gifts and offers to move in with him. He'd always thought sex would make up the deficit—he realized now it hadn't and never would.

He could see in her eyes she thought the same thing.

"I don't want us to break up," he said.

She gave him a sad smile. "Were we ever really together?"

He knew there was nothing he could offer her that would entice her to stay with him the way he wanted. There was one thing, though, that could prove he'd heard her. One thing he hoped would at least earn back her respect. "I have a story for you. An exclusive."

She perked up and flipped her notebook open, pen poised. That was his Quinn. He'd once thought of her as mercenary, but she was simply keen, intelligent, determined and motivated.

"I reread your article and looked into the unequal

pay figures you mentioned. We're overhauling the books and making sure all UFF employees are getting paid accordingly and equally. That means new HR standards for all employee assessments. We're also working on a cohesive sexual harassment policy and code of conduct to be implemented across the board in all the gyms and UFF facilities. I'm increasing maternity leave for female workers at all levels, and we're looking into on-site child care at headquarters, with subsidies for those in the international offices."

Her pen had stopped scribbling. She was staring at him openmouthed. "For real?"

"It's all on the record. Mrs. H. will provide all the details if you give her a call." He scrubbed a hand over his jaw. "Look, I know you don't want any kind of accounting or favors or anything, but hear me out. You've worked in this industry a long time, and I thought about some of the stuff you said. There's still lots of work to be done. Which is why I'd love to have you on board and hear more of your ideas— you'd be a huge asset to the UFF."

Her lips trembled. She reached out and placed her hand on his arm. "Thank you, Hadrian. But I do love my job. As much as I go through…"

He patted her hand but didn't let his touch linger. "I understand."

And he did. That was as much as he could do for her. He had to accept that and move on.

Quinn stared at him in surprise, at a loss for

words. Together, they watched the cranes hoist the UFF banners into the air.

Maybe one day, when she saw he was serious, they could move on together.

CHAPTER TWENTY-THREE

"LINE ONE," LIZ SAID. "It's Hadrian Blackwell."

Kyle closed his eyes as a slightly sick feeling swamped him. He'd been expecting this call since the day Bella had stormed out. Maybe he'd been expecting it for even longer. He tried to gauge the UFF president's mood from the look on Liz's face, but her expression was stone-cold.

He headed for his office and shut the door. Time to get this over with.

"Peters." Hadrian sounded like he was greeting a man at a funeral. "How are you?"

"Fine, all things considered." Not fine. Not in the least. In the two and a half weeks since Bella had left, all he'd been able to think about was how he'd screwed up. He hadn't even been able to find Bella to apologize.

A sudden horrible thought popped into his head: What if Hadrian was calling because Bella was hurt? What if she'd been hit by a car because she was so stubborn she'd started biking again? "Have you found Bella? Is she all right?" Panic seized him.

"She's training in a secret location with her brother Marco and her father, Carlos."

Kyle slumped back. "Good. That's good." Kyle was surprised and pleased by this bit of news. He knew her relationship with her family had been strained.

"Good?" Disbelief and ire torqued Hadrian's tone. "You think it's good that a star fighter has left an official UFF gym days before her first big fight? Do you have any idea how that looks?"

"That's my fault. I take full responsibility." He was prepared to pay for his mistakes. But he couldn't say he regretted his relationship with Bella.

He waited for the ax to fall. He could move back to California, maybe, and work as a private coach, or…

"That may be so, but I'm not firing you yet, Peters."

It took Kyle a moment to process his words. "Meaning what, exactly?"

"Meaning I happen to be in a good mood. If I'd left this to the board to decide, you'd be out. But as far as I'm concerned, what happened between you and Bella is a personal matter. That doesn't excuse your behavior, though. When your private life affects my business, it sure as hell isn't private anymore. You and I are going to have a discussion eventually, but not until the anniversary card is over."

So he had a reprieve. That was something, he supposed, but he was far from relieved.

"Did you see that piece Quinn Bourdain wrote last week?" Hadrian asked after a beat.

"No."

"She wrote that Bella insisted you were a good coach and a good gym manager. She said everything that happened was a misunderstanding. Personally," he added emphatically, "I think she's too blind to see that you don't appreciate her the way she appreciates you. You don't deserve her."

He wanted to puke. How could she defend him after all the crap he'd put her through? How could she forgive him? "I guess I don't."

"You're coming to Vegas for the fight." The UFF president jumped back to business. "You're going to show up and act like nothing's wrong. Payette's needs to be seen as supporting Bella all the way. According to Quinn, Bella's father and brother are going to be her cornermen. Imagine how that'll look when the graphics go up and they say 'fighting out of New Orleans' without a single rep from Payette's in her corner."

"If she has her family at her side, at least the world knows the Fiores are taking her seriously."

"I don't give a crap if they're a happy family, Kyle. I care about my business. I need Bella to be the champion. Kamino's great, but she's not the star I'd hoped for. If Bella loses, the women's division goes under."

Kyle scowled. "Bella can win. I have every confidence in her."

"Confidence gets you shit all right now. It should be you in that corner with her, Peters."

Hadrian was right. It should be him. Even after all they had shared, he'd still pushed her away. He'd be lucky if he ever got to be a part of her life again.

The thought that he might *not* squeezed the air from his lungs. They'd shared more than sex. He'd told her things he'd never told anyone. Hell, he'd cried in front of her. He'd never trusted anyone like that before. His father hadn't permitted it—emotions weren't something men expressed or felt.

Kyle ground his jaw. He'd do as Hadrian asked, but not for him or his career or the UFF. "I'll do what it takes, sir."

"Make sure you do. She might not want you, but she sure as hell needs you for this fight if she wants to be champ." Hadrian hung up.

IT WAS BRISK for February in Las Vegas, but Kyle was certain his reception would be even frostier than the temperature. As he made his way to the MGM Grand for the weigh-in, all he could focus on was Bella and how this would be the place where his future with her would be decided.

The sectioned-off portion of the arena bustled with media, cameras and cameramen. Fans swarmed the gallery, and the air buzzed with excitement. Officials hovered over a scale, testing and retesting it, while other techs moved microphones and other apparatuses.

Kyle wended his way backstage, spotting grim-faced members of Kamino's camp guarding a door. The young champion would be in her locker room, waiting for the weigh-in to start. This wait could be brutal because frequently, fighters would not eat or drink anything twelve hours in advance. They couldn't risk going a fraction of an ounce over the target weight. Every ounce over meant a percentage taken off their paycheck or, worse, disqualification.

He worried about Bella. She'd been working hard, and he'd had her on a strict diet, but he had no idea what she'd been doing since she left. Not having control made him crazy.

He shook his head. He'd given up control the moment he'd decided to have a relationship with her. Control of any relationship was an illusion.

Eventually, he found out where Team Fiore's locker room was. A beefy security guy stood outside.

"I'm Kyle Peters. I'm with the team," he said, but the guy put a strong hand on his shoulder and backed him off.

"Sorry, no visitors."

"I said I'm with the team."

"Bella's in there alone." Kyle recognized the voice. He'd spoken with Marco Fiore over the phone, but never met him in person until now. Kyle saw that they were about the same height, but Marco was leaner. He shared Bella's raven-black hair, but his eyes were a shade grayer than her brilliant emerald-green. "She wants to be left alone."

He stuck out a hand. "I'm Kyle Peters."

"I know."

He retracted his hand. "Listen, I'm just here to make amends and offer my help."

"I think you've helped her enough." Marco met him chest to chest. "If you know what's good for you, you'll leave before my father arrives. I have a lot more control than he does when it comes to guys like you."

"I'm not leaving." He folded his arms. "I'm waiting right here for Bella. I'll shout through the door if that's what it takes for her to hear me."

"Marco, o que está acontecendo?" An older man Kyle instantly recognized as Brazilian jujitsu master and seven-time world champion Carlos Fiore strode toward them. His eyes narrowed on him. "You."

Kyle put his hands up as the older man advanced. "Respectfully, Mr. Fiore, I'm here to apologize to—"

He didn't get another word out as Carlos grabbed him by the collar and slammed him against the wall. Someone gave a shout, and a ring of spectators formed around them. The bodyguard melted into the background, content to watch, it seemed. Even Marco backed away.

Kyle struggled to go limp. If he was going to take his licks, best make himself soft. They might be evenly matched, but he was not going to fight Bella's dad.

"You stay away from my family." His knuckles ground against Kyle's collarbone painfully. "You don't speak to my daughter ever again. You break her heart, I break your face. Understand?"

"I'm not worthy of her," Kyle gritted. "I know that. I never meant to hurt her, but I did and I was wrong to do it. I want her to hear that from me."

"*Papai,* what's going on?" Bella poked her head through the door. Kyle's heart lurched. Her lips pulled down in a steep frown and she stepped farther out. "What are you doing here?" she asked Kyle irately.

"I'm here to support you." Carlos dug his fists in harder, and he winced. "I got stopped."

The senior Fiore said something harshly to Bella in Portuguese, and she snapped back at him. Reluctantly, he let go.

"Come in, Kyle." Bella went back through the door. Kyle slid sideways past both Carlos and Marco, and he could feel the hostility radiating off them. If it ever came to blows, Kyle would be in for a hell of a knuckle-duster.

When the door shut, the hubbub subsided. The small locker room sported the usual wooden benches and cubbies. The floor had been padded with clean, new-smelling rubber mats. High up in one corner, a TV showed muted feed from the press area where the weigh-ins would take place. This would be the room she'd occupy for tomorrow's fight.

She sat on the ground cross-legged and glared at him expectantly.

"How are you doing?" he asked, suddenly nervous.

"Let's see. I haven't eaten anything other than green smoothies for the past five days, and have had nothing since lunch yesterday. Dad's made me spit into a cup for the past twelve hours to cut the last few ounces. I've got a headache and I have to face the crowd and the media looking like I've been wrung through a washing machine, and now you're here, getting into fights with my family. How the hell do you think I'm doing?"

If he was worried about being on her bad side, at least now he was reassured that he couldn't get on a side that was any worse. "What's your weight at?" That was not the question he wanted to jump to, but he couldn't help inquiring.

"Since this morning, 144.8." She closed her eyes. "I'm going to have a strawberry milkshake, a steak and fries with a fried egg and bacon on top right after this."

He chuckled. Her gaze snapped to him, her irritation clear, and he slammed his lips closed.

"Tell me what you came to say, Kyle. I'm not in the mood to be nice."

He sat on the bench on the opposite side of the room. "I came to apologize."

She waved a hand in dismissal. "You're forgiven."

"No. I can't let you forgive me that easily. I want you to know that I know what I did wrong. That I've been thinking a lot about...what happened to me—" he rubbed him palms over his knees, feeling the old ache creep back in "—and what happened between us. I was wrong to say the things I did."

"I got your note." The pause let him know she'd read it, probably more than once. And as the silence dragged on, it was as if she were acknowledging in her own taciturn way that she'd understood everything he'd meant to say, everything he'd striven to infuse in between the inadequate words and limp emotion twenty-six letters could produce.

Hope rose within him. She drew her knees up, refusing to meet his eye. "If I were in a better mood, I would say I'm sorry for calling you all those nasty things. But I don't have the brain space to feel remorse or dwell on anything else. I can't deal with drama right now. So I forgive you, and I hope you forgive me. Now, are you done?"

He felt a stab of pain lance through his chest. No. He wasn't. He needed to tell her she was right—he had issues. He wanted to tell her that he was willing to work through those issues—that he'd never be able to move on until he did. He wanted to tell her that when she won that belt he would do whatever it took to make her understand that his feelings for her—

Yes, he had feelings for her. Deeper than he'd first admitted. Being in Bella's inner sanctum now after what felt like an eternity apart from her settled something inside him. Made him feel…complete. Like this was the place he belonged. Dad would say that was just plain corny and probably would've smacked him in the back of the head. Nonetheless his emotions swelled, and with it, a flurry of words raced up his throat.

But he couldn't tell her everything right now—that would be selfish of him. Fighting Kamino was the only thing Bella had room for in her head. Any distraction could mean a quick and brutal end, like what had happened in the exhibition match in New Orleans. He couldn't risk being the cause of another humiliation for her.

And he couldn't stand in her corner.

"Yeah. Good luck out there, Bella," he said. "I'm glad your father and brother are here for you. You couldn't ask for better cornermen."

With that he left. There was nothing else Kyle could say right now—he had a whole host of issues to deal with first. He'd apologized, but that didn't make him worthy of Bella yet.

THE MOMENT THE door closed behind Kyle, Bella slumped over, chest aching, stomach hollowed out from more than hunger. *There. It's done.* Kyle had apologized, but that was it. He hadn't even said he still wanted to be friends. He'd come here to clear his conscience and then he left.

You're free now, a quiet, determined voice inside told her. *You have the biggest fight of your life in front of you. Kyle doesn't need to be a part of that—he never wanted to be in the first place.*

If she had any water in her body, tears might have

fallen freely. Instead, she felt achy all over, as if she'd taken a beating.

"Bella?" Her father stuck his head past the door. "You all right? It's almost time."

"Sim, Papai."

He scowled. "Did that Kyle Peters say something? Did he hurt you?"

"No, *Papai*. He said nothing." Slowly, she pushed to her feet. The rest of her life lay ahead. After tomorrow night, she'd never have to see Kyle again.

CHAPTER TWENTY-FOUR

KYLE HAD BEEN to plenty of MMA fights before. He'd been a spectator, absorbing the rush of sound and heat as combatants clashed in the cage. He'd dealt with the gut-wrenching nerves that went with being a cornerman, watching his trainees from the sidelines. But he'd never felt this urgency and nauseating nervousness before, as if he were heading into a final exam for a class he'd never attended.

It was a nightmare. The roar of the 16,000-strong crowd made Kyle's skin shiver and his ears ring. The audience wasn't as big as some other events the UFF had hosted, but the energy of the crowd could have lit up the Vegas Strip.

And he wasn't at Bella's side to share it.

The announcer made the introductions as lights flashed and flared. A taiko drumbeat started, overlaid with an orchestral arrangement of a hip-hop song. Ayumi "Kamikaze" Kamino marched in with her entourage, standing a head-and-a-half below her cornermen but exuding twice their menace and determination.

Kyle's passes gave him full access to the arena,

but he'd chosen a seat in the VIP section across from Bella's corner. It was the best seat he could get without spooking her. He wasn't even sure he should be sitting this close.

The lights went out again. Strobes flickered and a single, piercing note rang across the stadium before it exploded in a cacophony of sound. He rose to his feet.

"In the red corner, weighing in at 145 pounds, fighting out of Brazil by way of New Orleans, Louisiana—" the announcer dragged it out "—Bel-la Fiiiiiiioooooore!"

The crowd cheered raucously as she jogged out, flanked by her father and brother. The jumbotron overhead showed her stripping down to her trunks and rash guard. She looked mean, her game face set.

After an application of Vaseline to her face and a quick check of her gloves and mouth guard, she burst into the cage and the gate slammed shut behind her. Kyle's feet went numb as all his blood congealed.

Bella hopped from foot to foot, shaking out her limbs and stretching her neck while Ayumi eyed her from the opposite side of the cage, prowling like a caged panther.

That's good. Conserve your energy. Limber up. It was killing him to watch her from way over here.

"This is a five-round fight. I want to see a clean match, ladies. Do you have any questions?" The ref didn't get a response. The women were locked in a death stare match. The ref had them touch gloves, and with a definitive chop of his hand, the UFF's first female fight began.

Kyle was half-out of his seat the entire first round. They kept the match mostly stand-up, but Bella managed to use her superior BJJ training to get in a couple of takedowns. Ayumi was slippery, though. She had a strong guard, and was quickly adapting to Bella's preferred methods of attack.

In the second round, Ayumi got two strong blows in, one to Bella's thigh and the other to her chin. A hit like that could have ended the fight, but Bella only staggered back, then shook it off and launched herself at her opponent, delivering a few solid body blows. The audience hooted its approval.

By the third round, it was obvious the two were getting tired of dancing. So was the crowd. A stand-up game was great, but unless some major skills were displayed, it hardly mattered.

"C'mon! Finish her!" Kyle heard someone yell.

Recklessly, Bella rushed at Ayumi with a series of punches, hooking one arm around her neck, and the other over the elbow. In one swift move, she dragged her opponent to the ground.

The crowd howled as the two women scrambled for dominance. Bella almost had Ayumi in an arm bar, twisting her wrist in a painful-looking hold. Any normal human would have tapped out, and the audience cringed and moaned at the way Ayumi's shoulder and elbow torqued in horrific braids of muscle. But Kamikaze Kamino hadn't earned her nickname for no reason. Kyle watched in morbid fascination as she lifted her hips, twisted her torso up and flipped over.

Bella's grip slipped. Ayumi mounted, straddling Bella's chest, and she began a brutal barrage of hits to the side of her face.

All Kyle could see was blood. Bella's blood. The rushing sound in his ears melded with the roar of the crowd. He stuffed down the urge to scream at the ref to stop the fight.

Ayumi might have ended the match given four more seconds, but then the horn sounded and she hopped off as Bella struggled to her feet. Kyle rushed toward the red corner, flashing his badge and pushing through the forest of shoulders.

Sour sweat hit his nostrils—not Bella's, but everyone else's. She sat on a low stool, breathing deeply, the back of her head resting against the chain link cage. Marco bathed her brow with an ice bag, saying something in Portuguese to her.

Blood flowed from her nose and from a huge gash in her forehead. Her eye was swollen and darkening, the goose egg growing larger by the second. The cutman stanched the blood, fingers flying as he applied his various remedies, pressing an endswell that looked like a big metal stamp against the lump above her eye while pinching a cotton swab in her nostril.

Hanging over the edge of the cage, Carlos fanned her, his face pinched with worry. Bella turned her head side to side, winking and squinting out of her swollen eye.

The cutman shone a light into her face. "Can you see that, honey?"

"Don't call me honey." She spit a wad of blood into the bucket held out for her and rinsed her mouth. "I can see fine."

Marco frowned. "Bella, don't lie. I can't even see your pupil. If the swelling doesn't stop or gets worse, you could permanently damage your vision."

"It's not worth it, Bella," Carlos urged above her. She craned her neck up. "You're risking your whole future."

Her gaze seemed hazy, but then it slid toward Kyle. She smiled past her split, bloodied lip. "You here to give me pointers?"

"I'm here to give you my support." He gripped the vinyl-coated chain link, trying to telegraph his feelings past the barrier. "I believe in you, Bella. This is your fight, your choice. And no matter what happens, I want you to know…" *I love you.* "I'm here for you. Right here."

A clarity entered her previously clouded eyes, and she tossed her head to one side and chuckled. "You had to say that now when I don't have a lick of makeup on, huh?"

"Ten seconds!" the official shouted.

"This is your fight. Your life. Your choice."

She took a deep breath. "I'm good. I'll fight."

In a rush, everyone cleared the cage. Kyle took

his place in Bella's corner with her family. The bell rang and the fourth round began.

Carlos grabbed his wrist. "If she gets hurt—"

"Of course she'll get hurt," Kyle said, shaking him off. "But she'll pick herself back up. She made this choice for herself. We never had a say in it." He met the senior Fiore's eye and snatched the white towel out of the man's hand. "And we're not going to give up on her."

Marco glowered. "If you had any feelings for her, you'd be protecting her. That's your job. Her career could end tonight if she gets another blow to the head."

Of course, they didn't get that it would end no matter how she lost, whether they threw in the towel or not. But he couldn't share that information with them. "I believe in her," he said, and meant it.

Ayumi bounced around the cage. She knew like everyone else that Bella's right eye was her weakest point now, and that a few taps to the head would likely be her downfall. Bella was being careful, not getting too close.

You can do this, Bella. He was afraid to shout his support and distract her.

And showing up ringside and practically telling her you love her in the middle of a fight isn't distracting? His father's voice rang loudly in the back of his mind. *You always were selfish.*

"I'm doing this for her."

"I don't see you doing anything," Marco muttered. "What kind of coach are you?"

Ayumi feinted, trying to scare Bella into leaving an opening. One minute into the round and the crowd started booing. No one had landed a single blow.

Unable to hold it in any longer, Kyle banged his fist on the edge of the mat. "C'mon, Bella!" he shouted. "Surprise her!"

He thought he saw the twitch of her cheek, but it was hard to say. She shifted her footing and got into a staggered stance. It must have confused everyone because in that instant, Ayumi thought she had her. The GRRL Fight champion went for a high kick—

Bella ducked and lunged, grabbed her in a high single leg takedown, cut the corner and slammed Ayumi onto her side. She went for a full-frontal mount and just as Kamikaze Kamino had, began whaling on her face, both fists swinging.

The crowd went nuts. Three seconds of that and the ref called it. Ayumi lay on the mat, dazed, as Bella sprang to her feet and whooped.

Bella Fiore had won the first ever women's UFF championship belt.

EVERYTHING AFTER THE match with Ayumi went by in a daze, and it wasn't because of the hits Bella had taken. She'd remembered the enormous belt being wrapped around her waist, thanking her trainers, her family, the UFF and especially her opponent. Ayumi was fine. She'd hugged her tight in the cage after she'd gotten to her feet, thanking her for a good fight.

The press conference immediately following was a little harder to remember. Questions about strategy, training—they were all answered in much the same way.

"Kyle Peters and the crew at Payette's in New Orleans were a huge help to me. My father and brother and my family's support has been tremendous. I can't think of a better, stronger team than family *and* friends."

Hadrian Blackwell had seemed very pleased by her statement. That night, he declared he'd be signing ten more female fighters. The women's featherweight division would be well stocked for the next year or two. It meant Bella would be defending her title sooner than she thought.

After a visit with the physician, she went to the locker room where Carlos and Marco awaited her with champagne. As they were toasting her success, Carlos's cell phone rang and he answered. His expression firmed and he held the phone out. "Fulvio wants to talk to you."

A dark cloud obscured her victory for a moment. Was her grandfather going to yell at her some more? Tell her he was disowning her for good? *"Avô,"* she greeted neutrally, breathing deep.

"I watched your fight, Bella." She waited for his verdict, but he seemed to be expecting her to say something in return.

"Thank you for watching." It was all she could think to say. A mix of sadness and anger swirled through her. Her grandfather had taught her everything about the sport. He'd taught her how to be passionate about the family business. *He* should have been in her corner tonight, but some out-of-date, misogynistic, old-world ideals had them barely on speaking terms.

"I think you will have a lot of bruises," he said.

Was that supposed to be a criticism of her game? "They'll heal."

"Yes. I suppose they will." He gave a long sigh. "This is what you want, then? To fight?"

"I didn't spend half my life learning from you so I could stand by and make babies and cook."

"I thought you'd get tired of it eventually. I thought Antonio would settle you down."

"He didn't." She didn't feel the usual stab of hurt at the mention of Antonio. She didn't feel anything except a muted wistfulness. Apparently she was still cruising on adrenaline and euphoria. She'd achieved her dream. She'd fought for the UFF. She was a champion, and she had this man to thank. Though he didn't approve, he had been the reason she'd come to the sport in the first place. She softened her voice. "This is my life, *Avô* Fulvio. I know you don't approve. That you'll never forgive me."

"Forgive you? *Querida,* why would you say that? Of course I forgive you. I don't approve, it's true, but only because this is a hard life, and hard on the body. When you get to my age…" He made a gruff sound. "I have been hard on you, I think. Too hard. But I love you, Bella. You know that."

Tears filled her eyes. "I love you, too."

"Come home," he said. "We will not talk about *this* anymore. You are too much like me—too bull-headed to change your mind. But we will talk. I cannot decide your life for you, but I have some things I want you to consider for the future…."

THE UFF AFTER-PARTY was loud and filled with alcohol-soaked partygoers. Marco and her father stayed with her, intent on keeping her from over-indulging. There was no way she could have, any-way—she was way too tired. All she wanted was to soak in a hot tub and then sleep for a week.

But she had social obligations and had to make an appearance at the party. The rest of her career would be like this, she realized.

It was nearly three in the morning by the time she headed back to her hotel room, but Bella had yet to see Kyle and thank him. He'd disappeared after the post-fight interview. It wasn't until late the following morning that she finally managed to reach him on his cell phone.

"I'm at the airport," he told her over the buzz of flight announcements. "I have to get back to New Orleans. Hadrian asked me to get the place ready for a press event. He sprang it on me last night as we were leaving the cage."

"Oh."

"I'm sorry. I'd planned to be with you to celebrate, but things got kind of crazy."

"Yeah." She couldn't swallow past her disappointment. Tightly, she said, "I wanted to...thank you. For everything."

"Will you be coming back to New Orleans?"

She'd promised to stay until April, but after all that had happened between them, listening to her grandfather's proposal and then speaking with Hadrian about her future with the UFF, she wasn't sure she could. She had options, but only one choice really stood out for her.

She cleared the frog in her throat. "My grandfather wants me to return to Brazil and help with the new studio he's opening."

"Wow. That's great."

Was that all he had to say? Maybe she'd only imagined his cage-side confession of love. She had been beat around the head, after all. Bella clutched her pullover's collar and gave a forced chuckle. "Well, it's not the all-women's MMA gym I want to build, but it'll give me an idea of how to start."

"That's good. Listen, my flight is being called. I have to go. I'll talk to you soon, okay?" He hung up.

She bit her lip. Well, that was that. They were both moving on. As they should.

THREE DAYS AFTER Bella's fight, Kyle stood in the back of Payette's watching Hadrian work the crowd at the press conference. More than a dozen news outlets had come to take the UFF president's triumphant statement.

"I want to make sure we build up lots of talent to pad our female divisions," Hadrian said. "So I'm announcing new programming at all UFF gyms that will open up MMA to more women. Further to that," he added, "I want to say that the UFF is committed to fostering healthy attitudes toward women in general. We welcome fans and fighters of every creed, color and background. I want everyone to know that women are always welcome in the UFF, and that any comments I may have made contrary to that are ones I regret deeply."

Kyle was surprised by Hadrian's turnaround. Maybe it was just a company line; maybe his handlers had somehow managed to get him to tone down his attitude. Change didn't happen overnight. But when Hadrian had pulled him aside to talk about Karla, Kyle began to wonder exactly what the UFF president was trying to atone for.

"I can't turn back the clock and change the way I handled things," Hadrian said, "but I've had a lot of time to think about it, and I don't think I did right by you or Karla. The story never jibed with me, the way she told it. But I swept the problem under the rug instead of dealing with it. I mean, I thought it was clear what had happened. But I've realized I made assumptions. You're under no obligation to explain yourself, but I want to hear your side of the story again."

He should've been mad. The president had dismissed him once before, and had blamed him for the incident. But Kyle appreciated the opportunity to explain now.

So he did. He found it easier to talk about the whole fiasco with a couple of years' hindsight. And as he described the lead up to the "attack" in his office, he realized he was guilty of toying with Karla's emotions the same way he'd toyed with Bella's.

When he got to the part about Karla meeting him for farewell drinks, he stopped abruptly. That was more than he'd told others previously. Hadrian's brow wrinkled. "I don't remember hearing that part of the story."

"She left for Ireland after that. I didn't think it was necessary." He fidgeted, eyes cast down.

"So what happened?"

Kyle clenched his fists, biting the inside of his cheek. He didn't respond.

Hadrian sighed. "Listen, Kyle. I'd rather not drag this all out into public after all this time, but if there's more you're not telling me…if you want to bring this to court, I'd understand. It doesn't serve me or my business to stick my nose in your private life, but whatever happened to you outside of my gym is important to me because it involves you. And you should know I can get you help."

Help. He'd never expected it from the UFF president. He'd fully expected to be released from his position after Bella's match. He thought Hadrian was exactly the kind of guy who'd laugh at his ordeal, just like his father…

Your father is dead. Let him rest.

That strong, quiet, determinedly rational part of him that had kept him sane all these years suddenly had a voice. Bella's voice. Some part of him must've always been listening, too, because he knew in his heart it was true. He'd let what his father thought of him dictate his actions for too long, even in death. David Peters wasn't here now. He couldn't hurt him, and he couldn't run his life. He hadn't for more than seven years.

Strangely, he could imagine his father liking Bella. She was a lot like him in many ways, and could probably show him a thing or two on the mats.…

The thought set hooks in his lungs and pulled. He missed her. He missed having her in his arms. The spicy-sweet scent of her skin, the brilliant smile against her dark features, her snappy comebacks and hot temper. She was brash, provocative and stubborn—and he loved that about her.

It was time he dealt with his problems and became a man worthy of Bella.

"I might take you up on that offer," Kyle said, "but not yet. Not before I talk to my family."

Hadrian nodded and shook his hand. "When you're ready."

CHAPTER TWENTY-FIVE

"MOM, DO YOU have a flashlight?" Kyle shuffled the boxes in his mother's dank, gloomy basement. He could've sworn they'd multiplied since he'd left Modesto more than ten years ago.

"There's one at the top of the stairs," she called back. "Don't take too long down there. Dinner's almost ready."

He finally found the cardboard box marked "Kyle's Stuff," musty and slightly warped by age and moisture. He brought it up to the kitchen where his mother stirred a pot of spaghetti sauce. Jess tossed a salad at the island. She looked up and grinned. "Find it?"

"Yup." He set the box on the ground and opened it, rifling through the certificates, medals, photos and small trophies he'd accumulated throughout his wrestling career. He dug out the three velvet boxes holding the Olympic gold medals and opened each of them, laying them out on the kitchen table. Their beautifully etched faces winked up at him, reminding him of all the grueling training and sacrifice he'd endured to earn them. He didn't know why he'd hidden them away like this. They should've been on display.

"Seems like a long way to come for some mementos," Jess said, bringing the salad to the table at the same time his mother started dishing out pasta.

"I need them to remind me of something important." He released a long breath. "But let's eat before I tell you."

After dinner, he sat them down, keeping the medals close by, and he told them about what had happened with Karla. Including how she'd raped him.

Jess gasped and grabbed his arm, and his mother covered her mouth with both her hands, eyes wide.

"Why didn't you tell us before?" his sister demanded, her long nails digging into his forearm.

"I couldn't. Until recently, I couldn't even accept what'd happened or how it'd affected me. I thought I was fine." He rubbed his palms against his thighs.

They asked him if he wanted to press charges, wanted to know what they could do to help. Their love and concern and utter lack of judgment wrapped him in a cozy blanket of safety. He cried in his mother's arms for the first time since he was a child. But it wasn't so much for his ordeal as it was the way his secret had affected his family. Mostly, they just wished that he hadn't shut them out all this time.

"I'm sorry to dump this on you," he said with a shuddering sigh.

"Never be sorry for sharing your problems with your family," his mother said. "All I've ever wanted was for you to be healthy and happy. Now we need to focus on how to help you. I didn't do anything when your father kicked Jess out, and I'll never forgive myself for that." She grabbed her daughter's hand and squeezed.

They talked for a long time after that. Slowly, Kyle began to feel less heavy. Sharing a burden really did lighten the load.

It didn't mean the road to recovery would be a short one. He didn't want to think about filing charges—not now, anyhow, and maybe not ever. But he had to work through his feelings. He needed to get professional help.

Later he joined Jess outside as she sipped a lemonade. They sat in the worn old porch swing.

"Hey, squirt." She punched him in the arm. "You doing okay?"

"Weirdly, yeah."

"I watched Bella's fight last week," she said. "It was on at the bar I was at. I had them turn it up. Man, she's something."

"Yeah."

"She doing okay? I mean, her face looked pretty bad."

"It was, but I haven't seen her since."

"What? Why not? I thought you were training her. You were at the fight, weren't you?"

"It's kind of a long story." He gave his sister the Cliff's Notes version of everything that had happened between him and Bella. It felt like old times, when they were boys and best friends, before Dad had drawn a line in the sand and made Kyle choose sides.

Jess whistled and set her drink down. "So she knew about all *that* before we did, huh?"

"Yeah. Sorry."

"Don't be. You've spent too much time with regret. And I'm glad you told Bella. She must be something special." She gave him a knowing look. "So... you haven't told her the magical three words yet?"

Kyle shrugged, his cheeks heating. It was weird hearing it from his sister.

"C'mon, squirt. You keep this secret from your family and friends, but you tell a woman who scares the crap out of you? If that's not love, I don't know what is."

He chuckled and relented. "You have a twisted sense of what the *L* word is."

"Is it that hard to say?"

Yes. But he'd never said it to anyone before. "If she doesn't say it back, I don't think my ego can take it."

"Hey." Jess grabbed his shoulder and squeezed. "You know what really makes a man a man? Being strong enough to admit you're afraid. Having the balls to risk everything for love."

"Lame."

She punched him in the arm. "Cut it out. Dad

messed us all up with his super-macho chest-pounding man ideas. But he got one thing right. If you want something, you go after it. It takes a real man—or a real woman—to go after the things that make them happiest. Screw what other people think. Me? I wanted to wear dresses and feel pretty. I wanted boys to look at me and go 'Wow.' I wanted to be freaking Claudia Schiffer. It cost me, but I did pretty good in the end. I got what I wanted. Question is, what do you want?"

Kyle grinned. Jess was right.

That night, he slept. A solid ten hours without waking up in a cold sweat. He felt warm and safe and loved and cherished. He'd opened himself up to his family. And he didn't feel any weaker for it.

It was time to go after what he wanted most.

BELLA CHECKED HER apartment one more time. She couldn't shake the feeling she'd left something behind.

The furniture belonged to the apartment, so that wasn't going anywhere. She'd donated a bunch of her clothes to Reta to use at the youth center. Her bike had been shipped back to São Paulo with her father and brother, who'd left a week after the fight. All she had to take with her was the single carry-on duffel bag.

There was just one thing left to do.

She grabbed a cab to Payette's.

When she got there and walked in, Liz looked up, her eyes brightening with tears. "When's your flight?"

"Not until eight. Thought I'd make it an extra-long goodbye to torture you all."

Liz rounded the desk and hugged her. "I'm going to miss you. You'll come and stay with me when you visit, right?"

"Of course." Though she had a hard time imagining coming back here and letting the hurt sink its claws deep into her again. She needed to go home and be with her family while she healed. She needed to mend fences with her brothers and her grandfather.

She made the rounds, chatted with the guys, took turns giving Tito and Orville hugs and lifting them off the ground. Wayne practically sobbed as she held him. He kept patting her on the head, apologizing for the drama he'd caused, telling her how proud he was of her, how honored he'd been to work with her. Bella's eyes burned as he clasped her hands and said, "Don't let anyone ever give you shit about what you can and cannot do. You know yourself. Don't let them tell you otherwise."

"I never have." She grinned.

Finally, it was time to say goodbye to Kyle. She hadn't seen him around the gym, so she knocked on his office door. His desk chair faced the wall calendar. A big red check mark scored through her fight.

"Hey, Coach." Her voice sounded rough and she cleared her throat. Damn Wayne's waterworks.

She'd expected Kyle to spin around in his office chair like a Bond villain, fingers steepled. But there was no response. She walked farther in and rounded the desk. He wasn't in his chair.

"He's visiting his family in California," Liz said softly. Bella turned to her, stricken. The receptionist licked her lips. "We were expecting him back this morning, but his flight was cancelled. My guess is he's spending another day with his mom."

"Oh." Her chest ached. A tear slipped from the corner of her eye, and she wiped it away hastily. "I guess...I'll have to leave this here with a note."

She opened her duffel bag and took out the UFF championship belt. "Something to put in the display case up front."

Liz's eyes widened. "Bella, no, you can't give us—"

"I want you to have it. I couldn't have won it without everyone here. You guys deserve it."

Once Liz left the office, Bella sat down at Kyle's desk and pulled out a sheet of notepaper and a marker. The tip rested against the sheet, leaving a dark, spreading blot.

What was she supposed to say? *Dear Kyle, I loved being here, I loved the staff, I love—*

Another tear dripped from the tip of her nose and onto the sheet, leaving a big stain. She crumpled up the paper until it looked the way her heart felt.

She abandoned the letter. There weren't any words she could leave behind to express her gratitude, her love.

No sense in prolonging the pain. She'd go to the airport and grab a sandwich. Maybe it'd help fill the big empty hole inside her.

She paused at the office door and drank in one last look at all she had left of Kyle.

Then she turned and ran straight into his chest with a scream.

"Nice to see you, too." He rubbed at his ears.

She laughed to hide her sudden tears of relief. "Sorry. I was just on my way out. I thought you were stuck in California." She let him pass and walked with him back into his office.

"I was. And then I was stuck in San Antonio. And Dallas. And I think I was in South Keys at some point. I've been in the air for almost twenty-two hours."

"Smells that way." She made a face, hoping it would mask the emotions rioting through her. "But why? You could've stayed with your mom an extra night."

"No, I couldn't. I had to get back. I'd never forgive myself if I let you leave."

The air stopped up in her lungs. Kyle looked nervous all of a sudden and sniffed his armpits, scowling. "Sorry. I would've showered, but I swung by your apartment as soon as I arrived. You'd already gone. I thought maybe you were heading to the airport, but I hedged my bets that you'd come here first to say goodbye." His fists clenched as he looked down at the big shiny belt on his desk. "Bella, you can't give this to us."

She smiled to hide her tears. "I want you to have it. Don't argue with me."

"You know, there is something we'd rather have."

She quirked her lips. "Sorry, the prize money is mine."

"Not that, dummy. You."

Her throat got tighter. "I can't stay. My family needs me."

"I need you."

She glanced up in surprise. His dark eyes remained fixed on her as he took her hands. "I need you in my life, Bella. I need a strong, beautiful, drives-me-crazy kind of woman who won't take no for an answer and isn't afraid to call bullshit on me."

Her smile faltered. "That doesn't sound like it'd be a very happy relationship, considering how often I've done all that since I got here."

"But I needed to hear it," Kyle said. "I needed that swift kick in the ass to realize what I was doing to myself. You were right. I can't change in a day. I need help. A lot of it. I'm not afraid to admit that anymore."

She nodded. Everything he was saying was right, but it wasn't what she'd been hoping for. "You have lots of friends, Kyle. Lots of people who love you." *But not the way I love you.* "I don't want to tell you what to do, but since I'm leaving…I think you should start by telling Jess and your mother about what happened with Karla."

"I already did."

She did a double take. "You did?"

"I went home for the weekend and told them everything. You made me realize what I've been hanging on to and how it's affected me. I want to move on, but I don't want to move on without you. I don't know if I can."

She gave a half sob, half laugh. "You could have told me this a week ago, before I bought my plane ticket."

"So postpone it."

"Till when?"

"Till some future date when you want to go back to Brazil to introduce me to your family."

"Kyle—I'm going home. My grandfather wants me to help open his new studio. It'll give me good experience on running my own."

"I've got a better offer. Stay here and get firsthand experience. We'll go into business together and open a women's MMA gym in New Orleans—or wherever you want. I've had lots of time to think about it. I have start-up money stashed away. If you want to make sure the UFF keeps women on its cards, we need to build up the next generation of fighters."

The air rushed out of her. "Kyle—"

"Bella." He clasped her hands tighter. "I know I'm no good at talking about my feelings. I can be an irrational, pigheaded, self-centered douche bag at times. Everything that happened with Karla twisted me in ways I don't like, and I kept myself in the dark to make sure I didn't see it. But then you showed me how broken I was." His eyes watered. "I want to get better. I want to be a better person. *You* make me want to be better. You make me feel whole." He broke into a watery smile. "I...I love you."

Bella pressed her lips tightly together, trying to stem her tears.

She burst out laughing.

Kyle pouted. "That wasn't exactly the response I was hoping for."

"I'm sorry, I'm sorry." She put a hand over her mouth and gestured helplessly. "I'm just..."

When she didn't finish, he nervously supplied, "Exuberant? Ecstatic?" His face fell when she shook her head. "Confused? Sad? Mad? Hungry? Help me out here."

"Happy." She kicked her bag aside and threw her arms around Kyle's shoulders. He squeezed her tightly as their lips met in a deep, long kiss. Then she drew away and cupped his cheeks. "But I have to go home."

She watched the light drain out of his eyes as his silly grin faltered. Oh, she couldn't torture him any longer. "I have to go home because I can't live without my bike."

Kyle blinked, then laughed. "Forget the bike. I'll buy you a car."

"Hell, no. You're going to buy yourself a bike. We're going to bike everywhere from now on."

"Fine." He glanced out the door, where nosy spectators had gathered to watch. He didn't care. "I'll do it for you, as long as you promise to stick to the traffic rules."

"Wimp."

He rubbed the tip of his nose against hers. "But that's why you love me, right?"

She grinned. "I love you for a lot of reasons. Let me show you how much." And she kissed him once more. And again. And again.

* * * * *

LARGER-PRINT BOOKS!
GET 2 FREE LARGER-PRINT NOVELS PLUS
2 FREE GIFTS!

HARLEQUIN®

superromance®

More Story...More Romance

YES! Please send me 2 FREE LARGER-PRINT Harlequin® Superromance® novels and my 2 FREE gifts (gifts are worth about $10). After receiving them, if I don't wish to receive any more books, I can return the shipping statement marked "cancel." If I don't cancel, I will receive 6 brand-new novels every month and be billed just $5.69 per book in the U.S. or $5.99 per book in Canada. That's a savings of at least 16% off the cover price! It's quite a bargain! Shipping and handling is just 50¢ per book in the U.S. or 75¢ per book in Canada.* I understand that accepting the 2 free books and gifts places me under no obligation to buy anything. I can always return a shipment and cancel at any time. Even if I never buy another book, the two free books and gifts are mine to keep forever.

139/339 HDN F46Y

Name	(PLEASE PRINT)
Address	Apt. #
City	State/Prov. Zip/Postal Code

Signature (if under 18, a parent or guardian must sign)

Mail to the **Harlequin® Reader Service:**
IN U.S.A.: P.O. Box 1867, Buffalo, NY 14240-1867
IN CANADA: P.O. Box 609, Fort Erie, Ontario L2A 5X3

Are you a current subscriber to Harlequin Superromance books and want to receive the larger-print edition?
Call 1-800-873-8635 today or visit www.ReaderService.com.

* Terms and prices subject to change without notice. Prices do not include applicable taxes. Sales tax applicable in N.Y. Canadian residents will be charged applicable taxes. Offer not valid in Quebec. This offer is limited to one order per household. Not valid for current subscribers to Harlequin Superromance Larger-Print books. All orders subject to credit approval. Credit or debit balances in a customer's account(s) may be offset by any other outstanding balance owed by or to the customer. Please allow 4 to 6 weeks for delivery. Offer available while quantities last.

Your Privacy—The Harlequin® Reader Service is committed to protecting your privacy. Our Privacy Policy is available online at www.ReaderService.com or upon request from the Harlequin Reader Service.

We make a portion of our mailing list available to reputable third parties that offer products we believe may interest you. If you prefer that we not exchange your name with third parties, or if you wish to clarify or modify your communication preferences, please visit us at www.ReaderService.com/consumerchoice or write to us at Harlequin Reader Service Preference Service, P.O. Box 9062, Buffalo, NY 14269. Include your complete name and address.

HSRLP13R

LARGER-PRINT BOOKS!

HARLEQUIN *Presents*

PASSION GUARANTEED SEDUCTION

GET 2 FREE LARGER-PRINT NOVELS PLUS 2 FREE GIFTS!

YES! Please send me 2 FREE LARGER-PRINT Harlequin Presents® novels and my 2 FREE gifts (gifts are worth about $10). After receiving them, if I don't wish to receive any more books, I can return the shipping statement marked "cancel." If I don't cancel, I will receive 6 brand-new novels every month and be billed just $5.05 per book in the U.S. or $5.49 per book in Canada. That's a saving of at least 16% off the cover price! It's quite a bargain! Shipping and handling is just 50¢ per book in the U.S. and 75¢ per book in Canada.* I understand that accepting the 2 free books and gifts places me under no obligation to buy anything. I can always return a shipment and cancel at any time. Even if I never buy another book, the two free books and gifts are mine to keep forever.

176/376 HDN F43N

Name	(PLEASE PRINT)	
Address		Apt. #
City	State/Prov.	Zip/Postal Code

Signature (if under 18, a parent or guardian must sign)

Mail to the **Harlequin®** Reader Service:
IN U.S.A.: P.O. Box 1867, Buffalo, NY 14240-1867
IN CANADA: P.O. Box 609, Fort Erie, Ontario L2A 5X3

Are you a subscriber to Harlequin Presents books and want to receive the larger-print edition?
Call 1-800-873-8635 today or visit us at www.ReaderService.com.

* Terms and prices subject to change without notice. Prices do not include applicable taxes. Sales tax applicable in N.Y. Canadian residents will be charged applicable taxes. Offer not valid in Quebec. This offer is limited to one order per household. Not valid for current subscribers to Harlequin Presents Larger-Print books. All orders subject to credit approval. Credit or debit balances in a customer's account(s) may be offset by any other outstanding balance owed by or to the customer. Please allow 4 to 6 weeks for delivery. Offer available while quantities last.

Your Privacy—The Harlequin® Reader Service is committed to protecting your privacy. Our Privacy Policy is available online at www.ReaderService.com or upon request from the Harlequin Reader Service.

We make a portion of our mailing list available to reputable third parties that offer products we believe may interest you. If you prefer that we not exchange your name with third parties, or if you wish to clarify or modify your communication preferences, please visit us at www.ReaderService.com/consumerschoice or write to us at Harlequin Reader Service Preference Service, P.O. Box 9062, Buffalo, NY 14269. Include your complete name and address.

HPLP13R

ReaderService.com

Manage your account online!

- Review your order history
- Manage your payments
- Update your address

> *We've designed
> the Harlequin® Reader Service
> website just for you.*

Enjoy all the features!

- Reader excerpts from any series
- Respond to mailings and
  special monthly offers
- Discover new series available to you
- Browse the Bonus Bucks catalog
- Share your feedback

Visit us at:
ReaderService.com